Endless Road

*Other Five Star Titles
by John Lutz:*

The Nudger Dilemmas

Endless Road

and Other Stories

John Lutz

Five Star • Waterville, Maine

First Edition
First Printing: August 2003

Published in 2003 in conjunction with Tekno Books and Ed Gorman.

Set in 11 pt. Plantin.

Printed in the United States on permanent paper.

Library of Congress Cataloging-in-Publication Data

Lutz, John, 1939–
    Endless road and other stories / John Lutz.—1st ed.
        p. cm.
    Contents: Endless road—The truth of the matter—DNA—Image—S.O.S.
    ISBN 0-7862-5442-4 (hc : alk. paper)
    1. Detective and mystery stories, American.   I. Title.
PS3562.U854E53 2003
813′.54—dc21   2003052874

For Ed Gorman
Who has made so much of it possible.

Table of Contents

Endless Road

It was the dry season. A hot, brisk wind whipped out of the west, snapping taut the white cloth canopy above the verandah. Morgan Hoyt sat next to his aide, Langner, at a round wicker table in the deep shade of the canopy. The verandah was part of what had once been the main house of a large French rice plantation. The clapboard and stone mansion was in serious disrepair. Beyond the house's immediate grounds, the vast plain of now-fallow rice paddies remained, but it was tended by people other than the French.

Morgan sipped from his glass of quinine water and looked out over the sun-bright fields toward a stone building that had once been a guest house. It wasn't as badly damaged as the mansion and had been refurbished and even air-conditioned. It was where the negotiations were being held. Morgan had been using his arts of persuasion since early morning and was glad for this afternoon break before resuming the talks.

"We're down to the short strokes," Langner said. He was a tall young man with a hatchet face and a permanent forward lean, all angles inside and out. "Have you formulated the outlines of a recommendation?"

Morgan smiled slightly. Langner liked to speak bureaucratese, as did many of the people involved in the

9

process. "Not yet," he said.

"You're smiling," Langner pointed out.

"That Dengh's a charming bastard," Morgan said of the other side's chief negotiator. "We have to give him that. But I'm not sure if I trust him even within the context of what we're doing."

"I think he's trustworthy," Langner said, "in that he's bound by his word until his masters change their minds. And I believed him when he told us any kind of traffic on a long road from the North would be impossible to stop."

"I'm not so ready to accept his assessments," Morgan said. "But I do like the man. He reminds me of someone."

From across the fields a woman and two young children were walking toward the mansion, the half-caste wife and off-spring of the Frenchman who had fled. They remained and were allowed to live in the ruined mansion.

Morgan sat back in his wicker chair, narrowing his eyes against the bright sun, and watched the three distant figures wavering in the vaporous heat. It hadn't rained in almost a month, and blown dust made the woman raise both hands to shield her eyes. Perhaps it was her casual, elegant gesture, perhaps the dust, that made Morgan's mind travel back more than thirty years . . .

"Your mother's bringing back some Coca-Cola," his father said as they watched Morgan's mother walk toward where they sat in the overheated car. She was a tall, graceful woman, burdened by a large straw purse that she used for every purpose. The wind kicked up and blew across the sun-baked road, setting her loose skirt flowing about her legs and carrying a haze of dust that caused her to raise both hands to her eyes.

They'd stopped so she could use the restroom at the Stan-

10

dard Oil gas station; then Morgan's father had driven the car several yards beyond the building to a pump that supplied water for radiators. He'd hand-pumped water into a big bucket, used a funnel to add some carefully to the steaming radiator, then got back in the car with twelve-year-old Morgan and his sister, Julia, and waited.

"Here's two cold bottles," his mother said to both children as she slid into the front seat next to Morgan's father, whose name was Art. She drew two bottles from her straw bag, opened them with the notch on the can opener she carried, and handed them back.

"Nothing for me?" Morgan's father asked.

"Only this," she said, and kissed his cheek.

"Not bad," he said, smiling, "considering the country's in a depression and everything's scarce."

The starter ground, the motor turned over, and the car continued its journey along U.S. 66 toward Morgan's father's promised job with the government in Oklahoma City. He'd been selling ladies' shoes in St. Louis, but the company went out of business, just like the other places where he'd worked. It was an old friend who'd offered him this latest job, which would require passing some tests before it was a sure thing.

"There's a restaurant," Morgan's mother said, after another few hours of driving.

"Five o'clock," Art said. "Guess we oughta stop this side of Joplin, get us some supper, and let the car cool down."

They had water and cold sandwiches in a booth near a window. It was hot in the restaurant and there were a lot of flies. Morgan remembered there were several dead ones on a brown-stained white windowsill. Julia, who was seven, was out of sorts and deliberately jabbing her older brother in the elbow as she ate. An old woman in a flower-print dress smiled at them when they'd finished eating and were leaving, but

11

Morgan could tell she was glad to see them go and she wouldn't have to listen to Julia anymore.

He was looking forward to the car moving and wind rushing in through the open window. But his father stopped grinding the starter and said, "Damn! She won't kick over, and I'm afraid I'm gonna run down the battery."

He got out, slammed the door hard, and strode back into the restaurant. Morgan's mother sat stiffly, staring straight ahead and saying nothing.

When his father returned he said he'd called a mechanic who told him he'd drive out to the restaurant and look at the car, but it would take him a long while to get there and the Chevy was an old car so he wouldn't make any promises. Then Morgan's father stooped down like an old man and looked in at his wife and children, and Morgan would always remember the stricken, hopeless expression on his face. And his words: "It seems like God's mad as hell at us."

"We passed a motor court just before we stopped here," Morgan's mother said. "I'm sure there was a vacancy sign hanging out. So we're in luck."

And they were. The Do Dropp Inn was a motor court made up of a dozen detached cottages arranged in a wide circle around a small sand-and-earth playground with a swing set and sliding board. The cottages had sharply peaked roofs, ivy growing up their front walls, and inside each was neatly furnished with a double bed, chintz curtains, and thick window shades that kept the interior five degrees cooler than outside. There was a bed that rolled out from under the big bed, and Mom called down to the office from a phone right outside to get a cot brought to the cottage. Julia and Morgan both wanted the cot, so their father flipped a coin. Morgan got the cot. Things were looking up.

They settled in while their father left to walk back to the

restaurant to meet the mechanic who promised nothing. He would drive the car to the Do Dropp Inn when and if whatever was wrong with it was repaired. A tenuous plan to match the times.

The cottage on the left was empty. Morgan knew the one on the right was occupied because of the big Packard that was parked there. It was old, faded brown and starting to rust, but it was the largest car he'd ever seen, twice as long as his family's Chevy sedan.

He was outside, flipping his pocketknife to the ground so the blade stuck more often than not, when the neighboring cottage's door opened and two women emerged. One was tall and very thin, the other shorter and overweight with a huge wart or mole growing on one of her cheeks near the corner of her eye. Morgan politely answered them when they told him good afternoon, and they both smiled at him as the shorter and heavier of the two women opened the cavernous trunk of the huge car. They got a fancy valise and a leather suitcase from the trunk, closed the lid, and started to return to their cottage. Then the tall one, who had short brown hair and was pretty even if she was kind of stoop-shouldered, smiled and said hello to Morgan's mother, who'd stepped out of the cottage to check on him.

The three women talked for a while, and Morgan heard his mother explain about the car problem. Then Julia came out, letting the screen door slam behind her, and the tall woman, whose name Morgan later learned was Adelle, patted her on the head as if she were a dog. The grown-ups seemed to run out of things to talk about, so they were discussing the heat when tires crunched on gravel and everyone turned to see if Morgan's dad was returning with the Chevy.

But the car that had turned from the highway into the motor court's lot was a new black Ford coupe with a rumble seat. A dark-haired man wearing a sweat-soaked white shirt with a loosely knotted tie climbed out of the car, grinned, and said hello to everyone. Then he remarked on how hot it was as he pulled a small suitcase from the dusty coupe's passenger-side seat. He lifted a larger suitcase from the rumble seat and carried his luggage to the door of the cottage on the other side of Morgan's family's. After he went inside, Morgan saw him open the cottage's windows but leave the shades down.

"He's certainly a nice-looking young man," Morgan heard Adelle say. At first Morgan thought she was talking about him, then he realized she'd meant the new guest.

There was more crunching of tires on gravel. This time it was a tow truck that had braked to a halt just inside the driveway. Morgan's father got out, with the suitcase he'd left in the car, said something to the truck's driver, then trudged toward the cottage.

"The driver's going back to the restaurant to tow the Chevy," he said, looking distraught. "Says it needs a new distributor and the water pump's leaking. It'll be late to-morrow before he can get parts and get it fixed so we can drive on."

"You poor man," Adelle said, her sweet, lean face twisted with compassion.

"We have some watermelons we bought at a roadside stand," the short woman said. "Let us give you one to compensate for your bad luck."

Morgan's father looked embarrassed. "We don't need . . . I mean, I'm on my way to Oklahoma City, got a government job waiting for me."

"Of course," Adelle said. She smiled and made a back-hand motion, dusting away any notion of charity. "Some of the melons will rot anyway in this heat if we don't eat them," she called over her shoulder, already on her way to the

Packard to open the trunk again.

Behind the women's cottage was a small wooden picnic table. Morgan's mother used a knife borrowed from Adelle to cut the melon; then Adelle and her short friend, whose name was Ida, joined the family. Ida brought a salt shaker she'd found somewhere. Everyone ate watermelon, holding slices like ears of corn and taking lusty bites. Morgan spit the seeds to the side, but noticed that Adelle daintily removed each one from between pursed lips and tossed it away. Morgan decided he liked Adelle, and was even beginning to like Ida despite the mole with hair growing out of it on her cheek.

After the watermelon picnic there was still daylight left, so Morgan and Julia wandered over to the playground and used the swing and sliding board for a while. But Julia started to harangue Morgan the way she often did, and the playground equipment was for smaller kids anyway. So Morgan returned to play with his pocketknife again in a bare dirt area near the cottage.

He was resting the blade's point lightly on his index finger, then using his other hand to flip the knife so it rotated once and stuck in the hard earth.

"Mumbletypeg," a man's voice said. "I used to play that when I was a kid."

Morgan looked up to see the dark-haired man who'd checked into the cottage next door. He had a friendly smile, with a slightly crooked front tooth that made him look devilish and the kind who'd enjoy a good joke. He kneeled down next to Morgan, took the knife from his hand, and flipped it off his forefinger so it landed point down and stuck three times in a row.

Standing up again, he said, "I ain't lost my touch." He grinned down at Morgan. "You and your family traveling through to California?"

15

"Nope, just to Oklahoma. My dad's got him a job waiting there."

The man's grin got wider. "Jobs are hard to come by these days. I just left one and I'm heading up to Chicago for another." He wiped sweat from his forehead with the back of his hand and looked around. "Say, you ever done any fishing?"

"Sure."

"I got the stuff for it in the car and I seen a little lake down behind the motel. Clear it with your folks and you can come with me and we'll see what we can catch."

That sounded great to Morgan. He thanked the man and ran in to ask his father for permission. But he was taking a nap. It was his mother who came out of the cottage to size up the man from next door.

He gave her his grin. "I look upstanding enough?"

Morgan's mother returned his smile. "I suppose. And I see you and Morgan are already friends."

"He and I ain't been formally introduced, but I get a certain sense about some fellas, and I consider us friends. I'm Tom Blake. Headed up to Chicago for a job."

"My husband's traveling toward a job, only going in the opposite direction."

"That's what Morgan said. Lots of folks traveling the highway these days, heading for work or looking for it. A little fishing'd break up the long trip and make it more tolerable."

Morgan's mother shot a glance at him. "I noticed the lake out our cottage's back window. Could barely see it through the trees. But there's a dirt path. I suppose it's okay if you two walk down and fish there."

They both thanked Morgan's mother, then Morgan went with Tom to the car. Tom opened the rumble seat, reached in, and came up with a disassembled rod and reel and a bamboo pole broken down in four sections. He then reached down and handed Morgan a small steel tackle box. "We're off," he said breezily, and began striding toward the lake. Morgan fell in beside him.

The tackle box was locked and Tom had forgotten the key, so he used Morgan's knife to pry it open. It was full of lead weights, fishing line, cork floats, and all kinds of fancy lures. There was also a can of worms, but it looked as if the heat had gotten to them.

Morgan and Tom fished until it got dark, catching three small sunfish along with a measly crawdad they threw back in.

When they returned to the cottages, Morgan's mother and father were standing outside talking to Adelle and Ida. The warm night was just past dusk, moonlit, and filled with the ratcheting screams of crickets.

Tom introduced himself to the two women and Morgan's father, then offered the sunfish to anyone who was interested. When there were no takers, he smiled and said he'd clean and eat them himself. Before turning to go to his cottage, he ruffled Morgan's hair roughly and said, "This here's a good one, this boy. Gonna be one heck of a man." It was an offhand compliment from a man he'd only just met yet sensed was special, but Morgan would never forget that casual assessment of his character, the rough show of approval and affection. It had come just when he'd needed it most, sensing a weakening in his father that he'd never suspected he'd see.

"You like Mr. Blake?" his father asked, when Tom had disappeared in the dark and they heard his cottage screen door slam shut.

"He's the neatest fella I ever met," Morgan said. He was proud to know Tom Blake and figured he must have an important job in Chicago, probably more important than Morgan's dad's government job in Oklahoma.

Later that night Morgan awoke to the sound of his parents' voices.

"We got no choice but to wait for the car to be fixed," his father was saying. "But if we stay another night here, we'll barely have enough to eat and buy gas when we continue on our way."

"Like you said, there's no choice," Morgan's mother said. "Maybe you should have accepted Tom Blake's offer of the fish."

"The hell with Tom Blake and his new Ford and his job waiting in Chicago!" his father snapped, surprising Morgan with his anger.

Morgan was further surprised to hear his mother apologize for something. They made no further sound, and he drifted off again to sleep.

The next morning the mechanic phoned from Joplin and confirmed it would be another day before the Chevy was repaired. They were stuck at the Do Dropp Inn.

When Tom Blake heard the news about the car he told them how sorry he was, then said he'd hang around for a few hours and keep them company. Adelle and Ida, however, loaded their suitcases into the big Packard.

Then Tom surprised everyone by showing them some canned stew and a dozen eggs in a sack, and offered to make everyone breakfast if they built a little camp fire behind one of the cottages.

Adelle and Ida stared at each other, then Adelle nodded. "We have a small kitchenette in our cottage," she said. "We'll be glad to prepare breakfast and check out later."

Morgan's mother pitched in, and the three women soon had breakfast cooked up, which everyone ate at the picnic table in the shade of a tree between the cottages.

Afterward Tom offered Morgan's dad a Camel cigarette, and they smoked and talked while the women cleaned up after breakfast. The motor court owner, a gray-haired man named Ralph Dropp, and his wife, Alma, joined them, and everyone discussed the sorry state of the economy and the increasing car traffic on Route 66. The Do Dropp Inn was about the only business in or around Joplin that was turning much of a profit these days, Dropp said.

Tom Blake had drifted away from the conversation. Morgan, squatting on the bare earth off to the side and playing Mumbletypeg, glanced up and noticed Tom and Adelle talking near where the woods began. But the next time he looked that way they were gone.

"Seein' as you got stuck here against your will due to car trouble," Dropp was saying to Morgan's father, "we're gonna give you a special rate on the cottage. That 66 is a long, hard road, so that's our policy."

"It's a mighty nice policy," Morgan's mother said, before his father could protest. "And we thank you."

Morgan caught movement in the corner of his vision and saw Adelle stalking toward her cottage. Her blouse was half untucked and she looked angry.

A few minutes later there was the sound of a car starting, and the big Packard rumbled from the motor court lot out onto the highway. Everyone sat silently, listening to the accelerating motor and the gears changing.

"Why, they never said goodbye," Morgan's mother said. "How odd."

"They paid up, though," Ralph Dropp told them. "That's all I request of a guest."

Tom Blake was suddenly alongside them. "I think I still got time for a little fishing before I go," he said, looking at Morgan and winking.

Morgan folded his pocketknife and stood up, looking hopefully at his father.

His father laughed, but not with his heart in it. "Why not?" he said. "You two go ahead. I think I'll read the paper and wait for another phone call from the garage in Joplin."

The morning was still cool, and the fishing should have been good. But all Tom Blake and Morgan caught during the next two hours was a small catfish. Tom said they were the devil to clean so he tossed it back in the lake.

That was when Morgan heard his mother call his name.

He turned to see her standing halfway down from the cottage, her hands on her hips. "I need to talk to you for just a few minutes," she yelled. "You can come right back and fish some more."

Tom grinned down at Morgan and ruffled his hair again in that mock-rough way. It messed it up something awful but Morgan didn't mind at all. In fact, he was glad of it.

"Better do what your mom says," Tom told Morgan. "Man's best friend ain't a dog, it's his mother."

Morgan grinned back and used his fingers to brush his hair out of his eyes. Then he propped up his bamboo fishing pole with some stones and ran toward the cottage.

"I'll catch that big one for you if he takes your bait," Tom called after him.

When he reached his mother, Morgan was surprised to see the tight expression on her pale face. Yet she didn't seem angry. He'd never before seen that look on her and it kind of scared him.

As soon as they'd taken half a dozen steps toward the cottage she hugged him to her hip and began hurrying them along.

"What's going on?" Morgan asked. "What's the matter?"

As they turned a bend in the dirt path he saw at least a

dozen uniformed policemen standing around, along with lots of men wearing suits and ties despite the heat. Some of the men had shotguns or rifles; Morgan's father was there too, holding Julia's hand. The two of them walked toward Morgan and his mother. Julia looked blankly at Morgan and he could tell she didn't understand what was going on either.

"We're going over by the office," Morgan's father said.

He almost physically herded them to the edge of the gravel parking lot where there were lots of police cars parked, and about a dozen guests were standing with some policemen. Mr. and Mrs. Dropp were there looking worried. Everybody wore an expression similar to the one on Morgan's mother's face. Morgan noticed that one of the police cars was parked sideways across the driveway.

Another car drove up, and a big man with a thin mustache and wearing a dark suit climbed out, talked to two other men, then strode through where everyone was standing. He seemed to be in charge. Morgan still remembered the film of dust on the toes of his shined black shoes, the hard look in his eyes, and the way he barely moved his lips when he spoke: "Let's do him."

The big man and the two he'd been talking to disappeared in the direction of the cottages.

No one spoke. Several minutes passed. Then there were half a dozen shots that actually had sounded like fire crackers.

The uniformed police cautioned everyone to stand still. Three other policemen came up from where the cottages were. Their faces were pale as bone but one of them was smiling. He nodded to the men who'd stayed with the motel guests.

Then more men came from the direction of the cottages. Two of them were lugging a motel blanket that was half-folded around the soaking wet body of Tom Blake. Morgan

21

could see Tom's peaceful face clearly and knew immediately that he was dead. There was blood as well as lake water glistening in his hair and staining the blanket; and some blood darker than that on the blanket dripped onto the ground.

Morgan was stunned, numbed with anger and despair. "Why'd they shoot Mr. Blake?" he heard himself ask. His voice sounded higher than usual, strikingly like Julia's.

"He's no Mr. Blake," one of the uniformed policemen said. "He's Tommy-gun Blain, and he robbed a bank in Galena, Kansas, yesterday and was on his way to join his gang for another job in Chicago."

That was when Morgan glanced toward the highway and saw the big brown Packard parked on the shoulder. He remembered the look on Adelle's face when she'd come out of the woods after being there with Tom Blake.

"He killed a bank guard and four customers in Galena," the policeman said, "including a mother and her young daughter. Then he killed an old fella about to go on a fishin' trip, just so's he could steal his car. And he didn't have to kill nobody. Lucky we got a tip he was here. And you folks are lucky you're still alive."

Morgan felt his mother's grip on his shoulders tighten as she pulled him closer. He still remembered her scent and how warm her perspiring body had felt through her cheap, thin dress, his cheek pressed softly against the side of her breast.

The woman and children were near the main house now. Several members of the delegation from the north walked past them, including Dengh, who smiled warmly at them. The woman smiled back and made a kind of respectful bow.

"Dengh is a likable bastard," Langner said, standing to return to the negotiating table. "It's hard not to trust him."

As Morgan stood up from his chair, he saw Dengh pause

and grin broadly, and with mock-roughness bend over and muss the boy's hair. He saw how the boy looked up at Dengh.

"Hard not to trust him," Morgan agreed.

Later, on the converted Air Force plane traveling back to the United States, Langner set his martini down and looked over at Morgan.

"Have you made your decision?" he asked.

"I have," Morgan said. "I'm going to recommend to the Secretary of State that we commit ourselves to a major effort and introduce armed forces in much larger numbers to Vietnam."

"Could be a long, hard road," Langner said, not looking at Morgan but gazing out the window at wisps of gray cloud.

"Could be," Morgan conceded.

But he was confident he'd made the right decision. This time there would be no misplacement of trust and affection. This time there would be no second guessing.

The Truth of the Matter

PART ONE

1

Lou Roebuck sat poised on the edge of the bed. He could hear the whir of truck tires on the warming pavement outside the Jolly Rest Motel, early rising drivers who had someplace to go in a hurry. He stood quietly and slipped into his pants. It was barely past sunrise, and the tiny room was still dim and inviting more sleep. But Roebuck didn't have time for sleep.

After putting on his socks and polished Western boots, he went to the door and opened it a crack. The morning was empty. The broad highway lay gleaming dully in the sunlight a hundred feet or so from the motel room door, a quiet river of concrete. Roebuck stepped outside and walked across the graveled parking area to the station wagon, listening to the loud crunching of his footsteps in the brittle morning.

Within a few minutes he was back inside the motel room with a can of coffee, a cheap aluminum coffeepot, and the bag of donuts they'd bought the evening before. Going in someplace for breakfast was a risk they'd decided they didn't have to take.

Roebuck lit the burner of the tiny stove in the room and sat down again on the bed. He spooned some coffee into the pot, replaced the lid, and set the pot on the burner without even having to rise. Then he lay back with his hands behind his head.

He should be out of Missouri by morning. He wondered if they knew he was heading for the West Coast. They might know everything, they might know more than he ever dreamed they could know, or they might know less. The uncertainty was the hardest part of running. And if they did catch him, what could he do? They wouldn't understand about the murder (if you could call it that, if Ingrahm really was dead). Reporting Ingrahm dead might very well be a plot, Roebuck thought, a plot to get him to turn himself in. But he'd never give up. By God, he'd go out shooting like a goddamn John Dillinger!

The coffee began to percolate.

Outside, a bird began a persistent chirp, and Roebuck wished it would shut up.

He closed his eyes and tried to shut out the sound of the bird, concentrating instead on the perking coffee.

The inane phrase entered Roebuck's mind and stuck there: Perk, perk, perk, the—flavor buds at work. It repeated itself.

Ridiculous, Roebuck thought, but it might sell coffee. As it stuck in his mind it would stick in the mind of someone hearing it on radio or television. Now, if there were just some way to tie it in with the product, work in the brand . . .

Roebuck reminded himself that he didn't have to think about those things anymore. Now he wished he didn't have to listen to the perking coffee. It reminded him of Mr. Havers, and he didn't want to think of that man at all. He didn't want to think of Mr. Havers, so he wouldn't.

Roebuck got up and went into the bathroom, but he couldn't escape the gurgling cadence of the coffeepot.

"I'm sorry, Louis," Mr. Havers said, "but we're a small company. We don't have the money for that sort of thing."

25

Roebuck shrugged, settling his six-feet-two into the chair opposite Havers' desk. "What the hell, a little lie on an expense account . . ."

"Little lie!" Havers' normally pale face was flushed, his pencil-thin white moustache arced downward along the line of his bloodless lips. "You call three hundred dollars in one month a little lie? I'm surprised you even thought you could get by with it."

"You might not have noticed."

"You must be out of your mind." Havers leaned back in his padded desk chair and lit a cigarette. The impressiveness and security of his office was giving him confidence in a situation about which he'd been initially nervous. "I must say, Louis, even now you don't seem to be very concerned about it."

"Am I supposed to beg for my job?"

"Don't you care about your job?"

"I don't take anything off any son of a bitch," Roebuck said. "I don't care about my job that much."

Havers shifted the cigarette to the corner of his mouth and blew a cloud of smoke. "Just this once, Louis, spare me the corny B movie dialogue. Everybody in the office is sick of it. We put up with you for one reason only—we thought you could write advertising."

Roebuck purposely narrowed his eyes and stared at Havers. "Thought?"

Havers nodded. "I've done some checking, Louis, and it seems you lied to us when you applied for this job. You never were with Schnelling, Schnelling and King, you never had any magazine articles published, in short you really have little or no experience in advertising. And your war record . . ."

"What about my war record?"

"This about it, Louis. It doesn't correspond with the gov-

26

ernment's record. According to them you got a medical discharge, and the only decoration you received was rifle qualification."

"I can outshoot any son of a bitch."

"But that's not what it takes to write advertising. You're a pretender, Louis. You put in an impressive appearance. You look like John Wayne and you talk like you know what you're saying, but it's all a facade."

Roebuck was suddenly on his feet. "Listen, you hot air blimp . . . !"

"I'm done listening, Louis. Get out. Your money will be mailed to you."

"I have certain connections with the Mafia," Roebuck said, "and you better know that one word from me can bury you."

Havers was staring at his gleaming desk top.

"You ever hear of Johnny Palermo?" Roebuck asked in a cool voice.

"No, and neither have you, I'd wager."

"Well, he's gonna hear of you, Havers. He's a guy who doesn't take anything off of anybody, and he won't take kindly to one of his friends being treated like this!"

"For God's sake, Louis, leave!"

Roebuck strode to the door. "You'll be hearing from me," he said as he went out.

Downstairs in the street he took a deep breath. He hoped Mary, Havers' secretary, hadn't heard anything of what went on in the office. Roebuck had had his eye on Mary ever since that day she'd winked at him. He used to dream about her a lot, even at home lying next to his wife Alicia.

The buildings towered gray above him, into a gray sky, as Roebuck walked toward the Chase Hotel cocktail lounge. Then, tired of walking, he waved down a cab.

27

"Take me to the Chase right away," he said. "I'm late for a very important high level meeting."

"Right," the cabbie said, infected by the urgency. He pulled out into the traffic. "What kind of meeting is it, if you don't mind me asking?"

"I don't mind," Roebuck said stiffly, "but I'd appreciate it if you wouldn't spread the information around."

The cab eased into the left hand turn lane and picked up speed to make the traffic light.

Perk . . . ! Perk . . . !

Roebuck leaned with both hands on the wash basin and studied his reflection in the bathroom mirror. Crow's feet were beginning to appear around his blue eyes, and his hairline was starting to recede. What the hell, though, he was forty-five years old. That wasn't old and it wasn't young, but it was sure time for a man's hairline to start to recede. The wrinkles, the bags under his eyes, were from the running, from not sleeping enough. He turned his head and looked at his face three quarters, his features automatically set as he would like to see them. His was a noble face, sharp-featured, with a small, manfully hawkish nose and an aggressive, jutting chin. Roebuck smiled and turned back full face. We never see ourselves in the mirror as others see us, he thought, because we know how we are going to look. He stopped smiling and spat onto the mirror, watching the spittle bead and run down. Then he turned and went back into the motel room; He wished he hadn't had to recall that conversation with Havers.

No cups, damn it! Roebuck turned off the flame under the coffeepot and went back into the bathroom and got the paper cup from the toothbrush holder. It would have to do. The woman could use it when he was finished. As he poured the coffee he glanced over at her.

Still asleep, a shapeless mound under the white sheets, tangled wisps of blonde hair. He listened closely to the slow rhythm of her breathing, letting it calm him, steady him. Then he opened the bag of donuts.

They would have to be moving soon, he thought. The car he'd picked up in St. Louis would be safe for another day or two, no more. Then the police might be on to it. He'd get another car, maybe in Denver, maybe a convertible this time. Who'd ever think of looking for him in a convertible, behind sunglasses? Maybe he'd even grow a beard. But no, he looked better without a beard.

Roebuck sipped the bitter coffee, black, as he liked it, a man's drink. It helped him forget that he'd had the dream last night, even after he'd had the woman.

The dream wasn't about Ingrahm's murder (if indeed Ingrahm was dead and if you could call it murder). It was instead the dream of smoke, of flickering light and the hand, heavy on his shoulder. Why should he still dream about it after all these years? He knew the truth. He had convinced himself of the truth.

Outside a truck passed shrilly on the snaking highway.

The woman moaned in her sleep.

2

When Roebuck arrived home from the Chase Hotel cocktail lounge he was drunk. He was not completely drunk, he knew, not sick drunk. But he was drunk enough that he couldn't hide it from Alicia.

He closed the door behind him and looked around, as one might look about oneself in a dream just before waking. Everything spoke of wealth, though not pretentious wealth. Royal blue carpeting flowed over the floor and up the three low steps to the second level. The light fixtures were crystal, the stereo and television built unobtrusively into the paneled east wall. In one corner stood a muted gold sling chair, very modern, like the one that sat in Mr. Havers'—Fred's—living room. The shelf of leather-bound books, the surrealistic oils, the marble inlaid tables, all were the possessions of someone who had arrived at his particular plateau on the way to his somewhere. Seeing it all sway slightly before him, Roebuck stepped forward and slumped onto the long sofa.

Yet another possession of the successful advertising man came out of the kitchen with a martini in her hand. Alicia. She was quite pretty, as she should be, but not too pretty, as she shouldn't be. Like the furnishings of the apartment, which she had paid for, she was expensive but tastefully subdued. Roebuck had acquired her five months ago.

30

Alicia saw that he had had too many, and she casually sipped the martini as if it were hers, though Roebuck knew she had made it for him. Sometimes, through her almost total lack of imagination shone a certain cunning. "You're late," she said, smiling. "Working?" He looked at her without expression. She was at the peak of beauty in a woman, the ripeness; otherwise she wouldn't have been very attractive at all. The lines in her face were still easily softened by makeup, though nothing could soften the disillusioned eyes. Her figure was slender, lithe, like a tennis player's, and she possessed a tennis player's golden tan, for she spent most of her time sunning on the private balcony. She was thirty-five and alone when Roebuck had met her, and he knew that she was soon to be thirty-six and alone. "Not going to answer, huh?" she said. He continued to stare at her, knowing he was about to give her up, or, as he preferred to think of it, throw her back. She was now as unreal as the formless collector's items that hung on his walls, oil and canvas.

"Alicia, Alicia, blonde Alicia, bleached and manicured and sunned to a golden brown. Well done." He laughed and fumbled for a cigarette, lit it.

Alicia sat in the golden sling chair, where she belonged. "I'd say you were drunk."

"You did say it," Roebuck replied. "And if I'm any judge, you're about half right. You mad?"

She laughed. "No, I can forgive that in you once in a while."

"You can forgive me for anything."

"Almost," she said.

Roebuck drew on the just lit cigarette and snuffed it out in an ashtray. "You're dependent on me."

"I am," she said, draining the martini quickly, as if she didn't want him to get any. "I want to be."

31

"I suppose you do," Roebuck said.

"Do you want some coffee?"

"No."

Alicia set the empty cocktail glass on an end table and clasped her hands over a crossed knee. "Something's very wrong, isn't it, Lou?"

"I quit my job."

"How come?" No reaction, no flicker in those drained blue eyes.

"Because I knew that bastard Havers was about to fire me."

"But why would he do that? Your work?"

Roebuck snorted. "I'm one of the best and he knows it. Now it'll serve him right if his company never gets off the ground."

"I thought you got along well with him."

"I did," Roebuck said, "until he found out I was a middle man in a certain firearms deal a few years back."

"Firearms deal?"

"Just my luck," Roebuck said, "that Havers' family is Lebanese—and with a name like Havers! Must have been shortened."

Two fine lines of curiosity rose parallel from the bridge of Alicia's slender nose. "So what if he is Lebanese?"

"When he found out I was involved in a deal to sell guns to the Israelis he blew his stack. He said he'd blackball me from every advertising agency he could."

"That doesn't sound like Mr. Havers."

"Who'd have thought he was Lebanese?"

"Listen," Alicia said, "can't the government do something? I mean, we were behind the Israelis in that thing."

Roebuck shook his head. "The government will deny any knowledge of the deal if the question is put to them. That was

32

part of the arrangement. I wouldn't even be telling you if it weren't for this."

Alicia rose and walked into the kitchen. Roebuck knew she was going to get him some black coffee. She was so damned accommodating! Well, it didn't matter now. She was part of his world that was crumbling, and after paying for the co-op apartment and the furniture she had only about three thousand dollars in the bank. Roebuck's worlds had crumbled before, many times, and though he wouldn't admit it now, even to himself, he knew deep in the core of him that he would rise as before, phoenix-like from the ashes.

"Drink some coffee," Alicia said, returning with cup and saucer. She set the coffee on the table beside Roebuck and walked over to put some soft music on the stereo. The hell of it was that she knew he wanted the coffee.

Roebuck took one long sip and pushed the cup and saucer away. "I don't feel much like coffee," he said.

Alicia shrugged, and the soft Latin music that she liked began to drift from the six speakers spread throughout the apartment. "You can get a job in another city, can't you?" she asked.

"I doubt it. That damn Havers has some pull, even though it is a small company. They stick together. The bastards stick together against a man."

"So what are we going to do?"

"I don't know yet," he answered, and he was wondering where to go.

"Two men called today," Alicia said.

"Two men?"

Alicia nodded. "Bob—" she frowned "—Ingam, or something, and Ben Gipp. They said they were Army friends of yours and they'd only be in town a short while."

Roebuck knew at once who she meant. Ingrahm and Gipp.

He hadn't thought of them in a long time, not since Fort Leonard Wood. "What did you tell them?" he asked.

"I told them I was your wife," Alicia said, "what you were doing, and where you worked. The usual thing."

Roebuck stood and began to pace. "Usual thing! Usual thing!"

"They said they were at the Crest Motel."

"Usual thing!" Roebuck repeated. "Don't you know better than to talk to strangers who say they're out of my past?"

"You didn't say anything."

"You should have known better, after some of the things I've told you about myself."

"For Christ's sake, Lou, they said they were in the Army with you. The one even said he knew you in college."

"Ingrahm," Roebuck said. "You didn't even get his name right. He might not have even been Ingrahm. Did you think of that?"

Alicia sighed. "No. I'm sorry, Lou."

"Sorry, your ass!"

She sat looking at him, the anger whitening her face beneath the healthy tan.

The telephone rang.

Roebuck walked slowly over and answered it.

"Lou?"

Something stirred in the depths of Roebuck's mind.

"Lou Roebuck? This is Ingrahm, Lou. Bob Ingrahm."

"Well . . . how you doing, Bob?" Roebuck lapsed into his "telephone voice." "My wife said you called earlier."

"I bet you were surprised, hey?"

"You know I was."

"Benny's with me. Benny Gipp. You remember him, don't you?"

"Sure I do," Roebuck said. Was Ingrahm crazy? "How long you going to be in town?"

"Have to leave tomorrow. Benny and I are partners in a construction supply business, and we have to get back to Little Rock. We're here on business anyway, and we both shouldn't have come."

There was a pause.

"We went by where you work," Ingrahm said, "but you weren't there. We waited a while; then we had to leave."

Roebuck felt the blood rush hot to his face. So that was it! That's how Havers had gotten all those ideas about him.

"Lou?"

"Yeah, I'm still here."

"We're staying at the Crest . . . on Atkins Road."

"I know where it is."

"How about coming by tonight for a drink or two? We can meet you in the lounge. Old time's sake and all that."

Roebuck's grip on the receiver tightened. "Okay, Bob. About nine?"

"'Right. It's been a while. Maybe you better wear a red carnation."

Roebuck hung up.

"See." Alicia smiled from across the room. "No harm done."

Things were happening quickly, quickly. "Shut up," Roebuck said. He pressed his fingertips to his temples.

"Don't talk to me like that," Alicia said in an even voice. "They were who they said they were. It didn't matter what I told them."

"It might have."

"Listen, Lou!" Alicia was on her feet, moving toward him. "Don't take your frustrations out on me!"

"You could get me killed!" Roebuck almost shouted at

her. "Don't you understand that, you stupid bitch!"

"Oh, Christ, Lou, I'm fed up to here! You and your bullshit—"

He slapped her hard, high on the face across the cheekbone, before he even thought.

She stood staring at him, unafraid, very pale except for the red mark across her cheek, her eyes very steady.

Roebuck backed up a step.

"I don't hit women . . . you know I don't."

Alicia might have smiled—or was she trying not to smile? "You just did, Lou." She turned, walked into the bedroom, and closed the door softly and deliberately. He heard the lock click.

"I don't hit women," Roebuck repeated to himself in a low whisper. He stared at the blank expanse of closed door. "You go to hell!" he shouted suddenly. Then he remembered, that the expensive apartment was practically soundproof. "To hell with you!"

He spun on his heel in the soft carpet and went into the kitchen. The shaker-full of martinis was in the refrigerator. He poured himself a drink in a water glass from the cabinet above the sink.

"To hell with her," he said to himself as he leaned back against the breakfast bar. He finished the drink in three long swallows, picked up the shaker to pour another, then set it back down.

As Roebuck was walking across the living room toward the front door, he realized he still had the empty glass in his hand. He stood still for a moment, then in a magnificent flurry of rage hurled the glass at the closed bedroom door. Instead of shattering as he had imagined, it merely bounced off the wood with a dull thunk. He thought of picking it up and throwing it again, then he decided against it and stalked to the door.

None of his neighbors were in the hall. He walked swiftly to the elevator, stepped inside, and pushed the button for the garage. His hands clasped and unclasped on the steel wall rail as the elevator descended seven floors to the basement.

His black Thunderbird was parked where he had left it, shining jewel-like in the dim basement garage. Thirty more payments, Roebuck thought as he walked toward the car with echoing footsteps. He laughed to himself as he opened the door and settled back in the soft leather upholstery.

The engine caught immediately as he turned the ignition, and tires squealed as the big car shot toward the closed garage door, then braked to a halt. The power window on the driver's side lowered smoothly and Roebuck inserted the key with which all the building tenants were provided into the small metal box on the post near the door. The overhead door went up slowly as he twisted the key, and the Thunderbird roared out into the warm evening mist. As he turned the corner onto Twelfth Avenue, Roebuck hurled the key out the window and heard it bounce off the wet pavement.

Roebuck drove idly down Twelfth Avenue, listening to the rhythm of the Thunderbird's wipers as they swept the mist from the wide windshield. He looked at the dashboard clock. Seven forty-five. Not too early to drive to his meeting with Ingrahm and Gipp. The Crest Motel was way on the other side of town, almost an hour's drive if he stayed at the speed limit.

Making a careful left turn on the slick pavement, Roebuck thought of the last time he'd seen Ingrahm. It had been how long . . . ? Almost ten years ago in Little Rock, when Roebuck had been there and on impulse had looked up Ingrahm in the phone book. He hadn't seen Gipp in over twenty years, but

Roebuck remembered him. Gipp was one of those people who stuck in your memory, like a tiny splinter imbedded deep in the flesh of your hand, felt only when you bent a finger a certain way.

Twenty years . . . that was a long time. Odd that they even remembered each other, or cared if they did remember. The three of them hadn't really been friends in the true sense of the word. It was the Army that threw them together. The Army will do that to people. And the truth was that the three of them were misfits in one way or another, and misfits will band together, especially in the Army.

They were clear in Roebuck's mind now, Ingrahm, tall, slender, even-featured, with dark hair brushed straight back. Gipp had been a little man, with rimless glasses that were forever catching the light in front of his pale gray eyes. A little man, but with a curious hardness about him, in the sure movements of his square, bony hands, in his walk, in the muscular line of his jaw, but most of all in the way he looked at people. There had been an unyielding directness to Gipp's stare, as if he were looking at an inanimate object instead of a person.

Roebuck had known Ingrahm in college, where they were both journalism majors before the Army claimed them. They hadn't known each other well, and in fact from what Roebuck had seen of Ingrahm at college he hadn't liked him very much. There was a conceited self-assurance about the man, and a slyly depreciative way of talking that in a woman one might describe as cattiness.

Ingrahm had been like that in the Army too, always cutting people down in his subtle, smiling way. The only man who hadn't fallen victim to his cunning devaluation had been Gipp, and that might have been because Gipp practically worshiped Ingrahm, and Ingrahm needed that.

Gipp seemed to have admired Ingrahm's smooth charm, his ease with other people. Gipp himself was a strange type of man, remote. He had wanted to be an artist of some kind, Roebuck remembered, a sculptor. And then later he'd decided to become an accountant. That was damn odd, Roebuck thought, that a man who wanted to sculpt would suddenly turn to something as dry as accounting. But then Gipp was damn odd.

For all the time the three of them had spent together Roebuck never got to know Gipp well. Even when talking about the most personal subjects Gipp seemed to be drawn into himself, as if there were something about himself that he would not share or reveal. Roebuck had always had the feeling that Gipp vaguely resented him.

Eight months was all the time they spent at that miserably cold camp, with its lettered streets and its drab buildings with their hand-fired furnaces. The unit was transferred out then, just after Roebuck was given his discharge after cursing out that asinine colonel in the canteen.

Roebuck smiled as he thought of that. What had been the colonel's name? Tarkington, that was it. Colonel Tarkington had been surprised when Private Roebuck stepped right in front of him in the line to the cash register.

"In a hurry, Private?"

"If I wasn't, sir, I wouldn't have taken your place in line."

"That's not the way we act in this man's Army, Private."

"Your Army, sir, not this man's Army."

The canteen had suddenly quieted as everyone realized what was happening.

"What's your name, Private?"

"Duck, sir. Donald Duck."

There had been no laughter, no reaction at all from the rest of the men in the canteen.

The colonel had stared at Roebuck for a full half minute in disbelief and anger.

It was Roebuck who ended the silence.

"Screw you, Colonel."

The colonel started to answer, then spun and walked out the door.

Gradually conversation picked up again, with a few brief uneasy glances at Roebuck. Well, Roebuck knew what he could do, he knew how to get out of this man's Army.

At one of the tables sat a sergeant he had always disliked, a big, beefy ex-policeman with a tendency to bully. Roebuck purchased a chocolate malted milk, then he walked to the sergeant's table, from an angle where he wouldn't be noticed, and calmly poured the malted milk down the sergeant's back.

The sergeant sat very still for a moment, and Roebuck watched the back of his thick neck color. Then, with hardly a backward glance, the sergeant elbowed Roebuck once, hard, in the stomach as he stood. Roebuck crumpled.

"Sorry, Private," the sergeant said, standing over him. "I sure didn't see you there." The MPs had to carry Roebuck out. There had been a long confinement and long sessions with a battery of Army psychiatrists who didn't know enough not to disagree among themselves. Roebuck had refused to cooperate with them, of course, and he'd derived a lot of pleasure from observing their ceaseless disagreements. Then there had been a quick and formal court-martial, a suspended sentence, and a medical discharge. Roebuck had fooled them. He was free.

Roebuck noticed suddenly that he was driving faster, and he slowed and pulled to the inside lane. After a while he turned down the ramp to the section of state highway that led to Atkins Road. A green road sign told him he was driving toward the airport. The Crest Motel was very close to the airport. No doubt Ingrahm and Gipp had flown in from Little Rock.

A jet roared overhead, and Roebuck caught a glimpse of blinking lights above him through the mist. His hands tightened on the steering wheel. Driving the car was something like flying a jet, he thought, as he sat back in his bucket seat and read the softly lighted dials on the dashboard. He listened to the diminishing roar of the plane as he watched the wet road between swipes of the wiper blade. It was like flying on instruments, in a way.

The exit ramp to Atkins Road loomed ahead of him as he flicked on his highlights and prepared to make a careful, precision turn.

3

Roebuck backed the car into a space in the Crest Motel Lounge's parking lot and walked quickly through the dampness to the side door. He looked about him as he entered. There were perhaps a dozen people seated at booths or tables, and four or five men at the bar. Though he was sure they wouldn't appear as they had so many years ago, Roebuck was reasonably certain that no one in the lounge could be either Ingrahm or Gipp. The dampness outside seemed suddenly remote from the lounge's warmth and opulence. Roebuck walked to the bar and mounted a stool.

"Bourbon and water," he said to the bleached blonde barmaid who came to take his order. "And make it double strong, honey."

She glanced halfway back over her shoulder and he glimpsed the flattered look of mock annoyance on her heavily made-up face. She was about Alicia's age, her mid-thirties, and her figure was just beginning to go. She would look like hell in another five years, Roebuck thought, but she wasn't half bad now.

"Bourbon and water," the blonde repeated, setting the glass in front of him.

"Thanks, honey." He flicked a five-dollar bill from his wallet and laid it on the bar.

"You know, you look something like John Wayne," she said as she returned his change.

"Matter of fact," Roebuck said, "I used to be his double in a few movies. Of course, that was some years back."

"No kidding!" The blonde was obviously impressed, but she had to move off to take another customer's order. Then the red-vested bartender called her over to the other side of the large lounge where they sat in a booth and began talking about something in the evening paper. Another bartender took over behind the bar. An excess of help, Roebuck thought. Apparently the weather was hurting the Crest Lounge's business.

He sat sipping his drink, half listening to the drone of conversation around him, and his eyes were drawn to his reflection in the back bar mirror. Sad that a man had to get older, he thought, that the machine had to wear down. Things didn't change that much on the inside, or the outside, for that matter. Sometimes it came to Roebuck in brief flickers of thought that he had the same aspirations and dreams that he'd had as a boy, that the world was essentially the same, that nothing really changed while his reflection was aging in the mirror.

A hand touched his shoulder gently and he jumped, spilling part of his drink.

"How are things, Lou?"

It was Ingrahm, thinner-haired, older, more lined, but it was Ingrahm.

They shook hands. "You look good, Bob," Roebuck said.

"Thanks."

There was a silence as each man studied the apparition from his past.

"The Kid's over at a table," Ingrahm said, motioning with his hand.

So Ingrahm still called Gipp "the Kid." It had been a long time since Roebuck had heard that. They walked across the lounge toward the small, hard-looking man seated at a table by the wall.

Gipp stood as they approached and shook Roebuck's hand. Even the faint light of the lounge was captured in his rimless spectacles.

"You were right," Gipp said to Ingrahm.

"Sure," Ingrahm said. "I told you it was him. I recognized him by the boots."

"So you still wear cowboy boots, huh?" Gipp said, and all three men looked down at the polished toes of Roebuck's Western boots.

"Most comfortable thing there is," Roebuck said.

"I remember now." Ingrahm smiled. "They had a hell of a time getting them away from you in the Army. Threatened to throw you in the stockade or something."

"Good memory," Roebuck said. "A lieutenant and myself made a little deal about me giving up my boots. You didn't see me on KP too often after that, did you?"

"Come to think of it, I didn't." Ingrahm winked at Gipp, who was smiling mechanically.

The blonde barmaid came over and they sat down and ordered. Ingrahm and Gipp had martinis and Roebuck ordered another bourbon and water.

"You sure don't look like you did when you were eighteen or nineteen," Ingrahm said to Roebuck.

"A long time ago," Roebuck said. "But we saw each other in Little Rock ten years ago. That's probably why you recognized me so easy."

"Probably." Ingrahm sipped his drink, smiling around the rim of the glass.

Ingrahm would be about forty-seven now, Roebuck

thought, and Gipp about the same age. Both men a bit older than himself.

They made the usual small talk for a while, recalled the mutual memories, and then the mutual memories seemed to run out. There was a pause.

"We went by where you work," Gipp said.

"My wife told me."

"They didn't know who we meant when we asked for you," Ingrahm said. "They had you mixed up with some kind of war hero or something."

There was a cold feeling in the pit of Roebuck's stomach, and he suddenly realized how much he'd always hated Ingrahm. He cleared his throat. "You fellas didn't see any action, did you?"

"The war was almost over," Ingrahm said. "The story of my life. The Kid here got in on the Battle of the Bulge, though. Transferred out of the company and won himself a Silver Star, not to mention two Purple Hearts."

"That's right," Roebuck said. "You mentioned that in Little Rock."

Gipp was looking neither embarrassed nor proud as he lifted his glass to his lips. "What was your heroic act?" Roebuck asked.

"Surviving," Gipp answered flatly.

"Ah, modesty," Ingrahm said. "The Kid got mad over there and killed four Germans in a machine gun nest all by himself, then he took over the machine gun and he and a German tank had a run-in."

"You won, I take it," Roebuck said, wishing immediately that the envy and admiration hadn't sounded in his voice.

"I delayed the tank long enough for a bazooka team to knock it out," Gipp said.

"Where'd you go after you got your medical discharge?" Ingrahm asked.

"Back to school for a while," Roebuck said. "Studied advertising. I held several interesting jobs."

"You must have a good job now." Ingrahm searched his pockets for cigarettes, found them. Gipp lit one for him with a silver lighter. "We talked for a long time with that office manager . . ." He looked thoughtful. "What's his name?"

"George King?"

"That's it! He told us a lot about you when he found out we were old Army buddies."

And I'll bet you told him a pack of lies about me, Roebuck thought, taking a long swallow from his glass. "As a matter of fact," he said, "I quit that job today. Had my mind made up for a long time."

Ingrahm looked surprised. "How come?"

Roebuck shrugged. "Greener pastures. I've had a position offered me in the advertising department of General Motors."

"That's great."

"What's this business you guys have got going?" Roebuck asked, to change the subject.

"Construction supply," Gipp said. "We sell supplies to individual homeowners as well as subcontractors."

"Sounds profitable."

"It's growing," Ingrahm said. "Almost more than the Kid and I can keep up with." Ingrahm and Gipp exchanged glances and Gipp flashed his antiseptic smile.

Roebuck felt a strange current in the air, the old resentment, as if he were an intruder. He wondered why they had bothered to call him. There was something compulsive, something sadistic, in Ingrahm's personality. And as for himself, Roebuck, did he secretly enjoy Ingrahm's verbal lashings? Why had he bothered to come here if he didn't?

"I wish we had time to meet the wife," Ingrahm said. "She

sounded nice on the phone." There was a special emphasis on the word "nice."

Roebuck felt the hate for Ingrahm spreading in him as he sat calmly sipping his drink. "To tell you the truth," he said casually, "we're separated."

"A shame," Ingrahm said, and Gipp nodded agreement.

Roebuck made a futile gesture with his hands. "We weren't getting along; I wasn't home enough; she was jealous . . ."

"Anything we can do to help?" Ingrahm asked. "Money or something?"

"No," Roebuck said quickly, "I'm doing all right." He felt the blood rush to his face and he saw Gipp watching him from behind the thick glasses.

Roebuck cleared his throat. "Either of you fellas ever get married?"

"No," Gipp said, not smiling, "neither of us." He looked slowly away and raised his arm to glance at his wristwatch. "We've got that call coming," he said.

"Hey, that's right," Ingrahm answered. "Damn near forgot all about it." He turned to Roebuck. "We've got a business call due in five minutes that we'd better take in our room." There was apology in his voice.

"Sure." Roebuck drained his glass with finality.

"You want to join us in our room for a drink or something?" Ingrahm asked.

From the corner of his eye Roebuck saw Gipp shift uncomfortably. "Thanks, no," he said, setting down his glass. "I have to be going anyway. Got an appointment up in north county with a little gal whose husband works nights." He winked broadly as he stood.

"It's the same Roebuck." Ingrahm laughed as he and Gipp stood in perfect unison, as if they'd heard a silent command.

"Maybe we can get together later," Roebuck said without enthusiasm. "You fellas got a car?" He didn't think they would have a car, staying so near the airport, but Ingrahm nodded.

"We rented one," he said. He grinned. "Tax deductible. The thing is, though, that we have to leave tomorrow morning. That's why we called you this evening."

"That's too bad," Roebuck said. He stood awkwardly, leaning with one hand on the back of his chair. "Well, next time you're in town . . . call again." He began to back away.

"Sure," Gipp said. "Take care."

Ingrahm waved lightly with his right hand. "Do it once for me."

"What?"

"The little housewife in north county." Ingrahm winked.

"Oh, sure." Roebuck smiled and turned. He felt their eyes on his back as he walked toward the door, felt their silent laughter rocking the lounge. He hoped the back of his neck wasn't red, hoped they couldn't see that.

Outside, Roebuck sat in his car with the engine idling, watching the light rain drift downward onto the parking lot. The blinking neon sign shot glowing colors softly through the mist. Roebuck couldn't make himself drive away as he sat breathing quickly, feeling the hate for Ingrahm fill him. It was Ingrahm who had brought his world down about him, Ingrahm with his cutting voice, his evil, making things seem worse than they really were. Roebuck shut his eyes tightly and tried to calm himself. Only once before had he experienced such hatred, and it frightened him as well as enraged him. He let the hatred boil darkly in him, boil over until it was released through his rapid breathing and his trembling hands.

Then, for some reason, he opened his eyes.

Ingrahm was there, standing in the parking lot just outside the lounge's side door. He didn't see Roebuck as he flicked his cigarette away and began walking across the lot toward another line of parked cars, apparently to get something out of one of them.

He passed directly in front of Roebuck, and there was a sound, a grating, roaring sound in Roebuck's ears. Instantly, in a somehow unrelated way, Roebuck knew that what he was hearing was the spinning of the Thunderbird's rear tires in the wet gravel of the parking lot. Ingrahm turned curiously, and then the curiosity changed to surprise as the headlights flashed on, and he held an arm over his eyes. He grew larger and larger and he extended both hands, palms out, as if he could hold back the roaring tons of metal. Then he disappeared.

There was no sound, no feeling of arrested motion. Ingrahm had simply disappeared before Roebuck's eyes and the car was stopped a hundred feet from where it had been parked.

In a daze, Roebuck put the car in reverse and backed around so that it was pointed toward the exit. He looked out the side window and saw Gipp, poised in the lounge doorway, the neon sign glinting redly from his glasses. His heart pounding against his ribs, Roebuck stepped down on the accelerator. For a horrible instant the car sat motionless while the wheels spun, hurling pebbles against the insides of the fenders. Roebuck got an impression in the rear view mirror of Gipp running, of Ingrahm lying sprawled on his back, and as the tires dug deep enough for traction and the car shot way, Roebuck thought that through the mist he saw Ingrahm raise one leg slowly, almost lazily, and then lower it.

Roebuck turned off Atkins Road and made himself slow to the speed limit. He was trembling: his hands, his feet, his arms, even the flesh of his face. What now? What now? What now? he asked himself over and over in time with his racing heart.

It was a long time before he stopped trembling, and though it was warm outside he turned on the car heater. He hadn't meant to run Ingrahm down, not really. Why, he'd hardly seen him in the darkness. Anyway, the man wasn't dead, only hurt, only hurt. Didn't he move? Hadn't Roebuck seen him raise his leg in the rear view mirror? Maybe the wheels hadn't even touched him.

Roebuck felt a wave of relief at the thought that Ingrahm might not be hurt badly at all. Still, he was in trouble. He had run a man down and then left the scene of the . . . accident. Did it matter that much? Didn't Roebuck want to leave town anyway? He would run, tonight, now, and eventually it would be forgotten. There would be a tiny piece on page five of the paper, that's all—if it even made the papers.

Money was the question. Where could he get the money to run? He had only fifty dollars in his wallet, and he couldn't go back to the apartment. The police might even be there, making their routine inquiries. Then he remembered that he still had a key to the office of Havers Advertising, and that over two hundred dollars "emergency money" was kept in a box in Havers' secretary's desk. Roebuck turned toward the highway that led downtown, feeling better now that he had a plan of action. He knew that Havers might still be in his office, working late as he often did, but he chose not even to consider that possibility. Right now, to Roebuck, fifty-fifty chances seemed safe enough.

4

The woman sat straight up in bed. The white sheet hung for a moment, then slipped down to reveal her bare breasts. Through sleep-filled eyes she saw Roebuck, sipping his coffee from a paper cup, a half-eaten donut in his hand. Instinctively, but without a trace of embarrassment, she pulled the sheet back up and clutched it near her throat.

"What time is it?"

"Seven or so." Roebuck watched her as he washed down a mouthful of donut with his coffee.

"I better get up, I guess."

Roebuck nodded.

The woman turned and sat on the edge of the mattress, still clutching the sheet. She was facing away from Roebuck, and he could see her partially exposed round buttocks spreading and meeting the softness of the mattress. He could see the red marks on her that he'd made last night. She let the sheet fall and gathered up her underclothes from the floor. Nakedly slender, but without the grace of youth, she walked into the bathroom.

From behind the closed door came the squeak of a turned faucet handle and the abrupt splash of shower water onto the steel tub. Roebuck heard the tone of the splashing water change as she stepped beneath the shower.

51

When she emerged from the bathroom she was wearing her panties and bra, and she moved to the side of the bed and slipped still wet feet into her low heeled shoes. Her short blonde hair was combed roughly now, over a pretty, somewhat angular face, strongly boned yet very feminine. There was a strange serenity in the depths of her green flecked eyes, in the slightly upward curve of her wide mouth.

"We forgot to buy cups yesterday," Roebuck said.

She seemed amused as she went to the bureau mirror and began to apply makeup. "Breakfast here will still be better than at those roadside grease houses, with you all nervous and jumping every time somebody walks through the door. 'Course there's plenty to make you nervous, with the police after you and all."

"Plenty," Roebuck agreed.

As she spoke she applied eyebrow pencil carefully. "Too bad there weren't any more witnesses."

"My luck," Roebuck said.

"You sure you shouldn't turn yourself in, try to explain . . . ?"

Roebuck shook his head violently. "Who'd believe it was an accident? The only one who saw it was that damned Gipp, and he'd lie. He hates my guts because I didn't try to save his life at the Bulge, but I had to think of the safety of the platoon . . ." His voice hardened. "If Ingrahm really is dead, I wouldn't have a chance."

"I guess you're right."

Roebuck stood and paced to the window, peering out between the cracks in the Venetian blind at the heightening sun. The early morning sky was cloudless, and long shadows were beginning to form. Somewhere in the Jolly Rest Motel a door slammed and he heard the faint laughter of a child.

"Do you think this Gipp character is really after us too?"

"I know him," Roebuck said. "He's after us. I'll bet when he heard that bulletin about us being spotted in Collinsville he drove all night. I'll bet the bastard doesn't even sleep."

"He's why you bought the guns?"

"Among other reasons." Roebuck tucked his thumbs in his belt. "A man never knows when a revolver's going to come in handy." He'd bought the two secondhand pistols at a run-down hardware store in Illinois, and he wasn't even sure they'd fire.

The woman was replacing her makeup articles in a black purse atop the bureau. "I've been thinking," she said, "we could go to my brother's place in California."

"The guitar player?"

"He's a poet too," she said with a trace of indignation. "He's sensitive and smart; he'll understand and put us up for a while."

"Maybe we'll see him when we get to the Coast," Roebuck said noncommittally. "I've got some important friends there, though, and I was thinking about forged passports and a trip to the South Seas. Maybe your brother could even go with us."

She smiled, as if dismissing that as completely impossible.

Roebuck wondered why she'd decided to come with him. She was just a small town tramp, but still attractive. Why would she want to make herself a fugitive? He'd told her the hard facts, though he hadn't told her the only reason he wanted her with him was so he'd attract less suspicion. A man and his wife taking a trip, and if it came to a chase the police might think she was a hostage and not fire on the car.

"Ellie." He said her name aloud. "I told you what you were stepping into."

She snapped her compact closed. "I've stepped in worse. I don't have any regrets about coming with you. Anyway, I could walk right out that door if I wanted to."

With an uneasy feeling Roebuck realized that she was right. Maybe she did fall that hard for him. It had happened before. There were some women who got hooked on a man like that. And Ellie held an undeniable fascination for him. There was something about the way she put complete faith in him, obeyed him immediately and without question. He was glad now that he'd decided to bring her with him. It was the one lucky thing that had happened to him in the past week.

"Get dressed," Roebuck said suddenly, turning again to the window. "You can eat in the car. I want to put some miles behind us today."

She began to slip into the pink dress she'd bought in St. Louis. "I can be ready in two minutes."

5

Roebuck pulled to the curb in front of the building in which Havers Advertising was located. Glancing up and down the still busy street, he tried to look nonchalant as he walked toward the building entrance. Then he cursed and went back to put a nickel in the parking meter. There was no sense in leaving documented proof in the form of a parking ticket that he'd been here. He went back to the building entrance, drew his key case from his pocket, and, with the key that Havers had forgotten to ask him for, he unlocked one of the double doors and entered.

The lobby was deserted, the tile floor still littered with dark scuff marks and cigarette butts. The clank of a mop and scrub bucket sounded loudly from one of the downstairs halls. Roebuck walked quickly to the elevators and punched the "up" button.

As he closed the door of the anteroom behind him, Roebuck smiled. Mary's desk sat before him, everything in order, her electric typewriter neatly covered. There was no sound from the offices of Havers Advertising.

It was as easy as he thought it would be. Mary's desk drawer was unlocked, and he lifted the metal box from it and set it on the desk top. The box too was unlocked. The money was under some blank papers, neatly rolled and held by a thick rubber band. He counted. A hundred and fifty-two dollars. Not as much as he'd hoped for, but it would have to do.

He was closing the metal lid of the box when the door to the inner office opened with a slight sound and Havers looked out.

"Louis! What the devil are you doing here?" But even as he asked the question Havers' eyes went from the metal box to the open desk drawer to the stack of bills on the desk.

Roebuck was frightened, but he grinned as best he could. "I needed an advance on my salary," he said.

Havers was looking at him with disgust. "I told you I'd mail you your check."

"I needed it right away. Some bills to pay."

"I suggest you return the money to the drawer," Havers said, "and I won't call the police."

Roebuck stood very still. He was remembering the wall safe behind the bookcase in Havers' office. Perhaps it wasn't such bad luck that Havers had decided to work late. Roebuck picked up the stack of bills, folded them, and slipped them into his pocket. He could see Havers tighten.

Havers turned and walked back into his office and Roebuck followed.

"Open the safe," Roebuck said.

"There's nothing of value in it, Louis." Havers sat behind his desk, resting his hands lightly on the wide spread of polished walnut as if to give himself confidence. "I'd leave if I were you."

"Either open the safe or tell me the combination," Roebuck demanded, the edge of desperation creeping into his voice.

Havers' lips were quivering as he stood to face Roebuck across the desk. "Leave, Louis, or I shall call the police and have you arrested. Leave with the few hundred dollars. I'm giving you a chance."

"You'll give me the combination," Roebuck said, his voice breaking.

Havers' right hand moved toward the telephone as Roebuck's fingers curled about the heavy cut glass paperweight on the desk corner. As the tips of Havers' fingers touched the receiver, Roebuck hurled the paperweight with all his might.

The heavy paperweight caught Havers low in the stomach and he sagged to the floor without a sound. "Sorry, Private," Roebuck said, and he giggled. He didn't know why he giggled and he was immediately angry with himself as he walked around the desk and looked down at Havers writhing on the floor, fighting for breath. Roebuck picked up the paperweight, held it threateningly over Havers, and lowered his voice an octave. "The combination!" he demanded. "I've killed eleven men in my time, and I might as well make it an even dozen."

Havers struggled to speak, gasping, but no words forced themselves out.

"The combination!" Roebuck almost screamed.

". . . Thirty . . . right . . . seventeen, left . . . twenty-five . . . right . . ." Havers was sitting back against the wall, clutching his stomach, his face a sickly gray.

Roebuck went to the wrought iron bookcase and scooped the books from the third shelf to reveal the small wall safe behind them. He worked the combination.

Seventeen hundred dollars in cash, and some signed blank checks. The rest useless papers.

Roebuck stuffed the money into his pockets, then he sat at Havers' desk and filled in one of the checks for three hundred dollars. He blew on the check to dry the ink, folded it neatly, and put it in his shirt pocket. Now he needed time.

Roebuck pulled Havers to his feet and shoved him roughly into the desk chair. He removed Havers' tie and used it to bind his hands behind him. Havers' shoelaces were used to bind his feet. Roebuck went back to the anteroom and got some heavy sealing tape from Mary's desk, which he used to cover Havers' mouth. Then, as a precaution, he wrapped the brown tape tightly around the knots he'd tied and around Havers' ankles. Havers was sitting still in the chair, breathing deeply and evenly through his nose, his eyes open wide and following Roebuck's every move. Roebuck yanked the telephone cord from the wall and left.

They knew Roebuck at the Chase Hotel cocktail lounge, so they cashed his three-hundred-dollar check without question. He had a quick drink to avoid any suspicion, then walked out and got in his car. He drove for the highway, heading west out of the city.

Roebuck had driven for five hours without stopping, and he was tired. Once he'd even dozed behind the wheel, to awaken seconds later in the wrong lane with a horn blaring at him and headlights bearing down on him. He'd swerved just in time to avoid the truck, but the memory of the blinding lights and the rocking rush of air as the truck roared past was still very much with him. He had to rest.

He slowed the car as his lights picked up a side road ahead, dark and without a road sign. He turned up the road, drove for a few minutes to get away from the highway, then pulled the car off the road into some trees and turned off the engine.

Roebuck pushed the headlight switch and sat in the sudden darkness, the sudden silence. There wasn't much of a moon, and the night pressed softly against the windows of the car on all sides. Miles away, to his left, were a few tiny yellow lights, almost like stars but too low on the horizon. Roebuck was alone.

There hadn't been anything on the radio about him. Maybe Havers was still tied up; maybe Ingrahm was uninjured and hadn't even reported the accident to the police; maybe the police had made their routine investigation and then concentrated on more important crimes, on murders, rapes, bank robberies, and cunning embezzlements. Roebuck let himself slump sideways across the bucket seats and closed his eyes. He noticed now that the crickets were chirping, very loud, but somehow this only intensified the silence and induced him to sleep.

Roebuck was choking. Around him was a flickering reddish glare, an ebbing and flowing dark haze, and he was choking. And there was a horror, and a scream that he had heard, or was about to hear. On his lips? On someone else's lips? He was blinded, and he was choking, and the hand, large and with a talon-like strength, rested on his shoulder near his neck. The hand began to squeeze, gently at first, then with an increasing pressure that brought pain, pain that grew, cutting through the flesh and muscle of his shoulder, through the bone, paralyzing him, making him want to twist away—to scream!

He awoke.

The morning sun was high in a blue sky, beating through the windshield as if through a magnifying glass, hurting Roebuck's eyes, causing his head to throb painfully. The leather of the car seat was pressed into his cheek, and his neck was stiff from the unnatural angle of his head. Slowly, stiffly, he sat up in the driver's seat. He pressed his palms to the sides of his head, as if that would help the throbbing, then he rubbed his eyes and took a deep breath. Checking his hair in the rear view mirror, he saw that it was hardly mussed, that he'd slept so soundly he'd hardly moved. He opened the car door and got out to stand on the grass.

Roebuck stretched and looked around. He was behind a grove of trees, off a dirt road, on the edge of a large meadow that sloped gradually downward for about three hundred yards, then upward to end at the edge of some woods. Far away was a cluster of white buildings on a rise, probably farm buildings, the lights he'd noticed last night.

Roebuck looked at his watch, then stood quietly twisting the winding stem. Eleven-thirty. He'd slept later than he'd planned. It was time to move. Smoothing his wrinkled slacks, he got back into the car and started the engine.

As Roebuck turned back onto the highway he checked the gas gauge and saw that he was down to a quarter of a tank. Making a mental note to stop at the next service station, he flicked on the radio and tuned in some music.

He was listening idly to the radio, hardly paying attention, when suddenly he became aware of what a newscaster was talking about.

". . . After allegedly murdering Mr. Ingrahm, he drove to the offices of his former employer, Havers Advertising, and burglarized the safe, leaving Fred Havers, president of the company, bound and gagged in his office. Police say an intensive search is now underway for Roebuck.

"In Paris . . ."

Roebuck turned off the radio.

So Ingrahm was dead. Roebuck's eyes were fixed straight ahead on the road, watching the receding mirages of shimmering sunlight on the distant pavement.

Or was he dead?

It could be a trick, contrived by Havers. Ingrahm didn't have any close family. Before releasing such a story, the authorities could easily have contacted his friends and assured them that Ingrahm was really alive. It wouldn't be the first time the police had released a false story to capture a fugitive.

And Havers had the pull to convince them they should try things his way, for him.

But why would they want Roebuck to think he was wanted for murder?

Roebuck snorted, his mouth twisting into a faint grin.

So he'd give himself up, of course. No fool would surrender himself over a common robbery, but not many men wanted to run the rest of their lives from a murder charge; not many men had the nerve.

Roebuck cursed Havers as he drove. The old bastard was mistaken if he thought he'd have the last laugh. Roebuck would see to that.

A small service station appeared ahead, one of those one-pump combination grocery stores and stations that sat lazily on the edge of the highway. Roebuck turned in and stopped the car by a faded red pump.

A boy of about nineteen came slowly out of the white frame building. He wore an Army fatigue cap and there was a wrench stuck in the belt of his jeans. "Yes, sir?"

"Fill her up with ethyl," Roebuck said, getting out of the car.

As the attendant unscrewed the gas cap of the Thunderbird, Roebuck walked to the ever-present Coke machine and inserted a dime. Not much of a breakfast, he thought, but it might help his headache. He stood in the sun sipping the thick, cold liquid, listening to the measured rumbling of the ancient pump. As he raised the chilled bottle to his lips, it suddenly occurred to him that he was taking a big chance even stopping for gas in the Thunderbird. Had the young attendant heard the entire newscast? Had he heard a description of the car? He hadn't acted strangely. Or was he staring at Roebuck now, out of the corner of his eye as he wiped the windshield?

Roebuck drained the Coke and got back in the car. "Six-fifty, sir."

Roebuck slipped seven dollars into the grease-lined palm. "Keep the change. I'm in a hurry to address a convention of osteopaths."

"Thank you, sir." There was nothing unusual in the tone of voice.

As Roebuck drove away he watched carefully in the rear view mirror. The attendant didn't stand and stare after him. He was walking back into the frame building, tucking his shirttail into his jeans. Roebuck breathed easier.

Now he stayed off the highways as much as possible, taking instead the winding side roads, using a road map to navigate.

Just over the Illinois state line, Roebuck stole a car. It was amazingly simple. He parked in the lot of one of those roadside shopping centers, with a dime store, drugstore, grocery store, cleaners, and so on all in a row. Then he removed everything that could identify him from the glove compartment and put it in his pockets. In five minutes of walking casually about the lot he found four cars with the keys left in the ignition. He chose a late-model green sedan, the most unnoticeable car he could find. No one gave him a second glance as he pulled out onto the highway and sped away.

It was almost seven o'clock when he saw the flashing neon sign: FAY'S RESTAURANT AND LOUNGE. He had to stop and eat sometime, and he could use a drink for sure. Fay's was as good a place as any.

Remembering the stolen license plates, Roebuck took care to back the car into a remote parking space behind Fay's Restaurant.

6

Roebuck had eaten two roast beef sandwiches with the quick, sharp hunger of a hunted man. The food in Fay's Restaurant had been surprisingly good, making him relax for the first time since he'd begun to run. He had an after-dinner cigarette, savoring each deep inhalation, then he paid for his dinner and walked into the lounge half of Fay's establishment. He would allow himself the luxury of a drink.

The lounge was small, dim, with the mass-produced plushness of overstuffed vinyl booths and a long padded bar. Most of the illumination came from a lighted rectangular beer sign, with a pretty blonde in a bikini water skiing across the lighted panel in successive jerks, a fixed smile on her face, her arm raised in a fixed wave. As Roebuck watched she disappeared off the edge of the sign and reappeared at the other edge, moving jerkily in the same direction. Roebuck paid no particular attention to the other five or six customers in the lounge as he sat at the bar and ordered his drink from a friendly-looking fat bartender. He noticed a piece of friction tape covering a tear in the vinyl bar padding near his stool.

He was working on his drink slowly, listening to the soft music from the gigantic jukebox, when the woman approached with a faint rustling of skirt and nylon and sat next to him.

"Do we know each other?" she asked, unabashed by the ancient ineptness of the line.

Roebuck studied her short, carefully disarranged blonde hair, her strongly boned face with its pretty scimitar lips. She was about thirty-three, well-built and dressed to show it, and she had the resigned, amused, searching look of an experienced prostitute.

"I don't think so," Roebuck said, hesitant to get involved in anything just then.

The woman continued to appraise him with her gray-green eyes as the bartender approached and stood expectantly before them.

"What do you drink?" Roebuck finally asked the woman.

"Highball, sweet soda." The bartender turned without even having to listen to the end of her order. "I know what it is," she said. "You look like John Wayne enough to be his brother."

Roebuck grinned at her. "I used to double for him in the movies a while back."

"Doing what?"

"Stunt man," Roebuck said without hesitation. "My specialty was falls. I'd do falls no other stunt man would even go near."

"I'll be darned," she said as Roebuck paid for the drinks. "How do they do that, movie falls off roofs and all?"

"Mattresses," Roebuck said. "Sometimes trampolines."

The woman stirred her drink with a swizzle stick. "By the way, my name's Ellie Sanders."

Roebuck raised his glass. "Lou Watson."

She smiled. "So, glad to meet you."

There was a silence as Roebuck let his eyes wander slowly down the folds of Ellie's blue skirt to the shapely crossed legs, smooth and slender.

"What do you do now?" she asked suddenly.

"Uh, government work."

"What kind?"

"Classified."

Ellie lifted her shoulders in a shrug, as if apologizing for asking, "You're just driving through, I guess."

Roebuck nodded. "Going to California to do some research."

"I'll be! I've got a brother in California. Los Angeles."

"I'm going to Frisco."

"Oh . . ." She took a long sip of her drink. "There's a good motel just around the bend in the highway . . . if you're looking for a good place to stay the night."

Roebuck was warming to the idea. "What makes it a good place?" he asked, in a deliberate voice.

"I just know it is. I live there."

He put a dash of humor in his tone. "Ever think of subletting?"

Ellie turned her blonde head and smiled at him. "Why not?"

"I can't think of a good reason," Roebuck said, flashing a slow return smile to her. He motioned to the bartender. "Fifth of V.O. to go."

Ellie fished in her purse for a cigarette and allowed Roebuck to light it for her with the smoldering butt of his own. "There's ice at the motel," she said.

"Okay," Roebuck said. "What's my share of the rent?"

"Ten dollars."

He was surprised. "All night?"

Ellie finished her drink in one long gulp, and Roebuck noticed that she held her glass with her little finger extended, like a society matron sipping tea, only on Ellie it was strangely and completely unaffected.

"Sure all night," she said. "And into the morning."

7

"It does look like a comfortable place," Roebuck said as Ellie closed the motel room door behind them. The room was of medium size, with a tiny kitchen "L" supplied with a small refrigerator, stove, and table.

"Then make yourself comfortable," Ellie said through a smile. She took the brown paper bag containing the bottle of liquor from Roebuck's hand and walked with it into the kitchen. Roebuck liked the way she walked, no wasted motion, with all the right motion.

He watched as she mixed two drinks at the kitchen sink with the same economy of movement.

"Sit down," she invited as she turned and walked back into the room with a glass in each hand.

Roebuck sat in the room's one chair, and Ellie handed him his drink and sat down on the edge of the bed.

"Color TV, huh?" Roebuck motioned with his head toward the portable near the foot of the bed.

"Sure," Ellie said. "I like color in everything. Life's too drab sometimes."

"That's a fact," Roebuck agreed.

"That's why I liked you right off." She raised her glass to her lips. "You seemed different, you know?"

Roebuck laughed. "Yeah, I know. I'll bet you flatter your

66

other admirers by telling them the same thing."

Ellie wore a look of mock hurt. "But not at the same time."

They both laughed and Roebuck bent over and worked his boots off. "Ahhh!" He leaned back in the soft chair and stretched his legs.

"You been driving a long time?"

"All day . . ."

"You look tired."

Roebuck watched her through half-closed eyes. "I'm not as tired as you think." He was eyeing the level of her glass, waiting for it to become empty. The liquid was at the halfway mark now, and as he watched she took another long sip. Her eyes were dark and narrow and there was no firmness to her lips. She was either beginning to feel the effects of the liquor or the effects of her desire.

"Get undressed," she said suddenly.

Roebuck was pleasantly startled. "What?"

"Why don't you undress and get in bed?" She smiled slightly. "You said you weren't as tired as I thought."

Well, she's going to get my ten dollars, Roebuck thought. "That's right," he said. "I did say that."

Ellie looked him closely in the eye. "There isn't much coyness in me."

"Good."

She finished her drink and rattled the ice cubes in the empty glass. Then she reached into the glass and playfully tossed one of the cubes into Roebuck's lap. "I'll be back." She stood and walked into the bathroom. "Don't run off," she said as she passed out of sight.

"Never have yet," Roebuck called to her. He brushed the melting ice cube from his lap and stood. He undressed, laying out his clothes carefully. Then in his shorts he walked barefoot across the coarse carpet and made sure the blinds were shut tightly and the door was locked. He was sure he'd parked the car in a secluded enough spot. Leaning for a moment on the door frame, he cursed beneath his breath. The four walls of the motel room seemed as much a trap as a refuge. Trying to shake off that feeling, he walked back to the bed. Ellie's shadow danced tantalizingly over the section of bathroom wall visible to him as she removed her clothes.

"Still there?" she called.

Roebuck decided against answering. He flicked on the portable television and turned the volume all the way down, then he turned off the overhead light, bathing the bed in a soft and shifting glow from the TV screen. He lay on his back, deeply appreciating the softness of the mattress.

Ellie entered from the bathroom wearing a long blue robe.

"I thought there was no coyness in you," Roebuck said, uncomfortably aware of his nakedness.

Immediately the cords of the robe were untied and it settled to the floor at Ellie's feet. "There isn't."

She crossed to the bed and sat on the edge of the mattress, leaning over him with her breasts slightly swaying. She was as fine as she'd promised to be at Fay's Restaurant, he thought as he stroked her shoulder and let his gaze roam over her in the way men do with women they are seeing for the first time. Ellie was used to such scrutiny and didn't show the slightest embarrassment.

"You have a tattoo," she murmured softly, running her fingertips over the design on Roebuck's upper arm. The tattoo was of an eagle in dramatic full flight, an unfurled American flag clutched in its talons. "I thought only sailors got tattooed."

"I was on a ship for a while," Roebuck said. "Serving with Central Intelligence during the Korean thing."

"It's a pretty tattoo." She leaned forward and kissed Roebuck's forehead. "Do you have any more?"

"I don't need any more," Roebuck said. He closed his hand about the nape of her neck, and gently pulled her down to him.

Roebuck's lovemaking was sharp, violent, and quickly consummated.

When it was over Ellie lay back on the pillows, watching his face as he sank into deep sleep. She had been taken before in such a way, yet there was something in this man's rough, possessive lovemaking that did not quite possess her—as if he was preoccupied with something else, like a midnight safecracker somehow watching and listening all around him while he concentrated intently on the combination he was working.

She sighed and turned to gaze upward at the wide white ceiling. There was something in Roebuck's desperate lovemaking that had touched her.

It was well past ten that evening when Roebuck opened his eyes. He was lying on his stomach, his head turned, his perspiring cheek glued flat against the wrinkled linen. A siren was sounding far away. Too far away for him to worry about, he realized after a first few seconds of panic. He lay still, as if pressed to the mattress, listening to the rise and fall of the mournful, lilting sound. Whatever it was—police car, fire truck, ambulance—it was going the other way, fading into the night.

Roebuck was aware of the woman beside him, but he let his eyes lower to take in the television screen at the foot of the bed. The set was still on without volume. A gray-headed newscaster, suave, tight-lipped, a wry hint of a smile playing over his face, was speaking on the silent TV screen, spreading the bad news but unable to do anything about it. There was a resigned cynicism in that smooth visual delivery, a philosophical "what the hell!"

"You're being chased, aren't you?"

Roebuck was suddenly aware of Ellie looking at him, studying him.

He mustered a laugh. "Chased by what?"

"I wouldn't know," Ellie said. "Wouldn't care, if you didn't want to tell me."

Roebuck felt alarm. Was it that obvious? How did she know he was a hunted man?

"What makes you think I'm being chased?" he asked in what attempted to be a mildly amused voice.

"It adds up to that," she said. "The way you parked the car so it wouldn't be noticeable, the way you've got your clothes laid out with your boots by the bed, like you could step into them in a second and be gone. And the way you were just listening to that siren, all sad and lonely. Besides, it wasn't really loud enough to wake you up."

Roebuck tried to look her in the eye. "Maybe I'm on the F.B.I.'s top ten."

Ellie smiled. "Maybe you are. Maybe I wouldn't care."

"It could get you in trouble," Roebuck said, "housing a fugitive."

"Fugitive from what?"

Roebuck rolled over and sat up. "Damnit, Ellie, I'm only kidding!"

"No you're not. But like I told you, I guess I just don't care. It would be exciting, anyway."

"What would be exciting?"

"Being a fugitive. At least you're not like everybody else, stuck to a job like a machine . . . I guess I'm too romantic. That's what my family always said."

Roebuck lay back on the bed. Suppose she really didn't care if he was a wanted man? He could tell her. He could take her with him. The police wouldn't be as suspicious of a man with a woman in a car, a man with his wife out for a drive. And if it did come to a chase they wouldn't shoot; they might think she was a hostage. Then too, the last few hours had proven it would be much more pleasurable traveling if he could have a companion like Ellie. Any real man would want something like her.

"Can you keep something under your hat?" he asked in a serious tone.

"If you haven't noticed, I'm not wearing a hat, but I'll keep it somewhere."

"I am wanted," he said.

Ellie was silent, listening.

"But not exactly by the police." Roebuck folded his hands behind his head and expanded his chest. "Of course, you've never heard of 'Project N.' It's a government project designed to solve the nutrition problem. Did you know that nine-tenths of the world is malnourished?"

"I read that in the paper," Ellie said. "Were you working on this 'N' project?"

"As a civilian government employee," Roebuck said. "Then a month ago it happened. I figured out a formula that could solve the whole problem, and I'm the only man who has this knowledge."

"What kind of formula?"

"It's a system that enables us to extract raw protein from seawater and process it to powder form—from common seawater!" Roebuck stood and began to pace in the nude. "The world, the whole world, needs protein! And I discovered a way to give it to them! Why, if you wanted to, you could put one teaspoonful in a glass of fruit juice and you wouldn't really have to eat again for three days! Do you realize the possibilities?"

Ellie looked up at him from the bed and nodded.

"A power hungry group of politicians realized it too. That's why they want my formula, so they can sell it to the highest bidder." He looked shrewdly at Ellie. "And you know who that would be."

He began to pace faster, waving his arms. "They've got their whole crooked organization after me. They framed me for a murder back East so even the police will be hunting me, working for them without knowing it. And once they get me they'll fly me where they want to take me and use sodium pentothal on me. They have the power to do that. And any man will talk under the influence of truth serum—any man!"

"But why don't you take your formula to the right authorities?"

Roebuck let out one of his little snorts and stopped pacing. "You tell me who the right authorities are! You tell me who to trust!"

Ellie was subdued.

"All I can do," Roebuck said in a low voice, "is wait for the Secret Service to see what's happening and stop it. I have to run until then, do you understand?"

"Yes," Ellie said firmly, "and I told you I didn't care."

After neither of them spoke for a long moment she stood and slipped into her robe. "I'll fix you something to eat. There's some tuna salad in the refrigerator."

She walked slowly into the kitchen and began removing dishes from one of the cabinets. "You are hungry, aren't you?"

Roebuck grinned at her and nodded, feeling rather foolish not because he was standing before her stark nude but, oddly enough, because he had doubted her to begin with.

"Have I got time to take a shower?" he asked.

Ellie nodded. "Time for anything you want."

Beneath the soothing hot needles of shower water Roebuck relaxed completely for the first time. He reached out, turned the water on even hotter and stood with his head back, enjoying the pinpoint pressure of the fine spray, breathing in the steam that was rising around him. There was a strange security here, not only of the secret confines of the sliding glass shower doors but of the steady, beating sound. The entire outside world, sight, sound, smell, touch, all was cut off, held back by the warm, rushing, roaring privacy here.

It was with reluctance that he turned off the water, toweled himself dry, and slipped into his shorts. The outside room was cool as he walked quickly to the chair where his clothes were laid out and hurriedly put on his pants and undershirt.

"The food's ready if you are," Ellie said.

She had two plates with sandwiches and potato chips on them laid out on the small kitchen table. There was a bowl of tuna salad in the center of the table, and two glasses of milk. It looked delicious to Roebuck.

"Would you rather have something else to drink?" Ellie asked as they sat down.

Roebuck shook his head. "Milk is the most wholesome thing there is."

They began to eat slowly, occasionally looking across the table at each other.

"How long have you lived here?" Roebuck asked.

"Oh, maybe a year. How come you ask?"

"Curiosity. A scientist is curious. Were you born around here?"

"In Iowa, about a hundred years ago."

"Why'd you leave?"

Ellie shrugged. "I don't know, really. I quit high school after two years to go to work, but I decided I didn't like work.

73

The only job I could get was in a dairy, washing milk bottles. I quit after three months. They were going to get an automatic washer anyway."

"I can't see you washing bottles."

"Me either. Right after I quit, my older brother and I both left home."

"The brother in California?"

Ellie nodded. Her face glowed as she talked of her brother. "Ralph is a guitar player—he's played in a lot of night spots in California. And he's a poet, too. Now and then he sends me copies of those little poetry magazines he gets published in."

Roebuck took a bite of tuna salad sandwich. "That's great, a poet," he said with his mouth full.

Ellie leaned back in her chair and a dreamy look passed over her eyes. "We used to have an act together for a while, in Iowa. I'd sing while he played the guitar. I liked it but I just wasn't good enough. I knew it after a while, when the bookings thinned out and I heard people talk. But Ralph is great! You should see him, crooning, crooning away, making love to his guitar under the hot lights in front of all those people." She smiled. "That's how he put it once in one of his poems, and that's how I used to talk when I was younger, like a damn poet. You outgrow that, I guess."

"Most of us do," Roebuck said, and Ellie caught the sadness in his voice.

"Have you outgrown that poetic stuff?" she asked candidly.

"Most of it," Roebuck answered, taking a swig of milk. He decided it was time to get on another subject. "I've got an idea, Ellie."

She let her chair tilt forward and sat listening.

"Why don't you come with me when I leave?"

Mild surprise showed on Ellie's face, the kind of surprise

74

women show at being unexpectedly complimented. "You mean quit living here and travel with you?"

"I mean run with me," Roebuck said. "I never pulled any punches. You'd be in this thing with me all the way. They might even think I told you the formula and try to get it out of you. That's why I wouldn't tell you the formula, for your own sake. It's all up here." Roebuck touched his forefinger to his temple.

Ellie looked down at the table. "I don't know, Lou . . ."

"It might not be a picnic. Nothing worthwhile is a picnic."

Ellie leaned toward him. "All right, Lou, I'll come."

Roebuck hadn't expected her to be convinced so easily. "Like I said—"

"I know," Ellie interrupted. "I don't expect a honeymoon trip. But do you know how much happens around here, I mean really happens? Nothing. Boredom can be worse than anything."

"That's the only reason you're coming? Boredom?"

"No, Lou, I'm coming because for some reason I don't want to refuse you."

Roebuck nodded in the face of what he did not quite understand. "There's nothing in it for you . . ."

Ellie smiled across the table at him and laid her hand on his. She lifted his hand and brushed her lips on the back of his knuckles.

Early the next morning they rose, breakfasted, and Ellie began to pack her things in a small plaid suitcase. Roebuck observed that she had a meager wardrobe, inexpensive but not in bad taste.

"We can leave some of this stuff," she said, closing the last empty bureau drawer.

"How about the dishes?"

"They're the motel's. I've got a refund coming on my rent, too. I'll go check out with Mr. Lane soon as we're finished here."

Roebuck was drinking his second cup of coffee, gazing out the window through the partly opened blinds.

"You better make up a story when you check out," he said. "Why don't you tell them I'm your brother, and you're leaving because somebody in your family is sick?"

Ellie snapped the plaid suitcase shut. "I suppose that's a fairly believable fib." She went to the closet and opened the sliding doors one at a time to check the top shelf above the clothes hangers. "Funny," she said, "everything I've got will fit into one suitcase and a grocery bag. I guess it's funny, anyway."

There was a knock on the front door and Roebuck bolted away from the window as if someone had shot at him.

"Who is it?" he asked Ellie in a desperate whisper. "Who the hell could that be?" He hadn't seen the man approach from the window. He must have come from the other direction. Or had he crouched and passed under the window, the way they did in Western movies?

Ellie glanced at the electric clock above the refrigerator. "I think it's Billy," she said.

"Billy?"

"The bartender at Fay's. He comes by sometimes in the mornings on his way to work to drive me over there. You better get in the bathroom and shut the door."

"Get rid of him quick as you can," Roebuck said. He retreated to the bathroom and shut the door until only a narrow crack remained through which he could see. He turned his head and checked behind him to see if the small window was unlocked. If it wasn't Billy at the door he could make his retreat that way.

From behind the bathroom door Roebuck could hear

them talking but he couldn't make out the words. Then he caught a glimpse of a fleshy face in front of Ellie and he knew that it was the bartender to whom she was talking. He relaxed slightly. Ellie would know how to handle him.

They talked a while longer, then Ellie stood back, and closed the door. Roebuck waited in the bathroom until he heard a car door slam outside and the sound of an accelerating motor on the highway. When he stepped out of the bathroom Ellie was holding the curtains back a few inches, watching out the window. She turned.

"He's gone," she said. "I told him I wasn't going to Fay's today, said I had the flu."

"You don't suppose he saw me, do you?"

"If he did, he wouldn't think anything about it. That's one reason I'm going to miss Billy."

They finished getting Ellie's things together, then Roebuck waited while she walked to the motel office to check out and get her rent refund.

As he was putting her things in the back of the car he saw her returning slowly, buttoning the flap of her purse.

"Everything all right?" he asked.

"Sure, I told them what you said to." She went to the motel room door, and closed it so it locked from the inside. "I hate to leave anyplace," she said. "I guess I'm the kind that gets attached to things more than I should."

As they were getting into the car an old man stepped out of the motel office and waved to them. Roebuck raised an arm and waved back as he shut the car door.

"Mr. Lane?" he asked.

Ellie nodded, not looking up as Roebuck drove the car from the lot and out onto the highway.

He cranked down his window to let in the fresh morning air.

8

They had been traveling for two days along the side roads and the back highways, through the fertile plowed fields of Illinois, across the Mississippi into the lush, hot greenness of Missouri in summertime. Ellie sat beside Roebuck in the car, staring straight ahead at everything and nothing in that mild hypnotic state people fall into after hours of driving. Roebuck glanced sideways at her profile against the rushing scenery, and she sensed his glance.

"It's beautiful in this part of the country," she said, "all rolling and wild."

"Ever been through here in the fall?" Roebuck asked, watching the highway. "There's every color you can imagine in those woods. I was here sometime ago on a hunting trip."

"Do you like to hunt?"

"I've hunted everything from squirrel to lion."

They lapsed into silence, a silence with which Roebuck could be completely at ease. Ellie worked that way on him sometimes, soothing him. Perhaps it was his complete and uncompromising mastery over her, and her complete loyalty. Here was a woman who could be trusted, Roebuck thought, and he had not thought that about many women. Maybe that was the reason she inspired a certain degree of confession in him.

"I was born near here," Roebuck said, "Arkansas. But it's

not like it is here, not this pretty or this hot."

"Do you have those weeping willow trees there?" Ellie pointed to a roadside grove of the huge, graceful trees.

"Some."

"There's no prettier tree than a weeping willow," Ellie said, "or sadder, the way they thirst for moisture and grow all turned down instead of up."

Roebuck nodded. "You usually find them around septic tanks." He concentrated on his driving for a while. "We're going to have to steal another car sometime soon."

"It sure is less trouble to steal a car than I thought."

"You bet it is," Roebuck said with a tight grin. "People are fools."

Ellie sighed. "I hope the police are fools."

"They are," he assured her.

"How come we don't travel at night, Lou?"

Roebuck crooked his arm and rested it on the ledge of the open car window, flattening his bicep against the warm metal of the door as a group of young motorcyclists flashed by going in the other direction. "Less conspicuous during the day," he said. "There are fewer cars on the road at night and you can see their lights for miles. Besides, the police might be expecting me to travel by night. I told you they were mostly fools. In Intelligence it was all we could do to keep them from botching up our work when they were trying to help."

A brightly lettered restaurant sign, crying for their attention with a command to STOP AND EAT, appeared in the distance alongside the highway, and Roebuck slowed the car. "What about some supper?"

"If you want to stop, Lou."

"We have to eat soon," Roebuck said, "and that little place only has a few cars on the lot."

"I suppose we could use a good meal," Ellie agreed. "And

try not to be so nervous, Lou."

There was only one other customer in the small diner. They chose a booth in the far corner away from the counter and grill, a secluded corner near a plate glass window. Roebuck studiously avoided looking at the dead moths on the long metal sill as he and Ellie slid into the booth.

"Help you folks?" It was the cook who had been standing behind the counter when they entered, a fat, greasy man in a white shirt and apron. He placed two glasses of water on the booth table.

"What's good?" Ellie asked.

"Everything," the man answered flatly. He held a broken pencil poised over his order tablet. "Special's the best, and it's all cooked up. Roast beef and gravy."

"That'll be good," Roebuck said. "And two coffees."

The fat man made a quick notation on his tablet and moved off.

"No need to keep looking out the window," Ellie said. "We're safe here."

Roebuck smiled at her. He knew she represented the transition in his image from a hard-pressed fugitive to an average family man on the road with his wife. Of course, that was the image seen by the outsider. He knew he was a fugitive, and so did Ellie.

"There's something I'd like to tell you," Roebuck said confidentially.

Ellie waited, revolving her glass slowly in the spreading ring of water it left on the table.

"My real name's not Lou Watson, it's Lou Roebuck."

She looked up at him, her eyes unreadable.

"The seawater story, that wasn't true either. It was to test you, to see if I could really trust you."

"And can you?"

80

"Then you are wanted for murder?"

"It wasn't murder," Roebuck said quickly. "It was an accident." He swung into the outer lane to pass a station wagon loaded down with children. "You see, Gipp was taken prisoner and then released, and somehow he and Ingrahm became friends after the war. I saw them a couple of times, and I could tell that Gipp never forgave me for what I had to do. Then last week Ingrahm called me on the phone and asked me to meet the two of them at a motel where they were staying. I did, we had a few drinks, talked, and I left. Then, as I was driving out of the parking lot, it happened. Ingrahm came running out the door of the motel lounge right into the path of my car. Don't ask me why—he was always doing crazy things since he got that plate in his head. I ran over him, and Gipp was the only witness.

"He was mad with hate! He said he'd turn me in, say it was murder, that I'd threatened to run Ingrahm down! And it had happened so fast that there were no skid marks, nothing! I ran—I'm still running."

"You're not to blame," Ellie said, looking at him with compassion. "But you sure made it look worse when you ran."

Roebuck snorted. "I weighed the odds. It was all I could do. Anyway, I'm not sure Ingrahm is dead."

Ellie's voice was puzzled. "I don't get it."

"After leaving the scene of the accident I went to where I used to work to collect some money they owed me. My ex-boss was there. He refused to pay me and I didn't have any choice but to take the money by force. He's a very influential man who married the right woman. I think he convinced the police to fake a murder charge so I'd get scared and come crawling back. He didn't know me very well."

"But, Lou, could he do that . . . ?"

"He could and he would and he did! And if I go back and Ingrahm isn't dead, they'll still have me for attempted murder and robbery!"

Ellie said nothing. Roebuck slowed the car, parked on the shoulder of the highway and sat with his head bowed, his eyes clenched shut. "Sometimes I just don't know what to do," he said, squeezing the steering wheel with both hands so hard that his body trembled. "Sometimes things go so wrong and nothing fits and I just don't know what to do!"

Ellie placed a hand on his cheek, and with her other hand she caressed his shoulder until the trembling stopped. "You rest, Lou," she said softly, urgently. "It doesn't matter to me what you did. You rest and I'll drive."

Roebuck let out a long breath and opened his eyes, staring intently at the dashboard. "I'll go around," he said.

He got out of the car, walked around to the passenger's side, and got back in. As Ellie steered the car back onto the pavement and picked up speed, he slumped in the seat, letting the gentle motion and vibration relax him. After about five minutes he rested his head on the seat back and went to sleep.

As he slept, he dreamed.

A long, lonely scream. Light, flickering red light over everything, moving across the thin membrane of his closed eyelids, forcing its pulsating redness into his mind. The acrid odor of smoke was fading . . .

Roebuck opened his eyes and sat up violently. The car was stopped. There was a huge, red-tinted face outside the driver's window, a face beneath a silver-badged uniform cap.

"Didn't mean to scare you, mister," the face said, smiling a reddish smile.

"The officer stopped us because we only have one tail-light," Ellie explained sweetly. "It's a state law."

"There's a station about two miles down where you can get the bulb replaced," the highway patrolman said. He raised his eyebrows, and took in the interior of the car with a glance. "I noticed you people are from out of state."

"That's right," Roebuck said, regaining his composure. "We're going to visit my wife's family in Colorado. Her mother's sick."

The patrolman nodded. "Well, I guess there's no need for a citation if you get the light repaired right away."

"Thank you, officer." Ellie smiled. "It must have just burned out. I took the car to have it checked before we left on this trip."

"That's right," Roebuck said. "I'm in the auto repair business myself. I should have checked it over personally."

The patrolman shrugged. "That's how it always is. I get citations for burning leaves." He gave them a parting grin. "Have a good trip, folks. And I hope your mother's all right."

"Thank you," Ellie called after him as they watched him walk away, adjusting his cap in the wind from a passing car that might or might not have been going too fast.

The flashing red light atop the police car died as the patrolman swung sharply back onto the highway and drove away.

Roebuck and Ellie did stop at the service station down the highway, where they had the taillight bulb replaced and the gas tank filled before driving on.

"We better start playing it safer," Roebuck said as they pulled out of the station.

"I guess you're right." Ellie looked at the speedometer carefully. "Why don't we stop at a grocery and get something for our meals? That way we wouldn't have to risk eating in those greasy roadside places."

"I was thinking that myself."

"We can get some donuts or something for breakfast," she said, "and we can buy a coffeepot and some coffee. We can fix us something right in our motel room."

"We'll stop at the next town," Roebuck decided, slouching down and resting his head again on the back of the seat.

He closed his eyes, but this time he didn't sleep.

9

Roebuck drove the station wagon slowly out of the Jolly Rest Motel's lot, onto the baking expanse of concrete highway, and accelerated in a smooth and steady rush to seventy miles an hour. Ellie sat beside him, munching a glazed donut, sipping her coffee from the motel bathroom's sanitary paper cup. They drove away from the low morning sun, into the west, the green scenery rotating gently and sliding past them as they rode the snaking highway.

They drove for perhaps fifteen minutes before they passed a crude wooden sign almost obscured by dew-bent weeds. LAKE CHIPPEWA 5 MILES—it read in weather-beaten yellow letters—CABINS—FISHING—BOATS—REST—RELAX.

"Do you think we can run all the way to California?" Ellie asked, finishing the last donut and brushing sugar from her hands.

Roebuck grinned in his best desperado manner. "I'll tell you one thing. Nobody's going to stop us."

"I know you mean that, Lou, but do you think it's the smart thing to do? I mean, won't somebody somewhere figure out that we keep going the same direction?"

Roebuck had a vision of dozens of important-looking individuals gathered around a gigantic wall map, moving red-flagged pins and circling areas with red pencil. "Maybe," he said.

"We could stop," Ellie said. "We could fool them and hole up, rent one of those cabins."

Placing an unlit cigarette between his lips, Roebuck pushed in the car's lighter. "Yeah, I saw the sign."

"We could pretend we were a couple on a fishing vacation. Nobody'd suspect anything." Ellie was getting enthusiastic. "We could buy some fishing stuff and supplies and just take it easy."

Roebuck touched the hot tip of the lighter to his cigarette. "I don't think much of the idea. We should move, put miles behind us . . ."

"But that's what everybody does who runs from the law. It's just human nature, and they know it. But don't you know that they can radio ahead, that they're all across the country, that what we're running from keeps moving right along with us?"

That was sure as hell true, Roebuck thought. It followed, it waited ahead of them, like the sun, slowly passing them at thousands of miles an hour to wait for them on the other horizon.

"Anyway," Ellie said, "it'd be good for you. You're too nervous, Lou. Always worrying about who's behind us on the highway, where we're going to eat, how we're going to steal another car . . ."

"It would solve that problem," Roebuck said. "We wouldn't have to steal another car for a while." He'd been worrying about that.

"And nobody'd notice out-of-state license plates at a place like that," Ellie said. "They'd just think we came here to do some fishing."

"I don't like to be trapped, though," Roebuck said tensely.

"I don't like to be walled up."

"That's just a feeling, Lou. You'd be safer where nobody could see you than moving along out here on the highway in a stolen car."

"Understand," Roebuck said, "it's not just me I'm thinking of."

"I know, Lou." Ellie touched his knee with her fingertips.

Ahead of them was another wooden sign, like the first only bigger. The letters were freshly painted on this one, and beneath LAKE CHIPPEWA was an arrow pointing up a narrow dirt road.

"Whatever you want, Lou."

The sign flashed past.

After a few minutes Roebuck said, "It sure would be a relief not to have to keep looking in this rear view mirror."

Ellie was silent.

"We could go back," Roebuck said thoughtfully. "We could lay low for a while and listen to the radio, wait for things to loosen up."

"It's up to you, Lou."

Roebuck slowed the car.

"Lake Chippewa," Ellie said, "that's Indian."

"I know," Roebuck said absently. "My mother was half Pawnee."

He stepped down resolutely on the accelerator.

"What are we going to do, Lou?"

"We'll stop at the next place we see where there's a big store or shopping center and buy some fishing gear, then we'll go back to Lake Chippewa and look over those cabins."

They stopped at Millbrook, fifteen miles farther down the highway. There was a good-sized department store there, with a big sporting goods section. Roebuck and Ellie were examining some casting rods when a smiling sales clerk approached them.

"Those are the best for the price," the clerk said earnestly. He was a middle-aged man with a seamed face and horn-rimmed glasses.

"I like this one," Roebuck said knowledgeably, choosing another rod. "Plenty of whip to it. We'll take two of these."

The clerk beamed. "All right, sir, anything else?"

"Some fishing flies," Roebuck said, "and a tackle box—and I'll take one of those hats with the mosquito net hanging from the brim."

"Yes, sir! That'll keep the pesky devils away from your face and neck!" The clerk rushed to gather things up and display a case of colorful flies to Roebuck.

"Now this is the bait that gets results," he said, pointing to a particularly repulsive one. "Wonder Worm! We've had nothing but raves from our customers who've tried it. It's especially good for trout."

"I'll take two," Roebuck said, "and two of the spotted dragonflies, and one of the minnows that you put the little pill in to make their tail wiggle."

The clerk stared through his horn-rimmed glasses. "Do you do much fishing, sir?"

"Not freshwater," Roebuck said casually, "mostly swordfish."

The clerk hurried to get the flies Roebuck had requested.

Roebuck paid cash and watched as everything was wrapped. "Tell me," he said, "where's the best fishing around here?"

"There's Lake Manitoshi," the clerk answered, busily fighting the rustling brown paper. "Then there's the Great Horney River and Lake Chippewa about fifteen miles east of here."

"Where's Lake Manitoshi?" Roebuck asked. "I think we'll go there."

"It's about five miles west," the clerk said. "Good bass this time of year."

"Thanks," Roebuck said, taking the wrapped packages. Ellie carried the rods and he took the tackle box.

"You won't regret buying that Wonder Worm!" the clerk called after them as they walked away.

They got in the car, made a wide U-turn, and headed back the way they had come.

PART TWO

1

Lake Chippewa was more than Roebuck had expected. It was a large lake, with many coves, banked by hills of tall and full-branched trees. The water was a deep greenish blue, and there were a few motionless boats on it with motionless fishermen. Some of the small boats were tied up at the bank across the wide lake, near cabins that could be seen here and there at the edge of the woods.

"It's beautiful," Ellie said, as a stocky, red-faced man in a T-shirt walked toward them smiling. He was wearing an old gray hat covered with fishing flies. As he got closer Roebuck noticed a spotted dragonfly like the two he'd just bought.

"They all say that," the red-faced man said with a wider grin. "It sure enough is a pretty spot. I'm Hobey. Can I help you folks?"

"We'd like to see a cabin," Roebuck said.

"Sure enough. Just the two of you?"

Roebuck nodded.

"If you get in your car an' follow me in the Jeep," Hobey said, "we can scoot right over to the best cabin on the lake. Just vacated yesterday mornin'."

"Lead the way," Roebuck said.

It was a small pine cabin, with a kitchen, a comfortable-looking bed, and, to Ellie's delight, a real fireplace.

"Ain't too fancy," Hobey said. "But then the price ain't either."

"How much?" Roebuck asked.

"Fifty dollars a week suit you folks?"

"Suits us fine."

"How long you gonna be stayin' with us?"

"About two weeks," Ellie cut in.

Roebuck made no objection. "We'll pay in advance," he said, "if it's all right with you."

"I'll make you folks out a receipt," Hobey said with a smile. "What's the name?"

"Watson," Roebuck said without hesitation. "Mr. and Mrs. Lou Watson." He drew ten ten-dollar bills from his wallet as Hobey scribbled on a yellow piece of paper.

"Hope you folks enjoy your fishin'," Hobey said, handing the receipt to Roebuck and slipping the ten bills in his breast pocket without bothering to count them.

Roebuck and Ellie walked with him back to his Jeep.

"You folks done much fishin' around here?"

"No," Roebuck said, "mostly up north. Michigan, Canada."

"Say," Hobey said, "I'd like to go to Canada."

"It's great fishing," Roebuck said. "I caught one of the biggest catfish on record there. Had to fold it to get it into the trunk of the car."

"It was a little sports car," Ellie said.

Hobey laughed. "Still big enough." He pointed to various parts of the wide lake. "Over there near them dead trees is where they been gettin' a lot of bluegill; over there by them boats they're fishin' for bass and carp; your catfish you'll find in the channels and coves. We got some pretty good-size trout, too. That green rowboat tied up down there goes with the cabin."

"Thanks," Roebuck said.

Hobey squinted at them. "What kind of bait you folks usin'?"

"I had great luck with the Wonder Worm up north," Roebuck said. "Caught a nine-pound bass with it last summer."

"Say," Hobey said, "that's a bait they use a lot around here this summer. Guess it takes a while for the word to get around."

Roebuck smiled. "I guess it does."

"Well, catch some big ones," Hobey said as he climbed into the Jeep and gunned the engine. They watched him bump away in the squat vehicle down the uneven road that serviced the cabin.

"It looks nice," Ellie said, turning and surveying the cabin, "better than a motel."

"You won't get an argument out of me," Roebuck said. "Let's get our stuff from the car."

"Do you want to use the fireplace tonight?" Ellie asked as they were opening the back of the station wagon.

"Too hot for a fire."

"I know, but I've always liked to watch the flames dance in a fireplace. My mother's house had a real fireplace."

Roebuck reached into the back of the car for the fishing equipment. "We'll see," he said.

After they had moved their things into the cabin, Roebuck turned the station wagon around so the stolen license plate faced the thick woods. He filled a bucket with water from the outside tap of the cabin, then he returned to the car, poured the water on some bare ground, and stooped for a handful of mud. Carefully, he smeared the mud on the license plate to obscure the numbers, then he splattered the back of the station wagon with mud so the plate itself wouldn't be too conspicuous.

The voice behind him startled him.

"We forgot to buy some fishing clothes for you," Ellie said.

Roebuck stood slowly, in relief. "I'll wear what I have on today. Tomorrow morning we can drive to the nearest town and buy what clothes we need."

"I'll go myself," Ellie said. "That way you won't even have to be seen."

Roebuck walked with his hands cupped, idly squishing mud between his fingers as they returned to the cabin.

They spent the rest of the day getting used to their new surroundings. Ellie put things away in the cabin while Roebuck tried to relax by puttering with the new fishing equipment. He sat outside the cabin in a small webbed folding chair, stringing fishing line, attaching sinkers, looking up now and then to note with satisfaction that the lake was large and unsymmetrical, so that the cabin was quite secluded.

Just before noon Ellie made some coffee and opened a can of chili for lunch. They decided while they ate that they should do some fishing for appearance's sake even if they caught nothing. So, after lunch they carried rods and tackle box to the bank and set themselves adrift in the small wooden rowboat.

Roebuck rowed the boat to near the middle of the lake, where the sun-shot water was greenest. He looked the fisherman, with his pants rolled to the knees and his upper body bare. He wore his new hat with the mosquito net hanging from the brim, but he soon found that the net was rubbing a sore spot on the tip of his nose, so he ripped it off and wore the hat without it.

"I've never done much fishing," Ellie said, and for the next twenty minutes Roebuck showed her how to cast and reel the fly in slowly and unevenly. He showed her how to flip her wrist to get the maximum whip in the rod, and soon she was casting as far as he was.

For a half hour they sat quietly in the gently rocking boat, casting and reeling without success, Roebuck with the Wonder Worm, Ellie with the spotted dragonfly. Then Roebuck wedged his casting rod beneath a wooden seat and let his line play in the water. He slouched down on the dry, sun-warmed bottom of the boat and rested his head on the old cushion he'd been sitting on. Gazing up at the afternoon sky, he watched the clouds rock in perfect unison with the lazy waves of the lake waters.

"Looks like dinner will be out of a can," Ellie said, wiping the sweat from her forehead with her sleeve.

"You have to be patient with fish," Roebuck answered, and that's when the bass hit the Wonder Worm and jerked Roebuck's rod and reel into the lake.

Roebuck yelled and jumped up just in time to close his fingers about the handle of the rod six inches under water. He kneeled in the bottom of the boat and began to reel. "He's hooked! He's hooked!"

Ellie was squealing, clapping her hands.

The rod bent in a half-circle as Roebuck worked frantically with the reel. His thumb slipped and the line played out as he cursed and tried to keep his balance in the rocking boat. He got the fish under control again and began reeling more frantically than ever, feeling every movement of the unseen fish, every vibration of the desperate struggle for life.

The bass leaped and Roebuck saw its glistening silver flank as it hung for a moment above the surface of the lake. Then it was back in its cool world of silence with only the threadlike fishing line cutting the surface of the water in mad zigzag patterns to attest to its struggle below, pulling, pulling it back up to another world of heat and dry death.

"The net!" Roebuck yelled. "Get the net!"

Ellie fumbled in the open tackle box before she thought. "We didn't buy a net!"

"No net! No net!" Roebuck's voice was incredulous.

The battling fish was near the boat now, and Roebuck tried to land it without a net. He bent over and gripped the line, pulling it carefully toward him, feeling the pressure of the fish trying to change direction.

For a second he saw a silver head, a gaping mouth, magnified beneath the water. Then as he tried to lift the fish into the boat, the line snapped and he fell back to a sitting position in the boat bottom.

"No net," he repeated miserably, sitting with the wet, limp line in his hand.

They sat in silence as the boat rocked.

"He was a big one," Ellie said. "At least five pounds." And she began to laugh.

Roebuck sat looking down at the broken line for a while, then he began to laugh with her. "Chili again for supper," he said, wiping his eyes and struggling back up to sit on the boat seat.

"I guess I feel like having chili," Ellie said, still smiling, reeling in her line.

Roebuck closed the tackle box and reached for the oars. He drew a deep breath and began rowing toward the bank. "I think that fish was closer to ten pounds," he said.

There were still a few hours of daylight left after supper. Roebuck got the smaller of the two pistols he'd bought in Illinois, a .22 caliber, and looked about for a place to target shoot. He lined up four tin cans on a stump behind the cabin and backed off about twenty-five yards.

With four evenly spaced shots he cleared the stump.

"You sure can shoot," Ellie said admiringly.

Roebuck walked to the stump to replace the tin cans. "I can outshoot any son of a bitch!" He held up the punctured cans, turning them so Ellie could see light through the holes.

"Nothing cheap about any of those," she said.

Roebuck walked back to stand beside her. He raised the pistol and again cleared the stump with four shots.

"I'm going inside," Ellie said. "You coming?"

He looked closely at her. "You bet."

Tucking the revolver in his belt, Roebuck followed her into the cabin.

It was warm inside, so Roebuck opened all the windows a crack and a lazy breeze stirred through the cabin. He went into the bedroom behind Ellie. She turned back the bedspread and they both undressed casually, unhurriedly, without having to speak.

He made love to her then, taking her slowly, almost leisurely, giving something of himself as he felt her respond warmly beneath him.

"You were gentler that time," Ellie whispered, resting her tousled head on his chest. She had her eyes closed, her wide, flushed lips curved in a sensuous smile. "How come you were gentler?"

"I don't know," Roebuck said. He lay for a while longer, then he stood and slipped into his pants.

Ellie watched him as he walked to the bureau and reloaded his revolver. Without a word he crossed the cabin and went out through the screen door into the fading light.

She lay listening for a long time to the measured crack! crack! of the pistol as he took dead aim at his tin cans.

2

Idyllic was the word. Roebuck's tension and fear drained out of him, and the rest of the week with Ellie at the cabin was the most enjoyable week he'd ever experienced. Ellie soothed him with just her presence, as the glittering lake and rolling green scenery soothed him. Roebuck could rise now in the morning, dress quickly, drink a strong cup of coffee, and step outside to breathe fresh air instead of fear. Who would think to look for them here? Let the police, let Benny Gipp continue their wild pursuit while Roebuck fished, basked in the sun, and made love in his lakeside paradise.

In time Roebuck even came to enjoy sitting for hours with Ellie before the hypnotic flames in the fireplace. He always built a small fire, for effect rather than heat, for the days were healthy, sweltering hot and the nights were warm. But Ellie loved to sit curled on the worn hide-a-bed sofa before a fire, sipping a sweet soda highball, and it was Roebuck's pleasure to see her happy.

Roebuck occasionally wondered why this was so. Why did Ellie appeal to him and intrigue him more than any woman he'd met? Curiosity was part of the answer. Ellie possessed a calm strength and equilibrium that he did not quite understand. It seemed the more she was called on to do, the greater was her quiet, single-minded resourcefulness. She was self-possessed, and Roebuck possessed her. Did opposites attract in that manner?

The second week at the cabin was almost over. Roebuck and Ellie had lived an almost solitary existence. They had a waving acquaintance with a few of the other fishermen who passed them sometimes on the lake in rowboats or flat-nosed John boats with quiet outboard trolling motors. Once they had even shared some cold beer in the middle of the lake with a couple from a cabin on the opposite bank. But that couple had gone back to Nebraska now, and Roebuck's and Ellie's anonymity was again complete.

On Friday of the second week they had a long talk at breakfast and decided to rent the cabin for another two weeks. It suddenly occurred to them that their refuge might be reserved for the week after their scheduled departure, so immediately after breakfast Roebuck tucked his wallet in the hip pocket of his comfortable jeans, put on a clean sport shirt, and set out to find Hobey as quickly as possible to make arrangements for the cabin.

It was best to leave the station wagon where it was parked, he thought as he stepped outside. The car was seen enough on Ellie's occasional trips into Danton, the nearest town, to buy groceries and liquor. Whistling under his breath, Roebuck climbed into the boat, pushed off, and began rowing across the lake. The ascending sun felt marvelous on the back of his neck.

A half hour later Roebuck returned and called to Ellie as he pulled the boat part way up onto the bank and secured it with a loop of rope about a gnarled tree trunk.

"We're good for another two weeks!"

"Wonderful!"

They looked at each other in surprise at the sound of a car making its way up the dirt road to the cabin.

Roebuck felt the fear close on his heart. He turned instinctively to get back in the boat and push off into the lake, but he realized the car would emerge from the woods even before he managed to get the boat in the water. He moved toward the cabin, then froze in mid-step as a shining two-tone police cruiser with a huge red light flanked by two loudspeakers on its roof came bouncing slowly up the road, made a right angle turn, and braked to a precision stop facing the cabin.

No place to go, no place to run. Roebuck and Ellie stood motionless. There was one man in the car, and with racing heart Roebuck read the letters on the oversized gold shield painted on the door: SHERIFF'S CAR, CLARK COUNTY.

The man sat quietly behind the steering wheel for a moment before getting out and slamming the lettered door neatly behind him with an automatic, backward motion of his arm.

He stood straight and still in his spotless khaki uniform, looking at them unsmilingly for a second before walking toward them. Roebuck saw that he was a big man, about fifty, with angular but flesh-padded small features and the beginnings of a paunch that he seemed to be holding in. As he neared them, he removed his uniform cap to reveal iron-gray hair that appeared bent rather than combed to the side with a razor part. He was immaculately uniformed, and Roebuck noticed with surprise that even the bullets in his cartridge belt were buffed to a shine.

The voice was warm and affable, totally incongruous with the man's military appearance.

" 'Lo, there." He turned a handsome smile on them. "I'm Sheriff Boadeen, Rodney Boadeen, sheriff of Clark County."

A lump of fuzz lodged in Roebuck's throat. "Is there . . . something wrong?"

The sheriff folded his hands behind him, as if he were

103

standing at parade rest. "Nope, nothing wrong, just checking. I make it a habit to get to know people who spend time at the lake."

"I'm Ellie Watson," Ellie said. "And this is my husband, Lou."

"Glad to meet you folk." The sheriff shook Roebuck's hand with a curt, firm grip. "Catching many fish?" He addressed the question to Ellie, giving himself a chance to size her up in her tight blouse and hip-huggers.

"Some big trout," Roebuck answered. He saw that Ellie was aware of Boadeen's appraising eye, though she didn't blush or appear discomforted.

Sheriff Boadeen smiled at Roebuck. "Trout's good at this lake when the weather's hot."

Roebuck attempted to light a cigarette, dropped the pack as he was pulling it from his breast pocket, and had to stoop to retrieve it.

"You seem a bit nervous," Boadeen said, arching an eyebrow and peering down at him.

"I am," Roebuck said as he stood. "That's why I'm here, for my nerves. I'm a government test pilot and I just had a pretty bad crack-up in the desert. Damn near finished me."

The sheriff looked interested. "How'd it happen?"

"Flameout. New fighter plane with swept-back wings. Went down like a rock. The doctors said it was a miracle I escaped with only minor cuts and bruises, and the government gave me a month to get myself back together. Something like that shakes a man."

"Surely would," the sheriff said. "But I thought you fellas went right back up before you had a chance to lose your nerve."

"I did go back up," Roebuck said, "as soon as the doctors let me. I can still fly as good as the next man, but a test pilot's got to fly even better than that."

Boadeen stuck out his lower lip reflectively and nodded.

"Can we offer you something to drink, Sheriff Boadeen?" Ellie asked. She glanced toward the patrol car with its engine still running.

"Ain't got that much time," Boadeen said, looking her over with a smile. "But maybe some other day."

"Drop in whenever you'd like," Roebuck said in a strained voice.

"Surely will," the sheriff said. "I get up here to the lake pretty often. Like to see what I have to deal with in case we have trouble. You'd be surprised the calls I get to come up here. Young couples, honeymooners, and the like that rent these cabins are a big temptation to a certain type of mind, if you know what I mean." He looked again at Ellie. "We had an assault up here last year and you folk wouldn't believe what this scum did to the young woman. Caught her alone when her husband went into town for supplies and just purely gave her hell. I mean to tell you! Soda bottles, candles, anything that'd fit! I caught him myself, and you can bet I made him pay some for what he did to that poor girl. Laid my club on his head to the tune of twenty stitches!"

"At least you caught him," Ellie said, returning the sheriff's direct stare.

"Oh, sure," Boadeen said with disgust, "then he got a light sentence so's he could be paroled in a few years to do the same thing all over again." He straightened slightly as he looked from one of them to the other. "If I had the power to do things my way, the state wouldn't waste money on that kind of scum. One offense and the gas chamber. That way they wouldn't have a chance to prey on decent folk."

Roebuck cleared his throat. "It's good to know that somebody like you is here for protection, Sheriff."

105

"Why, I thank you, Mr. Watson. I don't get many compliments in my job. Most people aren't like you; they don't realize what this great country would be like if the thieves and rapists and murderers were allowed to exist with impunity."

"It wouldn't be much of a country at all," Ellie said, flashing a look at Roebuck.

"Going downhill as it is," Boadeen said with a frown of disgust, "with all them civil rights agitators and college demonstrators. Tell you what they ought to do—not to the kids, of course, the ones that really think they know what they're doing—but to the bearded long-haired commies and agitators. They ought to lay their long-haired heads open the first time they cause trouble. Then they wouldn't be so loud-mouth quick to cause trouble the next time."

"You've got a point," Roebuck agreed.

Boadeen hooked a thumb through the huge ring of keys that hung from his thick leather belt. "Well, it certainly is good to have folk like you here at the lake, somebody a man can talk to."

Ellie smiled. "Glad you feel that way, Sheriff."

"Good for the lake's reputation. Keeps out the—you know the type I mean."

"I suppose it does," Ellie said. "We enjoy the lake a lot."

Boadeen turned his head, gazing in a half-circle with pale eyes that didn't change expression. "Don't wonder you enjoy it here. Beautiful place. One of the prettiest in the country." He looked again at Roebuck and Ellie. "You folk catch lots of fish now." He threw them a military half-salute.

"We'll try, Sheriff," Roebuck said.

He watched Boadeen turn and walk away, very erect, keys jangling, swinging one arm wide to clear the holstered pistol and nightstick that hung at his hip. The sheriff stopped after a few steps and turned, as if in afterthought.

"By the by, Mr. Watson, I understand there was some shooting up here lately. It ain't hunting season, you know. We've had some trouble, people shooting squirrel from their boats."

"I was only target shooting," Roebuck said. "It's just a .22 pistol. The doctors recommended it, said it would be good for my nerves, keep my reflexes sharp."

"I trusted that was all it was," Boadeen said with a smile. He glanced at Ellie. "You folk need me, just run on over to the office and use the phone." He walked back to them, drew a card from his breast pocket, and placed it in Roebuck's outstretched hand. Then he threw them another half-salute, turned, and jangled away.

Roebuck looked at the card after the sheriff's car had disappeared down the dirt road. It was a white card, with a gold replica of the shield that had been painted on the car door, and at the bottom was the address of Boadeen's office in Danton and a phone number.

Slipping the card into his pocket, Roebuck turned to Ellie. "I thought we'd had it. I was trying to figure a way to get inside the cabin and get my gun."

Ellie looked toward the mouth of the road where dust still hung in the air from Boadeen's departure. "I don't think he suspects anything. He wouldn't have been so friendly and all."

Roebuck spat and kicked at the dirt. "Maybe we should move on, hide out someplace else."

"I don't see any reason we should," Ellie said. "He doesn't suspect anything—he couldn't. As far as he knows, we're just another couple renting a cabin at the lake. He probably pays a visit to everybody who rents a cabin for more than a week."

"Maybe."

Ellie walked over and rested her hand on Roebuck's arm.

"No 'maybes' about it. He's no worry. Every county in the state has got a sheriff."

"I just hope he doesn't come back." Roebuck looked out over the wide lake toward the opposite bank.

"He's no worry," Ellie repeated, "but I suspect he'll drop back here from time to time."

Boadeen was like a shadow over Roebuck's world. Days passed as before, the same activity, the same lolling in the sun during the day and making love to Ellie in the cooler hours of evening, but it wasn't the same as it had been before Sheriff Boadeen's visit. Roebuck felt again the heaviness in his chest, the furtiveness of the pursued man. Though Boadeen hadn't shown himself for two days, Roebuck had no doubt about him returning. The delicately balanced world had tumbled; a serpent was in Eden.

Boadeen appeared on the third day. Roebuck and Ellie were sitting in front of the cabin, sipping cool drinks in the dying hours of late afternoon, when they saw a small metal boat making its way slowly across the quiet lake toward them. The gentle throbbing of an outboard motor came to them as the boat neared, and they saw that it contained one man. They sat without speaking, waiting, and as the motor cut to silence and the metal bottom of the boat grounded on the mud bank, Sheriff Boadeen leaped nimbly ashore and secured the boat with a long silver chain and a spiraled stake.

The sheriff was out of uniform. He was wearing a white polo shirt, neatly pressed Bermuda shorts, and white tennis shoes that had somehow avoided the mud on the bank. In his right hand was a string of four or five bigger-than-average fish. Even dressed as he was, carrying a string of fish, he might have passed inspection.

Roebuck felt resentment and helpless anger churn inside

him. He and Ellie stood as the sheriff approached.

When he was about fifteen feet from them Boadeen's rigid expression changed abruptly to a smile, as if they were suddenly within range.

" 'Lo, there. How you folk doing?"

"Just fine," Roebuck said.

Ellie put her hands on her hips. "Nice catch you got there, Sheriff."

Boadeen held the string of fish up so they could examine it more closely. The last fish on the string, a big rainbow trout, had obviously just been caught. It was still flopping, its skewered gills pulsating for breath as it hung beneath Boadeen's handsome smile.

"I go fishing a lot up here on my days off," Boadeen said. "I found myself near here and decided to drop by and see you." He looked at Ellie. "Thought maybe we could fry up some of these beauties for dinner."

Ellie was taken partly by surprise. "That's nice of you, Sheriff . . ."

"Now, don't say no, Ellie." There was a touch of shyness in his voice. "You don't mind if I call you folk Ellie and Lou, do you?"

" 'Course not, Sheriff," Ellie said quickly.

"The fact is," Roebuck said, "that neither of us cares too much for fish. We like to catch them, but we usually give them away or throw them back."

Boadeen protruded his lower lip and nodded approval. "Why, that's sportsman-like conduct, Lou. I like to see that in a man." He grinned at Ellie. "And in a woman."

"I don't know if it's sportsman-like," Ellie said. "It's just that we're both steak and potato fans."

"I surely don't blame you for that." Boadeen ran a hand over carefully combed hair that seemed to fall back perfectly in place as soon as his fingers had disarranged it. "Say, though, I got an idea! There's a place in Danton called Angus House—best steak you'll ever eat. How about you folk running in there with me tonight and I'll treat? Least I can do after offering you a meal of something you don't like."

"Really, Sheriff," Ellie said, "we appreciate you asking but we can't go. Lou's doctor made him promise to stay completely isolated for at least a month. He's got to get well a hundred percent or he'll never fly again."

Roebuck waited now to see if Boadeen would have the nerve to ask him if he could escort Ellie into town for dinner alone.

The sheriff wasn't ready to go quite that far. "I'll tell you," he said amiably, "I got some connections with the fellow who owns Angus House. He was in trouble once and I helped him out, if you get my meaning. I can pick up some of his best steaks and bring them up here and we can let Ellie broil them right here in the cabin."

"I don't know," Roebuck said.

"Why not, Lou?" Ellie gave him her secret smile. "I don't mind cooking. It'll feel good to whip up a big meal again for more than two people."

"If the sheriff's furnishing the steaks," Roebuck said, shrugging, "how can we say no?"

"Fine," Boadeen said. "Settled, then! I'll turn up here tomorrow evening about this time with the juiciest sirloins you ever saw." He held his string of fish away from his body and looked at them. "I better be getting back and cleaning these."

"We'll see you tomorrow, then, Sheriff," Roebuck said.

They watched Boadeen get into his boat and push off into the lake. He jerked once on the starting cord and the outboard motor sputtered to life, spinning the boat in a slow half-circle to head for the opposite bank. Boadeen looked back over his wake and gave them his little half-salute half-wave.

"He's got a hell of a nerve," Roebuck said.

Ellie sighed. "We had to let him come tomorrow night. He might have started to get suspicious if we'd told him no."

"Maybe we should leave here," Roebuck said. "I feel like things are closing in again."

Ellie shook her head. "The worst thing we could do is leave real suddenly. He might get so suspicious, he'd start digging and find out who we are."

"Maybe you're right, but I sure as hell don't like him."

"So who does? But we have to be nice to him if he likes us. That's the safest thing we can do."

"That might be, but I don't want to be so nice to him that he starts hanging around here."

"Would you rather have him hanging around his office by one of those teletypes, or listening to his police radio?"

"He'll hear about us sooner or later anyway," Roebuck said with dismay. "He's got to."

"But he won't know who we are, Lou. We look like any other couple on a fishing trip. They didn't get a good description of me when we were spotted in Collinsville, and you don't have any distinguishing marks or anything."

"Just my eagle tattoo," Roebuck said, "and I won't let him see that."

"The only way he could suspect us is because of the car," Ellie said. "And there are thousands of station wagons that color. We just have to make sure he doesn't get a look at the license plate."

"He's not likely to. He'd have to scrape the mud off it."

"You got him outsmarted before he's even started to think," Ellie said, and she smiled invitingly with her generous mouth. Roebuck smiled with her, smiling the uneasiness from himself as they walked into the cabin.

3

Sheriff Boadeen arrived the next evening just as Roebuck and Ellie were returning from a luckless day's fishing on the lake. Roebuck watched as Boadeen braked the sheriff's car to a halt in exactly the same place before the cabin as he had the first time he'd visited them, as if invisible markings designated a parking space there.

Carrying rods and tackle box, Roebuck and Ellie walked up the mud bank toward the car. As they drew near and Boadeen opened the door and got out, Roebuck glimpsed a walnut stocked shotgun mounted with chrome brackets on the dashboard. The sheriff himself was resplendent in a powder blue uniform crisscrossed with black leather and displaying a formidable-looking gold badge.

"No luck, I see," Boadeen said as he shut the door behind him with that stiff, backward motion of his arm. "Or did you throw them back?"

"We threw them back," Ellie said, " 'cause they weren't worth keeping, anyway."

"Well, here's something worth keeping." Boadeen opened the package of butcher paper he was carrying to show them the steaks from Angus House. "Those are surely the reddest, juiciest cuts you'll ever see."

"I've never seen any better," Roebuck said, "except when

I worked as a cowboy in Wyoming. But that's been a long time ago."

Boadeen raised an eyebrow and looked at him with an intensity that made Roebuck uneasy. "Now you mention it, you look like you oughta be a cowboy. Something about you . . ."

"John Wayne," Roebuck said. "I was his double in a few movies."

"By gosh, you do resemble him. What kind of doubling did you do?"

"Stunt man," Roebuck said modestly. "Falls and things."

The sheriff clucked his tongue. "Learn something interesting about you folk every time I come up here."

"Those steaks'll spoil if we stand here much longer," Ellie said. "Why don't we go in and I'll put them on the broiler and make up a salad."

"Best idea yet," Boadeen said, winking at her.

They entered the cabin and Roebuck sat in a folding chair across from Boadeen while Ellie prepared dinner in the cabin's small kitchen. As he studied the stiff, authoritarian figure of Sheriff Boadeen, Roebuck wondered how such irony had happened. Here he was, running for his life from the law, and here sat the law across from him, waiting to exchange pleasant small talk.

"I noticed you carry a shotgun in your car," Roebuck said, trying to get comfortable in the webbed chair.

"Riot gun," Boadeen corrected. "I saw you admiring it when I got out of the cruiser. It's a twelve gauge automatic with an extra long barrel, and I have my own shells made up special, big pellets that'll stop a man in his tracks if just one or two hits him."

"Ever had to use it?"

Boadeen smiled. "Not yet."

Ellie came in from the kitchen and handed them each a

113

can of beer. "The steaks are on."

Boadeen looked at her, his smile lingering. "I can smell 'em cooking."

"Why don't you build a fire so it can get going while we're eating," Ellie called to Roebuck as she walked back into the kitchen.

Roebuck balanced his beer on the metal arm of his chair and went to the fireplace. He put in some tinder from the stack of wood alongside the stonework; then he placed a large log on top of it.

Boadeen noisily crumpled a piece of old newspaper that had been lying on the sofa and tossed it to Roebuck.

"This'll make it easier."

Without answering, Roebuck wadded the newspaper and wedged it under the log. He touched his lighter to the paper and stood, gazing down at the tiny but voracious flame. "A bit hot for a fire, ain't it?" Boadeen asked behind him.

"Ellie likes them," Roebuck answered, still staring at the growing flame. "She likes to sit in front of a fire in the evenings."

"Sounds like a real little homebody." Was there a knowing sarcasm in Boadeen's voice?

Roebuck turned away from the flame. "She is," he said. "We have a fireplace at home and during the winter you can't pry her away from it."

"Good to have a wife who likes to keep a fire burning." Boadeen laughed sharply at some inner joke. "Home fire, that is." He pulled on his beer and squinted at Roebuck over the uptilted can. "No offense, Lou, but it strikes me that you seem kind of old to be a flyer."

"Old?" Roebuck leaned casually on the mantel. "I am too old to fly combat, but for a test pilot they want a more mature flyer, one who's been through everything. That's why nerve and know-how are more important than reflexes. You have to be able to think while the wings are coming off."

"Sounds like a dangerous job."

"It is," Roebuck said, "but it pays well."

Ellie's voice came from the kitchen. "How do you like your steak, Sheriff Boadeen?"

"Rare and bloody!" He rested an arm on the back of the sofa and looked past Roebuck into the fireplace where the flames were licking at the base of the big log. "Looks like she's going to start," he said. "There surely is something about a fire that holds you, the way it turns and dances, always rising. You can see what you want in a fire, if you get my meaning."

"You can see things," Roebuck said in a low voice.

Ellie came in and sat down in the webbed chair, taking a sip of Roebuck's beer. "Should be ready to eat pretty soon. What've you two been talking about?"

"About what a homebody you are," Roebuck said. "How you like to sit by the fireplace back home—in Chicago."

"Sure," Ellie said. "We don't go out much."

"You folk got any kids?" Boadeen asked.

"One," Roebuck said quickly. "A boy in junior high."

"That's great," Sheriff Boadeen said earnestly. "We never had kids. Then my wife died nine years ago in a highway accident. Damn drunken driver doing a hundred miles an hour. He didn't even have insurance."

"That's too bad," Ellie said.

"Surely is." Boadeen nodded his head soberly. "She was a real good woman."

Ellie stood. "I guess that rare steak should be about ready. Excuse me."

Boadeen's eyes darted to watch her walk back into the kitchen, then he looked up at Roebuck. "You're a lucky man."

Roebuck was well aware of what the sheriff was really thinking, but he forced himself to smile. "Thanks," he said, and he could see the subtle mockery in Boadeen's pale eyes.

"Food's ready!" Ellie called, and they went into the kitchen to sit at the tiny Formica-topped table.

Roebuck saw that Sheriff Boadeen was one of those people who ate with impeccable manners, possessing the ability to hit his mouth with unerring accuracy without looking at his food.

"You surely do this steak credit," Boadeen said, looking admiringly at Ellie as he severed another piece of meat with his steak knife.

Ellie acknowledged the compliment with a brief smile.

Boadeen was still looking at her as he lifted his fork to his mouth.

"Do you really have much trouble out here?" Roebuck asked.

"You'd be surprised." Boadeen turned his gaze on Roebuck. "It ain't all in the big cities, the agitation and the commie inspired unrest. They have control of some of the newspapers and TV stations, you know, and folk out here read and watch TV."

"What kind of trouble have you had?" Ellie asked.

"Well, at the Danton high school not long ago they tried to have these lectures on sex education. Some of the things they went into I wouldn't tell you about because we're eating." He speared a bite of steak with a vengeance. "No, the commies and long-haired radicals haven't forgotten the folk in the small towns. I've got the statistics to prove it!"

"Do you think the communists were behind those sex education lectures?" Ellie asked, buttering a roll.

"I surely do! This Dr. Luther who was giving the lectures is from Detroit, and I know people there who tell me he consorts with suspected communists."

"The last communist I saw," Roebuck said calmly, "went down in flames while I was looking at him through my gunsight. Straight into the Yalu River. I almost felt sorry for him."

"I say good riddance to him. Pass the pepper please, Ellie."

"You sure don't like communists," Ellie said, handing him the shaker.

"Don't like lawbreakers of any kind. But these communist agitators are the worst I ever seen. Somebody's got to stop them from spreading their seeds of insurrection and their Maoist lies."

"You seem to know a lot about international politics for a county sheriff," Roebuck said. "It seems a little out of your line."

Boadeen laughed and looked down at his plate. "I'll tell you, Lou, this sheriff thing can be just a rung on the ladder. If the wind blows right I plan to run for County Supervisor next year, and then who knows what?"

"We wish you luck," Ellie said.

"Why, thank you, Ellie. By gosh, it's still a great country, and a man can go as far as his ambition will take him."

Roebuck saw the spark in the sheriff's eyes when he said this, and the rather wolfish grin. For a second Boadeen's ambition was naked before them, the covering of righteousness and small town affability stripped briefly from him.

"How far do you think you can go, Sheriff?" Roebuck asked.

"Far enough to do some good, I hope to God! I don't do things by halves, Lou. That's why you see me driving a brand-new high-speed cruiser, and all my enforcement equipment is top quality. The people of Clark County want first-rate protection, and they're willing to pay for it."

"They certainly seem to have it in you," Ellie said.

As they finished their meal Roebuck tried to accustom himself to the sheriff's presence. He was a big man, though not quite as tall as Roebuck, and his uniform seemed to dominate the tiny cabin. Suppose he found out about them before they left? Sheriff Boadeen, with his unyielding, hard-driving ambition, seemed to Roebuck the embodiment of the relentless lawman, a modern-day Pat Garrett, a yokel Mountie who would never give up.

As Ellie was clearing the table Boadeen pushed back his chair and lit a long, expensive-looking cigar. He offered one to Roebuck, who declined and lit a cigarette.

"Why don't I fix some drinks," Ellie said, "and we'll go into the other room."

"Sounds fine," Boadeen said from behind a bluish cloud of smoke. "Make mine a Scotch and water if you have any."

"I think we've got a little," Ellie said.

"Bourbon for me," Roebuck said, resenting the odorous haze Boadeen was exhaling.

When they went into the main room of the cabin Roebuck opened a window. "Gets hot in here sometimes with a fire."

Boadeen stuck out his lower lip and nodded, then clamped the cigar between his teeth. Roebuck realized that he knew the smoke was bothering him, and that the sheriff was secretly enjoying it.

Ellie came in with their drinks, holding the three glasses bunched together between the spread fingers of both hands.

Boadeen quickly took two of the glasses from her and handed the bourbon and water to Roebuck.

"Can't overwork the little lady," he said. "Unless she likes to be overworked." For her he politely ground out his cigar in the glass ashtray.

They sat before the lazy, flickering fire, Roebuck and Ellie on the sofa, Sheriff Boadeen in the webbed chair.

"Yes, sir," the sheriff said idly, gazing into the fire, "a man can go far in this world, far as his nerve'll take him. Don't you think so, Ellie?"

"Could be."

"Wha'd'you think, Lou?"

"That's true to a point," Roebuck said, looking down at his drink. "The fact is, though, I've seen some men overstep themselves because of their nerve. I did a stint with the C.I.A. in Japan. One of my best friends in the agency took it on himself to try to steal the famous purple machine from communist agents in Tokyo. They caught him and he lost his nerve; he talked when they poured hot coffee in his ear through a funnel. I had to get out of the country."

"Purple machine?" the sheriff asked in an interested voice. "What's that?"

"Still classified," Roebuck said curtly, looking into the fire without expression. "I shouldn't have mentioned it."

"But did we ever get hold of it?" Boadeen asked.

"Six months later," Roebuck said, "when I went back to Japan." And he refused to say more.

"I don't mean to pry," Boadeen said, catching Ellie's eye while Roebuck was looking the other way. "Least not in matters of national secrecy."

Ellie caught the meaning in his look. She drew a deep breath and turned her head.

"Maybe if the sheriff gets elected governor you can tell him about it," she said to Roebuck.

Roebuck flicked his cigarette butt into the fireplace. "Not even then."

Three drinks and two hours' conversation later, the sheriff left, and Roebuck sat gazing morosely at Ellie as she casually tidied up the cabin.

"You were nicer to him than you had to be," he said.

She stopped what she was doing and turned to face him with the dirty glass ashtray in her hand. "We have to be nice to him. The nicer we are, the less likely it is he'll be suspicious."

"Isn't it obvious to you what he's got in mind?"

" 'Course it is. But the worst thing I could do for us would be to tell him to get lost." She set the ashtray back down and turned on the small table radio. "He knows how long we rented the cabin for," she said as the radio warmed and began to emit soft music. "It'll look funny if we leave sooner, even though we want to."

That was true, Roebuck had to concede. Right now the police had no exact idea as to their whereabouts, only the vague knowledge that they were headed west. If they left here unexpectedly and Boadeen got suspicious and started making inquiries, it wouldn't take long for him to find out who they were. Of course they could make up some lie to leave early, something about Ellie's mother getting sick, or their imaginary teen-age son getting into trouble, but Boadeen wasn't a complete fool—a lie might make him more suspicious than if they simply packed and left.

And Benny Gipp. Roebuck had hardly thought of him since they'd rented the cabin, but Gipp was still looking, he was sure. The lakeside cabin provided a refuge from Gipp as well as the police. While Roebuck and Ellie stayed here, Sheriff Boadeen was a problem, but he was their only real worry.

If it came to a choice between Sheriff Boadeen and Benny Gipp, Roebuck would have to say that he feared Gipp the most. Boadeen was a professional zealot, but Gipp was a fanatic. Roebuck wondered now as he had before about the relationship between Gipp and Ingrahm, about the bond between the two men that made him so sure Gipp would never give up, would pursue him around the world if necessary to avenge Ingrahm's death. Gipp was like a capable and deadly slave, carrying out with unquestioning loyalty the last unspoken command of his dead master. It was an unnatural dedication, damned unnatural, and it was a dedication that frightened Roebuck.

"See if you can get some news on that thing," he said to Ellie.

"The news'll be on that station pretty soon," she said. "It's the one we always listen to."

She was right. It was almost eleven o'clock, later than Roebuck had thought. He and Ellie nightly tuned in the eleven o'clock news on the local station, listening for some gleaning of information about themselves. In the two and a half weeks that they'd been there the news broadcasts had mentioned once that they were still being sought, but that was all. The stolen station wagon apparently had not been connected with them, and no one seemed to have recognized them since that time in Collinsville.

Roebuck sat back and watched Ellie move about the cabin in unconscious time to the soft music. It was easy to understand why Sheriff Boadeen was interested in her. He probably made it a practice to size up all the women who stayed at the lake, and it was no wonder he'd decided blonde, slender Ellie was the most attractive. Roebuck didn't tell himself that the sheriff might also have decided she was the most likely.

"I want you to be careful with Boadeen," Roebuck said. "Don't let him get too close."

"Don't worry," Ellie said. "That kind of creep is easy to handle."

"I don't want him to ever do anything to you. If I assault a county sheriff, they'll be looking for us twice as hard as they are now."

"Let's go to bed," Ellie said with a smile that Roebuck had learned to interpret. "And while I think about it, see that I get up early. Tomorrow's the day I go shopping in Danton."

4

Ellie was pushing a wire grocery cart easily over the smooth cement floor of Blatkin's Foodliner when she happened to glance out between the LOW, LOW PRICES signs on the wide plate glass window. The glass had just been washed by a young man in a white shirt and was still smeared where the squeegee had glided over it, and at first she wasn't sure it was him. But the smears disappeared almost immediately under the hot sun and she could see Sheriff Boadeen quite clearly. He was standing near the curb, examining the front of the station wagon.

Ellie pushed the cart over by some shelves of canned goods and stood watching as the sheriff looked toward the store as if trying to make up his mind whether or not to enter. He drew himself up, looked from side to side, and advanced on the store with wide, purposeful strides.

There weren't many customers in Blatkin's, so Ellie knew she couldn't get out without him seeing her. She pushed the grocery cart forward and pretended to concentrate on the merchandise that lined the narrow aisle. The electric-eye door hissed as Boadeen entered, and Ellie moved slowly along the aisle toward the back of the store as she examined the rows of dog food and soap powder.

She turned the corner and moved down the next aisle, stooping to pick out a bottle of catsup. When she straightened there he was, looking at her from the next aisle over the dietary peaches with a sugary smile on his clean-shaven face.

" 'Lo there, Ellie." The overhead light from the fluorescent fixtures glinted off the gold badge on his cap. "Odd running into you at Blatkin's."

"I suppose, Sheriff." Ellie returned the smile. "I come in here about twice a week to do the shopping."

The sheriff disappeared for a moment, then walked around the corner of the aisle, glancing into her grocery cart as if to make sure she was indeed shopping as she'd claimed. Ellie saw that he carried a jar of instant coffee as an excuse to have entered the store.

"Well, what do you think?" Boadeen asked.

"Of what?"

"Why, of our little town of Danton. Best place to raise kids in the whole state."

"I really haven't seen much of it," Ellie said. "I just drive straight in here and straight back. But it does look real nice," she added, as an elderly woman bumped her in the rear with a cart. Ellie moved to the side to let her through and Boadeen nodded to the woman as if he knew her.

"Where's the husband?" Boadeen asked, making a big show of waiting until the old woman was around the corner. Ellie could take that as she wanted.

"Fishing, I suppose," Ellie said. "He doesn't like to shop."

"Well now, I don't see how he can't like to shop with you." Boadeen fixed what he thought to be his confidential stare on her.

"Maybe because we've been married a good while," Ellie said smoothly, reaching for a can of beans. As if giving it some thought, she suddenly reached for a second can. Boadeen watched her knowingly.

"How'd you like to take a little ride around town in the

cruiser?" he asked in a soft voice. "I could show you a few things—if you don't think your husband'd mind."

"Oh, he wouldn't mind," Ellie said, "but he expects me back pretty soon."

Boadeen gave her his wolfish smile. "Didn't think he'd really mind. Lou doesn't strike me as the jealous type. I mean, he seems to me the type to figure what he don't know won't hurt him."

"I guess he's that type," Ellie said. She wanted to keep the sheriff on a long string, but a taut one.

"Since he's that kind," Boadeen said, "suppose the next time you come into Danton I show you around. I can even show you my office. All the latest equipment."

"I guess that'd be okay," Ellie said.

They looked at each other without speaking. At the far end of the aisle a cash register went Grrrrlunk, racking up a sale as a customer checked out.

"After I show you the office," Boadeen said, "maybe I can show you where I live."

Grrrrlunk! Grrrrlunk!

"I live above the office."

"That's interesting," Ellie said, playing dumb, "living close to your work, I mean."

"You're interesting, Ellie," the sheriff said seriously. His smooth, small-featured face was blank.

Grrrrlunk!

"You and your husband are interesting folk, if you understand my meaning."

"I think I understand, Sheriff."

"You struck me as the type that'd understand things. When do you next intend to come into Danton?"

Ellie smiled wistfully. "When the food runs out, I guess."

Grrrrlunk!

The sheriff ran his fingertips over his gleaming cartridge belt. "I'll see you then," he said, backing away. "When you get hungry." He winked at her and was gone around the watermelon display.

Grrrrlunk! Grrrrlunk! Grrrrlunk!

Ellie pushed her cart forward to check out, past a bright pyramid of cans as eternal as the two-day sale price.

Roebuck recognized the sound of the car. He stood inside the screen door of the cabin and through the trees he caught a glimpse of it laboring up the bumpy road. When Ellie had parked the station wagon, backing it into the shallow ruts that the rear wheels had made, Roebuck stepped outside and walked toward it to help her carry in the groceries. He opened the tailgate as she turned off the engine and got out.

"Anything happen?" he asked, as she walked toward the back of the car.

"Nothing," she said. "I saw Sheriff Boadeen."

Roebuck pulled a heavy bag out of the station wagon and stood holding it.

"He came into the store where I was shopping. He saw the car parked outside."

"Did he act suspicious?" Roebuck rested the bag on the tailgate.

Ellie shook her head. "He wanted me to go for a ride with him in his police car. That's why he came into the store, though he did buy a jar of coffee."

"Did you go?"

" 'Course not."

Roebuck grabbed the bag and walked across the hard earth toward the cabin door as Ellie followed.

"I don't like this," he said, "the way he keeps chasing you."

"Maybe it'll keep his mind off other things."

Roebuck carried the groceries inside and set them on the kitchen table, then he went quickly back outside into the sunlight where Ellie was waiting.

"He's got to get onto us sooner or later," Roebuck said, walking back toward the car with Ellie at his side. "I'll bet the bastard stays up late every night going through old wanted posters and reading crime textbooks. I'll bet he has a subscription to *Law and Order Magazine*. He's a nut on his job."

"We'll only be here a little over a week more," Ellie said. "I don't think he'll figure out anything that soon."

"He's making a pest of himself," Roebuck said angrily. "A pest! Do you think I like having a goddamn sheriff hanging around trying to make you when I'm wanted for murder?" He dragged the last two bags out of the car and lifted his knee to slam the tailgate.

"Let me take that light bag. I don't like it any more than you, but while he's chasing me he's not gonna be paying much attention to us in any other way."

Roebuck followed her into the cabin, and the screen door slammed behind them with a long reverberating bang.

"You're right," he said, lowering the groceries onto the table. "But I'm sure as hell getting tired of being nice to him when he comes around."

Ellie got two cans of beer from the refrigerator and opened the pull tab tops with two skillful yanks. "Only a little while longer, Lou." She handed him one of the beer cans. "Anyway he'll cool off some."

"You're underestimating yourself," Roebuck said, taking a swallow of ice-flecked beer.

And Roebuck was right. Sheriff Boadeen showed no signs of "cooling off" toward Ellie. With feigned friendship toward Roebuck, he visited them almost every evening in the cabin, where they'd sit before the fireplace to drink and talk. The sound of his cruiser's powerful engine became as much a part of their evenings as the croaking of the frogs by the lake. He came with the setting of the sun.

Boadeen now barely concealed his growing interest in Ellie as he barely concealed his growing disdain for Roebuck. Time was running out on the sheriff, and this one would get away at the end of the week if he didn't hurry.

"When you going into Danton to do some more shopping?" he asked her late Wednesday evening as he sat sipping his Scotch and water before the fire.

"I don't know," Ellie answered. "I suspect tomorrow or the next day."

"I should think you folk would be running out of food up here," Boadeen said thoughtfully. "I should think you'd be getting hungry."

"As a matter of fact," Roebuck said; "we get by all right."

"Still and all," Boadeen said, "small town store like Blatkin's sells cheaper than stores in Chicago." He smiled with half his mouth and looked at Ellie. "Wouldn't hurt for you to stock up, take advantage of it while you can."

"I don't like her going into town alone too often," Roebuck said. "Something's liable to happen."

"Not in my town, Lou. Nothing can happen to her that I wouldn't be there to take care of."

"Nothing can happen, hell! One time in one of the nicest neighborhoods of Chicago a man walked right up to her and tried to drag her into an alley. He didn't know I was across the street and happened to see the whole thing reflected in a shop window. I ran across the street and got there just in time. Grabbed him and shook him till his teeth rattled. That's how Ellie and I met."

"I'll be damned," Boadeen said softly. "Frighten you much, Ellie?"

"Sure," Ellie said. "I didn't know him from Adam."

Boadeen chuckled, a sudden machine gun chuckle. Then he ran a finger thoughtfully along the ridge of his narrow nose. "Speaking of things in Chicago, I take it you folk have an unlisted phone number. I got a phone directory from every major city in America in my office and when I looked in Chicago I didn't see your number. Checked on some that might have been yours, but they were always somebody else's. Hope you folk don't think I'm nosy."

"Why would you check on us, Sheriff?" Roebuck asked in a voice a shade too high.

"Just happened to have the Chicago directory out," Boadeen said, "and I got curious. Part of my job to be curious."

"We do have an unlisted number," Ellie said smoothly. "We were getting crank calls."

"What kind of calls?" Boadeen leaned forward into the light of the fire. "Sex maniac or something?"

"That's right," Ellie said. "He'd call me and tell me things before I could hang up."

Anger crossed Boadeen's handsome, fleshy face. "They oughta catch people like that and fry them before it's too late. Who knows where something like that could lead? Next time he'll be following women and knocking on their doors and God knows what all!"

"There's no way to catch a crank caller," Roebuck said. "That's why we have an unlisted number." He watched Boadeen settle back on the couch, the firelight shimmering over his polished sheriff's boots. It was odd how sitting before the fire hadn't bothered Roebuck until the sheriff started making his frequent visits. Now Roebuck had to put down an increasing desire to leave the room when the flames were dancing, and last night he had dreamed his dream for the first

129

time since he and Ellie had come to the cabin.

"While we're on the subject of communications," Boadeen said suddenly, "I couldn't help but notice something else about you folk. I checked at the post office and old Mr. Gardner tells me you haven't received any mail at all. That's funny, especially with you having a young boy back home."

"He's not much for writing letters," Roebuck said.

"And not many people know where we're at." Ellie spoke up. "The doctors want Lou to rest and demanded that we wouldn't tell anyone where we were going. That way there wouldn't be any phone calls or letters to disturb him."

"You must be a pretty valuable man," Boadeen said.

Roebuck folded his arm across his chest. "There's no substitute for experience and they know it."

"Reckon not," Boadeen said. "Right, Ellie?"

Ellie was looking at the sheriff closely, rolling her highball glass between the palms of her hands. "That's right, Sheriff."

"Tomorrow's sale day at Blatkin's Foodliner," the sheriff said, looking at Roebuck but talking to Ellie. "Sure hate to see you folk miss it."

"I'll check and see what we're out of, Lou," Ellie said. "Maybe we can buy some canned goods and take them home with us. It'd probably be worth the trouble."

"Why, people come from miles around to shop at Blatkin's," the sheriff said. "Best prices in the state."

"If you go into Danton tomorrow," Roebuck said, "it might be a good idea if I go with you and drop by the post office. Remember, your mother was going to write us and tell us how she was."

"That's right," Ellie said. She laid a hand on Roebuck's knee. "But you'll stay here and rest like the doctor ordered, Lou." She smiled fondly at him. "They made me promise to see that you wouldn't do anything but relax for a month. You remember what Dr. Gipp said."

"That's right." Roebuck turned pale and took a quick, final swallow of his drink. He set the glass on the floor. "Can't go against doctor's orders."

"I see your glass is empty too," Ellie said to Boadeen. "We'd offer you one for the road, Sheriff, but we're clean out of Scotch."

Catching the hint, Boadeen looked at her and grinned his predatory grin. "That's okay," he said, standing and placing his uniform cap carefully on his head. "If I'm in town same time you are tomorrow, maybe we'll run into one another." He smoothed his trousers where they were tucked into his high-topped boots and adjusted the holster and long nightstick that hung at his hip. "See you folk." He turned and strutted jangling from the fire-lighted cabin, like some slighted Prussian Cavalry officer going back into the past.

Roebuck and Ellie sat listening to the fading rumble of the cruiser's powerful engine.

"I told you he suspects something," Roebuck said, kicking his empty glass across the room. "We've got to get out of here!"

"He suspects something," Ellie agreed, "but we don't know what and neither does he. If you ask me, I think he did all that checking on us to find out more about me."

"Yeah," Roebuck said, "but what's to keep him from checking further?"

"The next time he says anything to me, I'll tell him right off he doesn't have a chance. Then maybe he'll lose interest in us."

"Lose interest!" Roebuck stood and paced to the other side of the cabin. "Lose interest! He'll probably gain interest! I knew an MP like that once. Career cops like that don't lose

131

interest—they have to be satisfied!"

"He knows we're leaving this weekend, Lou. He's not that suspicious of us that he'll start checking all over the country. He thinks we have an unlisted phone number in Chicago now, so maybe he'll forget all about it."

"Maybe he will," Roebuck said, wanting to believe it. "I hope you're right. If it weren't for the fact that I know they'd be hot after us if we left here suddenly, we'd pack and leave right now."

"We'll go now," Ellie said, "if you say to."

Roebuck walked to the center of the room and stood with his thumbs hitched in his belt.

"No," he said, slowly and evenly, "it's worth the risk to stay until the end of the week. Then when we leave it'll be a clean break."

5

Ellie sat in the station wagon in front of Blatkin's Foodliner and waited. Within fifteen minutes Sheriff Boadeen's cruiser turned into the small blacktop lot and came to a rocking halt beside her. The sheriff looked over at her and smiled.

Ellie took her purse and got out of the station wagon. Sheriff Boadeen said nothing as she walked around, and he reached over and unlocked the passenger's door so she could get into the cruiser. As the powerful car pulled back out into the street, Ellie looked at the neat blank tablet and clipboard lying on the seat, the shortwave radio, and the shining walnut stocked shotgun mounted the length of the dashboard on silver brackets.

Boadeen saw her looking at the gun and smiled. "Husband know you're here with me?"

"I don't know," Ellie answered truthfully, "I think so."

"I think so too," Boadeen said. He made a right turn and they went down one of Danton's side streets.

It was a typical small Midwestern town, new brick buildings next to old white frames, gas stations, a confectionery, hardware store, bank, post office, and here and there a glimpse of nothing behind them.

"I knew you'd meet me," Boadeen said casually.

Ellie didn't answer.

"You and Lou ain't like most couples that come to the lake. I spotted it right off. So, according to my job, I did a little checking. You're not really from Chicago, are you?"

"We are," Ellie said. "We told you we had an unlisted number. Lots of people have unlisted numbers."

"Still," Boadeen said, looking ahead as he drove, "you two just don't fit right. Like the fact that you get no mail, and the way you're all nervous and wanted me to leave in a hurry the first time I met you."

Ellie turned her eyes on him honestly. "We're not law-breakers, Sheriff."

Boadeen gave his precise chuckle. "Why, I didn't say you were. But I do believe you're hiding from something."

The cruiser's engine broke into a deeper roar as they took a hill.

"You're right, Sheriff," Ellie said in a defeated voice. "We're hiding from my ex-husband. He doesn't want me to leave him and he hates Lou. He even tried to kill him once, run over him with our car."

"Why didn't you have him arrested?"

"You should know, Sheriff; it takes proof. Trouble is, we probably won't have proof until Lou or myself is dead. That's why we decided to hide from him a while, to let him get used to the idea of me being gone, of Lou and me being together."

The sheriff digested that story slowly while Ellie hoped he believed her.

"This ex-husband of yours following you?"

"We think he might be. That's why we didn't tell anyone where we were going."

Boadeen patted her on the knee, then let his hand rest there. "Don't be too upset, Ellie. That kind of thing happens all the time, but the husband seldom does anything about it. I've got the statistics to prove it."

Ellie made no attempt to remove his hand. "I hope you're right, Sheriff. But you can see why I was frightened."

"Surely can."

They were out of Danton now, surrounded by fields of ripe corn, tall green stalks that stretched away on either side of them. It was like a bug's eye view of a gigantic carpet. Dragonflies flitted now and then across the highway, and one struck the windshield with a loud smack that made Ellie wince.

Boadeen lifted his hand from her knee, slowed for a clearing that he must have known about and veered off the highway for a quick U-turn to head them back toward Danton. The hand returned to her stockinged knee, resting higher up on her thigh this time. She sat quietly.

"Would you like to go by the office?" Boadeen asked.

"Sure," Ellie said, "why not?"

"I thought you'd see it that way," Boadeen said. "I thought so the first time I saw you there at the lake."

"I know," Ellie said.

"You knew it would happen, didn't you?"

"I did."

They reentered Danton on a side street that ran parallel to the main highway and drove for about five minutes before stopping at the rear of a two story brick building. There was one set of yellow lines leading to the building, and Boadeen ran the car between them, facing a metal sign with his name and a gold shield painted on it mounted on the brick wall. They got out of the car and Boadeen reached without looking for the correct key that hung on the huge key ring on his belt. He swiveled his hip and inserted the key in one motion and they entered through the rear door.

There was no one in the office and the Venetian blinds on the front window were closed. A massive desk sat cater-corner facing the door. There were two telephones on the desk and that was all. Beneath a bulletin board decorated neatly with wanted posters was a table with a shortwave radio transmitter and an electric coffeepot on it. The walls by the desk were lined with filing cabinets, metal bookshelves, and a cherry wood gun rack with a padlocked chain running through the trigger guards of the dozen or so rifles and shotguns it held.

"Looks efficient," Ellie said. She knew what to say.

"It is efficient," Boadeen said proudly. "It's a firm step upward."

"Will you remember me when you get to be governor?" Ellie asked with her quiet smile.

Boadeen smiled back. "Why, I reckon that sort of depends on you, Ellie."

"I suppose you'll remember me," Ellie said. She walked to a bookcase and examined the leather-bound books. There were titles on law enforcement techniques, legal decisions, judges on the Supreme Court, firearms, civil liberties.

"Did you read all these?" Ellie asked, running her fingernail across the bindings of the books as a small boy might run a stick along a picket fence.

"They're reference works," Boadeen said. "All written by experts. I'm a self-educated man. I never wasted my time with the tripe they're teaching in colleges."

"You must know a lot," Ellie said, taking in the book-lined walls with a toss of her head.

Boadeen's professionally bland face broke into a smile. "I make what I know work. I campaigned myself to get a bond issue passed that'd buy all this equipment, so I could do the job right to the letter."

"That's wonderful," Ellie said.

Boadeen cocked his head at her. "You want to see the holdover?"

"Holdover?"

136

"The cell block, where I keep dangerous criminals until the State Patrol transfers them to prison. It's through that door there."

Ellie hesitated. "Is there anyone . . . in there now?"

"No, no," Boadeen said reassuringly, walking to the thick wooden door and opening it. "If there was, I surely wouldn't take you in there."

A few feet beyond the wooden door was a door lined with sheet metal and held shut by a sliding bolt lock. Sheriff Boadeen slipped the bolt and switched on a light.

The cell block was windowless, odorless. Steel and concrete bounced back the sound of their footsteps. Boadeen turned another light switch to reveal harshly shadowed rows of gleaming steel bars forming an aisle that led to a blank cinder block wall.

They took a few steps forward and Ellie saw that each cell contained a porcelain wash basin, a toilet, and a small bunk covered with a gray woolen blanket.

"It looks escape proof," she said admiringly. She'd decided to do a good job of alleviating the sheriff's suspicions, of making him not want to be suspicious. It wouldn't be all that hard for her to put her heart into her work.

"No one has ever got out," Boadeen said, the echo taking the softness from his Midwestern drawl. He stepped forward and opened the section of bars that was the door of the cell nearest them. His free hand pressed on the small of Ellie's back and he drew her to him. He began to kiss her warmly on the ear.

Ellie didn't struggle. "I thought you lived upstairs."

"Why, I do," Boadeen whispered, "but this is better. This is the most private place in town. Bars are made to keep people out as well as in, you know."

"If you say so, Sheriff."

137

Practiced fingers ran down the buttons on the back of her white blouse and unfastened her brassiere strap. She gasped involuntarily as one of her breasts was suddenly cupped in Boadeen's broad hand. He fondled her for a moment and then let go of her, nudging her gently into the cell. Ellie let her blouse and bra fall to the cement floor as she turned and sat down on the edge of the bunk.

Sheriff Boadeen stepped into the cell. On his face was a vague smile that came and went with his heavy breathing as he stood looking down at Ellie. That stiff, backward motion of his arm, and the cell door slammed shut loudly with an echoing, metallic clank.

"Makes a hell of a sound, doesn't it?" Boadeen said, and he began to undo his belt buckle.

For Boadeen it was conquest; for Ellie it was mere expediency.

Roebuck stood and watched from the cabin as Ellie parked the station wagon, watched her sit for a long moment before getting out and looking toward the lake to draw the fresh breeze into her lungs. He let the screen door slam behind him as he sauntered off the plank porch and walked toward her.

"Get your shopping done?"

"Sure." Ellie smiled and nodded.

Roebuck opened the tailgate of the station wagon. "Only one bag?"

"Our sheriff was exaggerating about the low prices at Blatkin's," Ellie said, "but I had to buy a few things just in case he did some more checking on us. Besides, there were some things we needed."

They went into the cabin and Roebuck sat at the kitchen table while she put the groceries away.

"Did you happen to see Sheriff Boadeen?"

Ellie squeezed a head of lettuce experimentally. "I saw him, but he was on the other side of the street and he didn't see me. I was glad to leave it that way."

Roebuck felt a bead of sweat run down the inside of his arm, zigzag to a stop, then continue toward his elbow more slowly. He clenched the fist of that arm with his thumb inside his fingers. He wanted to believe her, but there was just no way to know for sure. He should believe her, he told himself; there was really no reason not to believe her. Roebuck turned the whole thing over and over in his mind like a mental diamond, choosing his facets. Again he was at that most agonizing of crossroads, the pause of the pendulum, the moment of noncommitment.

It would be dishonorable and unreasonable not to believe her, he told himself at last. To not believe Ellie would be betraying his faith in her, his faith in himself. She was sure as hell happy with him, and it would be stupid to throw unfounded suspicions at her. It was natural to feel a little jealous with a woman like Ellie. Not that Boadeen wouldn't want to . . .

Ellie flipped the refrigerator door shut and turned to him. "What would you like for lunch?"

"How about hamburgers," Roebuck said, "and a salad from that head of lettuce you bought."

"Be ready in no time." Ellie started to fold the empty grocery bag, then stopped. "Darn it, I forgot cigarettes! The one thing we needed bad."

"I reckon you better stop at Blatkin's on the way back to the lake and buy something, just to make it look good," Boadeen had said when she was getting dressed. "But I want you to forget something important, like cigarettes." He'd turned his eager smile on her. "You better forget your ciga-

139

rettes and drive back into town tomorrow and buy some."

"That's okay," Roebuck said, looking down at the table top. "We've got enough to last this afternoon and evening. You can drive back into town tomorrow and buy some."

6

In the remaining week that she and Roebuck stayed at the cabin, Ellie had driven into Danton on some pretext to meet Boadeen three times. Saturday now. The day before Roebuck and Ellie were to leave the cabin.

Sheriff Boadeen awoke early that morning, did his sitting up exercises, and then breakfasted on toast and coffee before going downstairs to his office. He pulled the Venetian blind cord on the front window, blinking at the burst of morning light. Still unable to see clearly, he stood before the wall mirror to adjust his tie and place his cap on his head at just the right angle. Then he unlocked the front door and sat behind his desk to thumb idly through the latest *Law Enforcement Magazine*.

But he found his mind wandering to Ellie, to her warmth and her tight softness. Damned if she wasn't a hot one! And one who had been around, one who knew things . . . Boadeen turned a page of his magazine and chuckled. He bet there were some things that husband of hers didn't know about her.

The sheriff finished glancing through the magazine and slipped it carefully into a drawer. He sat drumming his fingers on the desktop for a moment before picking up the receiver of one of his phones.

141

"This is the sheriff," he said with authority. "Get me the post office."

He listened to the clicking, buzzing mysteries of the switchboard.

"I want to talk to Jack Gardner," he said, when someone at the post office had answered the phone.

"Jack? How about running over here with those wanted circulars from the East if they came in yet. They are? Good. I'll be waiting for you in the office."

The sheriff hung up the phone and smiled. There was no regular mail delivery until this afternoon, but he desired his weekly portfolio of wanted posters now. Old Jack Gardner would bring them to him as he did almost every week. He would do Sheriff Boadeen that favor because the sheriff had something on him, from long ago. The sheriff had something on almost everybody in Danton. Cutting into a town, he mused, was like cutting into a malignant cancer patient; the deeper you cut and explored, the more disease you found. And if they had made mistakes without covering them up, that was their tough luck. That was the game.

Boadeen leaned back in his desk chair and visualized the governor's mansion. After all, life was politics and politics was life. He wondered if the governor had ever made the mistake of not covering a sin. For now, wondering was all he would do; that would be thin ice for a county sheriff to fish on.

Old Mr. Gardner delivered the plain brown envelope addressed to Sheriff Boadeen and made his exit with deference.

Boadeen opened the envelope and studied the first three circulars: An armed robber from Washington D.C., a counterfeiter, and a murderer who had abducted and killed a twelve-year-old schoolgirl in Cairo, Illinois. The sheriff looked at the murderer's picture, at the insolent mouth and heavily lidded eyes. How he would love to get his hands around that one's neck! How he would love to make him feel what that poor schoolgirl felt! How he would love to do that!

The telephone rang and Boadeen dropped the circulars to the desk and lifted the receiver.

It was Ben Slattery, from Slattery's Diner. Boadeen knew about Slattery's wife, and he was watching Slattery's daughter.

It seemed that last night some kids had vandalized the back of the diner, tipping over trash cans, splashing paint, scrawling obscenities on the brick wall.

Wondering if the young schoolgirl in Cairo had been raped before she was murdered, Sheriff Boadeen got his fingerprint kit and went right over there.

It was past noon when he returned, because he had drawn out the investigation and accepted a free lunch from Slattery. The sheriff was walking to a filing cabinet to get paper to write a report on the Slattery vandalism when his eye fell on the wanted circulars still lying on his desk. The fourth circular, the one he would have looked at next, was half-exposed at an angle.

Boadeen stopped cold and cocked his head. Then he jumped to the desk to study the photograph on the fourth circular carefully. It sure as hell looked like Lou Watson, a younger Watson, with fewer lines and more hair, but the face had the same look about it. Boadeen read beneath his breath as his eyes skipped over the circular: Wanted for murder and robbery . . . last seen in Collinsville with a woman companion described as blonde, average height and weight, in her thirties . . . believed to be heading West.

A murderer! Sheriff Boadeen sat down behind his desk and tilted his cap back on his head. A murderer right here at the lake—in his jurisdiction!

He told himself to slow down. The wanted man's name was Lou Roebuck, not Watson, and he couldn't be sure from the photograph, not completely sure, anyway. But they did act peculiar. And that would explain why Ellie had been so accessible to him—to keep him from getting suspicious, and to have something on him if he did get suspicious. Not that it mattered, he thought with a chuckle. She couldn't prove they had ever been together; it would sound to the court like a desperate, vengeful lie. No, she could prove nothing. He'd seen to that. The sheriff was careful of his reputation.

Boadeen wasn't exactly hurt by Ellie, or angry about how she'd tried to play him for a fool. After all, he'd gotten what he wanted, and it looked like he'd have the last, best laugh.

He reached for the phone to call Will Clacker, his sometime deputy, and the State Patrol. Then he withdrew his hand. What a feather in his hat if he could bring them in alone. What a hatful of feathers! He could say he'd suspected all along, that he'd been working on the case for three weeks.

Again he told himself to slow down. He still wasn't sure, not absolutely sure. And there was only one way to find out. He walked to the cherrywood gun cabinet and opened the drawer near its base. Withdrawing some extra shotgun shells for the riot gun, he slipped them into his pocket and closed and locked the cabinet drawer. Then he checked the .38 Special that hung at his hip and made sure every loop in his thick cartridge belt contained a bullet. He knew that Roebuck, or Watson or whoever he was, was armed. But hadn't he said that day at the lake he was only firing a .22 pistol? He would be able to see at a glance that the sheriff had him outgunned even if he did decide to play hard to bring in.

Boadeen reached for the wanted circular to study the photograph once more, then he folded it in four equal parts and slipped it into his breast pocket. As his hand rested on the door knob, he again considered phoning his part-time deputy. But that would be dividing the glory and the political property in half—maybe more than half. Who knew what might happen up there if Lou Watson really was Lou Roebuck?

The sheriff stepped outside, locked the door behind him, and walked around back to where the cruiser sat baking in the early afternoon heat. He got in, started the engine, and rolled down all the windows before driving away.

There was no reason the cruiser shouldn't have air conditioning, he thought as he cut onto the highway and accelerated past the speed limit.

Roebuck and Ellie were rowing back from their last morning on Lake Chippewa. Roebuck dug deeply with the oars, enjoying the resistance of the clear water, shattering the mirror-like surface of reflected sun with each stroke. He watched the thousands of sunlit planes of water shimmer out behind the boat, then gently lose their watery motion to settle back into one smooth crystalline surface, as if the boat had never passed.

"I'll be real sorry to leave," Ellie said, looking beyond him, over his right shoulder at the pine cabin that was moving closer with each stroke of the oars. "I get more attached to places than I ought to."

"The sooner we leave the better," Roebuck said. "People like us shouldn't stay long in one place."

Ellie let her hand trail in the water. "Oh, you're right, I guess. But we're still probably safe here. I think you worry too much about Sheriff Boadeen."

"He's not as stupid as he looks," Roebuck said in a clipped voice.

"No matter now. We'll leave tomorrow without attracting

any attention and never see him again."

"I want to leave early in the morning," Roebuck said. "Before most people are up."

"I guess we might as well get used to leaving places early in the morning again," Ellie said.

It occurred to Roebuck that he was getting hungry. On the backstroke of the oars he looked at his watch. It was past noon already. Time was moving on. Soon they would be gone from a place that he didn't want to leave but would be glad to get away from. And they were traveling to what? Could they find another place like this, ever? Or would Boadeen's presence be with them? Roebuck was sure that eventually the law would discover that they'd taken refuge here, and they would put that fact in their files. Would fear of the law and Benny Gipp be a part of any new paradise they found?

With one last satisfying burst of strength, Roebuck pulled back on the oars and propelled the boat up onto the mud bank. He climbed out, not minding the warm mud on his bare feet, and looped the rope around the damp tree trunk.

"We might as well take the fishing gear," he said, helping Ellie out of the boat. He stepped past her, with one foot in the water, and reached into the boat for the tackle box and rods.

Ellie took the rods from his hand and they walked toward the cabin.

It would be the last time they made that walk, Roebuck thought. One small portion of contentment gone from his harried life.

In the cabin they changed out of their fishing clothes. Roebuck watched Ellie slip into her slacks and zip them up the side without a trace of false modesty. He felt the desire to make love to her stir within him. Then he decided to wait until tonight, to make everything right for the last time here. They were sipping a cool drink when they heard the now familiar sound of Sheriff Boadeen's cruiser approaching.

One last time, Roebuck thought as he and Ellie caught one another's eye. One last time to put up with that bastard. They stepped out onto the porch and waited, their drinks in their hands, watching the mouth of the dirt road where it emerged from the woods.

Boadeen parked the car in its customary spot and got out. Roebuck felt a twinge of uneasiness as he saw that the sheriff was carrying the walnut stocked riot gun in his right hand. Sheriff Boadeen smiled. " 'Lo." He walked toward them casually. "Knew you folk were leaving tomorrow and thought I'd just stop by to wish you a safe trip."

"We thank you, Sheriff," Ellie said brightly.

Roebuck nodded toward the riot gun. "Why the weaponry?"

"Why, I noticed you admired this," Boadeen said. "Thought you might want to take a closer look at it before you go. Not another gun like it in the county." He turned the long barreled shotgun sideways and tossed it to Roebuck. "It ain't loaded."

Roebuck checked the breech and found that the gun was truly empty. He didn't see Boadeen studying him as he lifted the gun to his shoulder to test for balance and sighted in on the top of a tree limb.

"Feels good," Roebuck said. "Like a gun I hunted with once in the Black Forest."

"It's accurate at long range," Boadeen said proudly, "but it throws a pattern that'll stop a crowd."

Roebuck tossed the empty shotgun back to him. Sheriff Boadeen caught it absently and looked up at the sky. "Hot today," he said.

"C'mon in," Ellie said. "We'll have a last drink before you go."

Still carrying the riot gun, Boadeen followed them into the cabin, noting as he had more carefully before that Ellie could be described as blonde and of average height and build. Average, he thought with a secret smile, until you saw her with her clothes off.

"You know," the sheriff said as they entered the cabin, "I lived in Illinois myself for a while. Collinsville. You ever been there?"

"No," Roebuck said, his heart picking up a beat, "never."

Boadeen sat down on the sofa and stretched out his legs. "Sure glad you folk had a good time at the lake. Word-of-mouth advertising is the best kind there is."

"I'll make us some fresh drinks," Ellie said. She went into the kitchen and Roebuck followed her. Boadeen had figured that Collinsville remark would get them off alone together.

While they were in the kitchen, he drew three shotgun shells from his pocket and fed them into the riot gun. Then he leaned the gun against the sofa cushions in its former position.

Roebuck and Ellie returned, and Boadeen stood to receive his Scotch and water.

Then they all sat as they had many evenings before, in a rough semicircle, only this time around the dark cavity of the cold fireplace.

"I sure am going to miss you folk," Boadeen said amiably as he took a sip of his drink.

"We've enjoyed your company too," Ellie said.

Roebuck had the feeling the sheriff was scrutinizing him, studying his features with those flat lawman's eyes, despite Ellie telling him in the kitchen not to worry about the reference to Collinsville. "Lots of people have been in Collinsville," she had whispered, "lots of people!" But Roebuck knew that more people hadn't.

Sheriff Boadeen sighed, as if making up his mind to something, and beneath the smooth fleshiness of his face his jaw clenched.

"Here's a little something you folk might want to see before you leave," he said in a friendly voice. He withdrew the wanted circular from his shirt pocket, unfolded it carefully, and handed it to Roebuck.

The sheriff watched them study the wanted circular, saw the flitting expression of fear on Roebuck's face before he'd had a chance to adjust to the shock. And in that moment Boadeen was sure.

Suddenly all three of them were standing, and the riot gun was in Boadeen's hands and pointing exactly between Roebuck and Ellie.

"Don't move now, Louis Roebuck," the sheriff said, forming his words carefully. There was remarkable menace in that drawling command.

Roebuck stammered as the wanted circular with his picture on it slipped from his hand and fluttered to the floor. Then he remembered that the riot gun had been empty when he'd examined it. "You've got the wrong man, Sheriff," he said in an easier voice.

Boadeen grinned from behind the long barrel. "I loaded the riot gun while you two were in the kitchen."

Roebuck stared at the cavernous dark twelve-gauge hole with renewed horror. He had never before had a loaded gun pointed at him, and he found that his knees were trembling so that he was having trouble keeping his balance. Ellie was moving slowly to the side while Boadeen was concentrating on Roebuck, until she was standing about three feet from where she'd been.

"What's going to happen now?" Roebuck asked, not looking at the yawning end of the shotgun.

"The electric chair if I have anything to say about it," Boadeen answered with a sneer. "I was on to you all along, feeling you out." He waved the gun barrel slightly to take in Ellie as he talked. "How long did you two think you could evade justice?"

"We're not running from justice," Ellie said in a confident tone. "You've made a mistake, Sheriff."

Boadeen's own confidence was shaken for an instant. Suppose he had made a mistake? It would be the end of his career . . . the end of everything. He planted his feet farther apart and stood his ground. "We'll let the courts decide who's made a mistake."

From the corner of his eye Roebuck saw that Ellie's right hand had moved up so that she was leaning on the mantel, with her fingertips very close to the ends of the two fishing rods propped against the stonework.

The radio in Boadeen's cruiser was a citizen's band type, unable to cut in on the State Patrol's frequency, so his plan was to make a dramatic entrance with his prisoners at the lake office and phone the Patrol. "I want you folk to march outside now," he said, waving the gun. "We're going to get in that boat and cross the lake to the office."

They stood still, and Sheriff Boadeen's face set in determined lines. "Let's move!"

Roebuck saw Ellie's fingers curl about the thin end of one of the casting rods, then suddenly she stepped to the side and was swinging the rod with both hands as if it were a baseball bat.

For a horrifying instant Roebuck saw that as she was swinging the slender end of the rod, the thick end with the reel seemed to be standing still, as if held fast by a wall of air. But Ellie had learned well the value of wrist action in casting. Boadeen started to turn, perhaps because he'd seen Roebuck's widening eyes or perhaps because of the swishing sound. He opened his mouth to speak as the heavy reel flashed through the air in a lightning arc and struck him on the side of the head.

Boadeen's cap slipped down over his eyes and he sank to his knees, supporting himself crutch-like with the butt of the shotgun. Ellie gripped the casting rod further toward the middle and struck him again, and he fell forward onto his face, the riot gun beneath him.

Instantly Ellie was hurrying about the cabin, cleaning out drawers and cupboards, tossing canned goods into an open suitcase.

"You better pack our clothes, Lou," she said in an even voice.

But Roebuck was bending over the prostrate Boadeen, feeling for a heartbeat. "He isn't dead!" he said, looking up at Ellie. "He isn't dead!"

"And he might have help coming," Ellie said, walking in from the kitchen with another armload of nonperishable food.

Roebuck straightened and backed away from Boadeen's outstretched body. "We better get out of here right away," he said in a gruff but shaky voice. "I'll pack our clothes."

Within minutes they were in the station wagon, heading down the dirt road that branched off toward the highway.

"Just our damn luck," Roebuck said as they bounced along. "Only a quarter tank of gas! Just our damn luck!"

"We can stop at a station and fill up," Ellie said. "We oughta be fairly safe until Sheriff Boadeen comes to."

Roebuck glanced in the rear view mirror and saw nothing but their settling dust. "I thought you'd killed him at first, but he wasn't dead. We left him alive."

"He probably has a very hard head."

As they turned onto the smoother section of road that led to the highway Roebuck felt calmer. What had happened was behind him. Not far behind him, but behind him.

Just at that time Sheriff Boadeen was regaining consciousness. He rolled onto his side and lay there, cursing and beating the floor with his fist. Between the stabbing pains that shot through his head he tried to stand, but he only got to his knees and fell forward again.

He would still find them, he swore to himself, mustering his strength for another attempt to rise. He would get to a phone and call the State Patrol to set up roadblocks, and if that didn't catch them he would search every inch of Clark County himself.

Again he tried to rise, and this time he made it to one knee, rested there for a moment, then gained his feet and staggered out of the cabin. He was making his way to where the boat was tied at the bank when he heard the hum of an outboard motor. Standing still, swaying in the agonizingly hot sun, he waited until the boat came into sight. Then he drew his revolver and fired three shots in the air in quick succession to attract attention.

There were two men in the boat. The beat of the motor slowed and the boat drifted in a lazy half-circle as the men looked toward the sheriff with their hands shading their eyes.

Blast them! Didn't they see the uniform?

Boadeen fired another shot and waved them toward the bank impatiently. The longer it took him to get to a phone, the more foolish he would look.

Roebuck held the station wagon at seventy on the level stretch of dual lane highway. The side windows were open and the steady boom-boom of air pressure in the back of the car throbbed in his ears. Every mile, every foot and inch they traveled, away from Lake Chippewa was that much closer to safety, he thought, and glancing into the rear view mirror he caught a glimpse of his own two wild eyes and his hair streaking with gusts of wind across his forehead.

"I suppose the sheriff has come to and called for help by now," Ellie said, the backwash of rushing air whipping the collar of her blouse.

Roebuck bit his lower lip. "We should have torn the radio out of his car before we left."

"It doesn't matter," Ellie said. "He can't get the State Patrol on that radio anyway."

Roebuck looked sideways at her out of the corner of his eye, half his attention still riveted on the road. "How do you know that?"

"He told me about it once."

"Oh, Christ!"

Roebuck braked the car to half its speed so violently that Ellie had to brace herself with her forearms against the dashboard. The highway stretched in a straight line ahead of them, and near the crest of a hill a mile or so away they saw sunlight glinting off the steel of several cars. Roebuck pulled to the side of the road and backed up a few yards, until the distant cars were once more visible. They could see some men walking among the half dozen cars stopped on the highway, and two cars on the shoulder of the road had red lights mounted on them.

"Roadblock!" Roebuck spit the words out. "Already a damn roadblock! Boadeen must have a thicker skull than either of us thought."

"Now what are we going to do?" Ellie asked.

"Going to do?" Roebuck looked at her as if she were something to be destroyed. "Going to do? Why, we'll go back! What else can we do?"

He spun the car around and headed back the way they had

come, toward a side road he remembered seeing.

"Do you think they saw us?" Ellie asked, twisting in her seat to look behind them.

The thought made Roebuck begin to sweat. Without answering he stepped down harder on the accelerator. They probably hadn't spotted them, but they might have. The thought of a State Patrol car speeding after them now with a silent siren terrified him.

They reached the side road, Alternate Y, and he turned onto it with relief. The odds had increased in his favor now if they were being followed.

"Get out the map and see where we're going," he said to Ellie.

She opened the glove compartment and unfolded the service station road map. "This takes us to Highway 30 after about two miles."

She laid the map on the seat between them and they drove in silence for a while.

"I was thinking," Ellie said as they turned onto an empty Route 30, "maybe we oughta drive slower, in case we run up on one of those roadblocks and don't have a chance to turn around."

Roebuck said nothing but he forced himself to hold their speed at about fifty-five. He'd been thinking the same thing, but until Ellie had put it into words he'd been unable to do anything about it. All the weight of his fears had been pushing down on the accelerator with his right foot.

Again they came upon some cars backed up on the highway. This time the entrance to a state park was handy, and they turned into it as if that was their actual destination.

"Do you think it was a roadblock?" Ellie asked.

"It had to be." Roebuck followed the road to where it made a circle around a concession stand, drove back out the park exit and turned the other way on Highway 30.

"We'll have to go east," he said in a tense voice. "They might not expect us to be headed that way. We might have a chance."

He ran their speed up to sixty-five and headed the car away from the sun, into its own lengthening shadow on the rushing pavement.

They drove for some time before passing another car, and Roebuck wondered if the light traffic was a good or bad omen. A side road with a sign flashed by them, telling them to turn to visit Lake Chippewa, and Roebuck shuddered. They were dead center again, headed away from the scene of their attempted arrest in the opposite direction.

"If we drive east far enough," Roebuck said, "we can double around and head west again south of the roadblocks."

Ellie folded her hands in her lap. "It's a good thing we stopped for gas."

Roebuck had been watching the odometer. They had driven east for exactly fourteen miles when they ran into another roadblock.

Screeching to the side of the highway, Roebuck stopped the car and pounded on the steering wheel. "They're all around us! The bastards have set up a ring of roadblocks so we can't drive out no matter which way we go!"

A van sped by them in the opposite lane. "Let's get off the highway," Ellie said. "Let's go back and try to find some kind of turnoff."

Roebuck knew she was right. They had been run to ground. He turned the car around and drove slowly to a barely discernible road overgrown with weeds. It didn't even really join the highway but began on the other side of a small drainage ditch. Probably it led nowhere, but at least it would take them off the highway, into the shelter of the deep woods.

The station wagon bumped across the drainage ditch and Roebuck steered it slowly up the winding, uneven rut marks in the brush.

The road didn't exactly end; it disappeared. Soon Roebuck and Ellie were surrounded by woods and there wasn't even a shallow depression in the undergrowth to tell them which way the road might have one time gone.

Roebuck turned off the engine, leaned back in the seat, and sighed.

He thought of the noose of the law that would soon be drawing tight around them. And he thought of Gipp. Oh God, Gipp would rush to the scene like a wolf closing on wounded game.

"Where do you suppose we are?" Ellie whispered through the silence.

Roebuck muttered with his eyes closed. "In the circle is where we are. In the net."

Heat waves rose from the hood, distorting the view of the woods before them.

"Listen," Ellie said. "Is that the wind?"

Roebuck held his breath and heard a soft rushing sound, too steady for wind.

"Water," he said. "Moving water." He opened his door and got out of the car.

Ellie came around to stand beside him. She pointed. "It sounds like it's coming from over there."

They began to walk through the woods, and with a suddenness that surprised them they found themselves on the bank of a small river about a hundred feet wide. The water was cluttered with debris, murky and moving slowly except where it turned to flow over some large rocks.

They stared at the current for a moment before either of them spoke.

"Too bad we didn't bring our boat," Ellie said.

Roebuck didn't know if she was serious or not. "The State Patrol's not stupid. They'd be watching this river if it'd get us out of here." He looked up at the clouding sky. "I wouldn't be surprised to see some helicopters pretty soon."

"Do you think they can spot the car through the trees?"

"They can spot it," Roebuck said. "In the service I could spot camouflaged tanks from thirty thousand feet."

Uneasy with the wide expanse of sky above the river, they turned and began walking back to the car through the woods. Roebuck felt strangely sensible and collected. Desperate as things were, they had come to something of a standstill. He had time to think now, and he was thinking.

By the time they got back to the station wagon it was firmly fixed in his mind. "I know what we have to do," he said.

Ellie opened the car door and sat sideways in the seat with her feet on the ground, listening.

"We're going to walk," Roebuck said.

"Walk?"

Roebuck nodded. "We'll hike through the woods, around that roadblock we just saw, to the nearest town. Then we'll steal another car and circle back around west."

"But won't they search for us?"

"They might think we slipped through the ring of road-blocks and we're a hundred miles away."

"They'll spot the car, though, sooner or later," Ellie said, "with their helicopters."

Roebuck's lips twisted in a smug little smile and he nodded toward the flowing sound off to his left. "The river. It looks deep and the water's dirty."

"I guess we don't have any other choice," Ellie said.

Roebuck tucked his thumbs in his belt. "Get the road map out of the glove compartment."

They spread the map out on the warm hood of the car and set their destination at Ironton, a town about fifteen miles away, twenty miles after they made their curve around the roadblock. Quickly they chose what they would take and what clothes they would wear. Roebuck changed into the Levi's and sport shirt he'd bought for the lake, and Ellie wore slacks and a long-sleeved blouse to protect her from scratches and insect bites. Into the plaid suitcase they put one extra pair of shoes each, some canned goods, some extra clothes and part of their money. Roebuck placed one of the pistols on top of the clothes before latching the suitcase and slipped the other pistol, the .38, into his belt.

"Think of anything we're forgetting?" he asked, folding the road map and putting it in his hip pocket.

Ellie looked at the car and shook her head.

They both got in and with difficulty Roebuck drove the car to the river's edge. Twice Ellie had to get out and signal him with her hands, and once squeezing between two trees they had left a vertical streak of green paint on each trunk. But at last the station wagon was parked facing the slowly moving water. A beer can went drifting past, lazily revolving in the gentle but irresistible current.

Roebuck snapped a fairly straight branch from a dead fallen tree and waded into the dirty water, testing for depth. He walked out until the water was well above his knees, then he threw the branch into the air like a javelin so that it struck the river's surface at a right angle. It cut down into the water over half its length before bobbing up, and Roebuck decided that the river was probably deep enough at that point to conceal the car.

He waded back up on the bank, and he and Ellie rolled down all the car windows. Then Roebuck started the engine and laid a stone on the accelerator.

The engine's roar was deafening in the still woods, and almost in a panic Roebuck slammed the car door shut, reached through the open window and flipped the automatic gear shift lever into low.

The station wagon's rear wheels spun on the soft earth as it moved forward slowly. Then in a bouncing burst of speed it shot off the bank out into the water with a tremendous splash. The engine died immediately. Roebuck watched in horror as the car settled about five feet from the river's bank. Then the station wagon gave a sudden lurch and drifted farther toward the center of the river, sinking slowly, evenly.

Roebuck thought the car might sink like a ship, with the rear end lifting into the air before taking the plunge to the river bottom. Instead the station wagon drifted downstream about twenty feet as the water rose in a perfect horizontal line around it. The long roof went under levelly, with a sucking rush of water.

Roebuck and Ellie stood on the bank and watched as the car gave out one last dying gasp of huge bubbles, then the quiet river rolled over the spot where it had sunk as before, leaving them alone.

They turned to face the ominously beautiful, silent woods, and they began to walk.

PART THREE

1

Roebuck and Ellie walked at a steady pace through the sun-dappled shade of the deep woods. Occasionally they would break into a small meadow, a green circle of sunlight with tall grass and wildflowers bent gracefully where the wind had passed. Then they would be back into the shadowed woods, trudging loudly through last winter's dead leaves, stepping over fallen, rotting logs teeming with insects. Around them was the stench of decay, and the fresh scent of things growing out of decay.

As they walked they glanced frequently behind them at the sun, winking at them through their roof of thick foliage. It was the sun that was leading them east, and by whose setting arc they were fixing their path to take them around the State Patrol roadblock.

Roebuck felt an odd exhilaration in the woods, a feeling of solitude and safety. Here the two of them walked in a world that demanded nothing but survival, that most important object of life that society had permitted man to place low on his list of concerns. And as they crossed a leaf-filled dry creek and he helped Ellie up the eroded bank, he felt the primeval protective instinct of man for his mate. He felt a closeness to Ellie that he'd never before experienced, and he wondered if she too felt their solitude and oneness.

160

"I bet I have a million chigger bites," she said, scratching beneath the elastic band of her slacks.

"Coal oil," Roebuck said. "Coal oil is the best thing for chiggers." He picked up a stick and began beating the sparse foliage that jutted up at wide intervals from the dead leaves to brush against their legs. A wonder that anything could grow, he thought, in the fetid sunlessness beneath the trees.

Ellie clapped her hands at a mosquito. "How far do you think we've gone?"

"Maybe a mile," Roebuck said. "It's rougher country than I expected. Another hour and we should be past that road-block and we can walk straight east."

"You don't think they'll be able to find the car, do you?"

"Nope. That water's so dirty they wouldn't even be able to look down and see anything under it from a plane or heli-copter. In a few days they'll probably think we drove past the roadblocks somehow and kept heading west."

"I hope you're right."

Roebuck was pleased to see the hint of uncertainty in Ellie. He threw away the stick he was carrying and switched the small plaid suitcase to his other hand. "We'll make camp about sundown," he said in a voice of authority.

"I never thought about that," Ellie said. "I mean, sleeping in the woods."

"Nothing to be afraid of. During the war five of us got shot down in a bomber and walked all the way across France, keeping to the woods all the way. We lived like animals."

"What will we sleep on?"

"Dry leaves," Roebuck said. "We'll make a bed of dry leaves."

"Won't they be full of bugs and things?"

"We'll shake them out."

Ellie accepted that but didn't seem too happy with it. "At

161

least we brought water and something to eat."

"Maybe we'll see a rabbit and I can get us some fresh meat," Roebuck said, and he wondered if it was the voice of his hunting ancestors speaking through him.

They walked on. Sunlight above, darkness below. Even the undersides of the tree leaves, Roebuck noticed, were a drabber, paler green than the upper sides which faced the sun.

"I've gotta rest pretty soon," Ellie said from behind him, so Roebuck stopped by the trunk of a large oak and laid the suitcase on the ground for her to sit on.

He'd noticed she was falling back, and he'd wondered when she would begin to complain.

Roebuck stayed on his feet, his hand resting lightly on the handle of the revolver that was stuck inside his belt against the warmth of his body. He wasn't tired; he could walk another twenty miles without getting tired. His Western boots, dusty and scuffed now, were perfect for tramping through rough country, but he reminded himself that he would have to polish them when they got to Ironton.

"Do you think we're past that roadblock yet?" Ellie asked wearily.

"We oughta be." Roebuck pulled the map from his hip pocket and slowly unfolded it. "We should be able to head straight east now, and in fifteen miles or so we'll come to Highway R. We can walk parallel to the highway then, right into Ironton." He traced his fingertip over the crinkled map, like a general going over his battle plan for the final time, then he folded the map and put it back in his pocket.

"I'm ready to go," Ellie said, "if you want to keep walking." She wiped her forehead with the sleeve of her blouse and Roebuck could see that she was still worn out.

"We can wait a while," he said gallantly. "You catch your

breath or you'll want to rest again in five minutes."

Ellie smiled at his thoughtfulness and leaned back against the tree trunk.

Roebuck lit a cigarette for each of them and they smoked leisurely, enjoying each deep inhalation.

"It's peaceful here," Ellie said. "I don't see how they can ever find us among all these trees."

"There are ways," Roebuck said ominously. "Sometimes they use dogs." He rather frightened himself with that sudden thought. But then they'd have to know where to pick up the trail even if they did happen to resort to that tactic.

"I'm ready to go now, really," Ellie said. "If you are."

"If you're sure you've got your wind back."

Ellie ground out her cigarette and stood, and Roebuck picked up the plaid suitcase again. He glanced over his shoulder at the sun, floating like a globe of dull fire above the treetops, and they began walking slowly due east.

The terrain was hillier now, and the going was slower than before. Roebuck began to worry. At this rate it would take them a long time to make Ironton. Around them birds flapped to the air and squirrels scurried away at their approach. Roebuck continued to lead the way, his high-topped boots smashing with noisy precision through the dead leaves.

Hours passed, and the shadows in the woods were deepening with the coming of dusk.

"I think I've gotta rest again," Ellie said for the third time, and Roebuck was more than ready for her suggestion.

He squatted on the ground beside her and rested his back against the rough bark of a tree trunk. Sweat was rolling down his face and his entire body itched.

"It'll be dark soon." There was a touch of apprehension in Ellie's voice.

Roebuck was too tired to answer. His legs ached and the

soles of his feet felt as if they were burning.

They sat listening to each other's breathing.

Roebuck was scratching his chest beneath his shirt when suddenly his hand stopped, and his breathing was suspended. The hand withdrew from inside his shirt and moved slowly to his belt.

The revolver was out in a slow, steady motion, and three shots rang through the dim woods. In their still aftermath the scurry of life rose up around Roebuck and Ellie and then was still again.

Roebuck was on his feet, walking toward a patch of high weeds. He picked up the bloody carcass of a small rabbit and turned to see that Ellie was standing and had moved back about ten feet from where they'd been sitting.

"Rabbit," he said reassuringly. "We'll have it for supper." He saw proudly that the rabbit had been hit twice, one bullet passing all the way through its ruined head. By God, two out of three wasn't bad for such a small target!

"What about all that noise, Lou?" Ellie glanced worriedly about her. "What if they're looking for us in the woods?"

Roebuck hadn't thought of that. The bastards might have sent out search parties, and they'd move toward the sound of the shots like columns of ants closing in on a doomed caterpillar.

"Come on," he said, holding the rabbit by one hind leg. "If we move on for another hour they'll never find us even if they are in this area. Hard to tell which direction shots come from in country like this."

This time Ellie carried the suitcase as they began trudging east.

Roebuck flushed as he heard her scraping through the leaves behind him. "Damn mosquitoes!" he almost shouted, turning up the collar of his shirt.

When they thought they had walked far enough, they crossed a small clearing and stopped at the foot of a heavily wooded hill.

"This will be a good place to camp," Roebuck proclaimed, turning in a circle to survey the surrounding countryside. "We can build a fire and it won't be noticeable from the hillside, and we can shield it from the west."

"Are you sure it's safe to build a fire, Lou? I mean, if they might just happen to be following us."

"Safe?" Roebuck snorted. "Of course it's safe, or I wouldn't have shot this rabbit for supper. Thick as these woods are, you can't spot a small fire from over two, three hundred yards."

"If you say so." Ellie smiled at him from her weariness. "I could use a good hot meal."

"While it's still light," Roebuck said, "I'll build us a lean-to in case it rains. The knife from the tackle box is in the suitcase."

They found a suitable spot to camp at the foot of the hill, and Ellie opened the suitcase and handed Roebuck the knife. In the failing light he set out to whittle off the small branches of some nearby trees.

Within a half hour he had a flimsy but serviceable affair made, framed with larger branches, roofed with small branches and twigs with a layer of leaves covering them. It would keep the rain off.

Roebuck cleared a spot for a fire, scraping the leaves beneath the small lean-to to form their bedding. Then he stacked some branches for the fire and found two forked sticks that would support a spit. All he had to do now was clean the rabbit, and they would be set for a pleasant evening in their camp.

Ellie watched as he laid the rabbit on a flat stone about

fifty feet from where the fire was going to be and inserted the point of the knife beneath the furry flesh. He had expected her to feel sick when he peeled the hide off, but she gave no sign of emotion. The truth was that it was Roebuck who felt slightly ill. He hadn't cleaned a rabbit since he was a boy.

Ellie brought the thermos of water from the suitcase and they poured a small trickle over the skinned rabbit where it had come in contact with the ground. Then they took the rabbit, along with the flat stone, back to their lean-to.

"We can have supper in no time," Roebuck said, eyeing the darkening woods. He found two branches and stuck them in the ground near where he'd built the pyramid of sticks for a fire. Quickly he peeled off his shirt and draped it over the tops of the two branches to form a curtain that would help shield the fire from the view of anyone approaching from the way they had come.

By the time it was dark Roebuck had a small fire going. Using the flat stone he'd cleaned the rabbit on for a carving block, he dismembered the rabbit and skewered the choice pieces with the straight stick he was going to use for a spit.

"I'll open a can of something," Ellie said, moving from where she was sitting beneath the lean-to.

Roebuck heard her fumbling in the suitcase as he placed the rabbit over the tiny fire and began slowly revolving the spit between his thumb and forefinger.

Ellie came and sat down cross-legged next to him. She had a can of beans and a can opener in her lap, and she handed Roebuck his spare shirt from the suitcase.

"Your nightgown," she said.

Still sitting on the hard earth, he slipped the shirt on and began buttoning it while Ellie turned the rabbit. He thought she might become frightened when night settled into the woods, but she seemed instead to be adapting very quickly to

166

the forest, like a domestic cat suddenly turned loose to make its own way.

"If you hear a plane," he said, "tell me right away so I can throw dirt over the fire. They can spot it from the air."

"Sure." She let him resume turning the spit without a break in the slow rhythm.

After supper Roebuck built the fire up and he and Ellie sat back in the lean-to and smoked a final cigarette. The woods were silent. The thousand subtle noises they had taken for granted during the day had one by one ceased with the approaching gloom of night. Then night had rushed in, like a victorious army rushing into the vacuum of its enemy's retreat, irresistible and gloating.

"We better go to sleep," Ellie said when the fire had almost died. "I guess you want to start early in the morning."

"Yeah, the earlier the better." Roebuck leaned over and worked off his boots. He considered putting out the fire, but he saw that it had only a short while to live anyway.

They settled into their bed of leaves with a great rustling and sighing of tired relief. Roebuck lay on his side, curled spoon fashion against Ellie with his arm draped across her. He felt her kiss his hand as his relaxing body gave a little jerk, and with the swiftness of complete submission he sank into deep sleep.

The fire gave a last popping flicker, and the towering darkness that had been ebbing and flowing about their circle of firelight fell in on them.

Roebuck was still curled on his side when he awoke in the middle of the night. He blinked his eyes to make sure they were open, so impenetrable was the blackness around him. Though he could hear Ellie's even breathing, he reached out a cautious hand and touched the small of her back to reassure himself that she was there.

What had awoken him? The pressure, he groggily realized, the intense, almost sensual pressure in his groin that told him he must relieve his swollen bladder.

With great reluctance he sat up and looked about him at the darkness, drawing the outlines of his surroundings in his mind. There was the fire curtain that was his shirt, there the suitcase and flat rock, there the unusually thick trunk of an oak tree where his knife was stuck, and there must be the ashes of the dead fire.

The throbbing pressure in his groin was almost unbearable, pulsating, as he slipped his boots on. He stood, brushing his head on the low roof of the lean-to, peering into the black night. A few steps and his outstretched hand felt the rough bark of a tree. A leaf brushed his cheek and he jumped, swatting at the empty air.

Far enough, he thought, taking a few more steps. His hand found the support of a tree, and he leaned and unzipped his pants to stand listening to the splatter of his urine on the dry leaves as the pressure within him was relieved.

He zipped his fly and stood straight with his hands on his hips, aware of the deep silence around him now that his urgent need was fulfilled. But the woods weren't completely silent. He heard something move off to his left, a gentle movement among the leaves as if a breeze had stirred them. He wheeled about suddenly as he heard a dry snapping sound behind him, but he was facing only the darkness.

Roebuck moved hurriedly back toward the lean-to, feeling his way among the trees. Beneath the roof of leaves there wasn't even a moon or a feeble star to lend its faint light.

He stopped.

Had he gone this far? He couldn't have; he must have somehow passed the campsite.

He began retracing his steps as best he could. Then he stopped again and stood motionless. To his left. He had turned to his right when the branch had brushed his face, so the campsite must be to his left.

Roebuck began moving in that direction, slowly, futilely straining his eyes against the night. Things were moving in the woods, all around him now, and he could hear his heartbeat. If there was anything near him, anything large, it would know. Animals could tell when a man was afraid. Something—a bear, a wild dog—something could be on him in the darkness before he knew it, crushing his bones with powerful jaws, churning his flesh with its claws. "Ellie?" he called softly.

No answer, only that soft rustling sound, behind him now, closer.

He took three quick steps and bumped his forehead on a tree.

"Ellie!"

He stumbled forward, one hand against his forehead, the other groping ahead of him. He was moving as fast as he dared in the darkness now, thrashing noisily through the leaves, ignoring the branches that brushed his face and plucked at his clothes.

Then he stood still.

He was making too much noise. If anything was out there it would find him by his noise, sense his panic.

Now he was afraid to move. He stood breathing faster and faster, his fear welling up in him.

"Ellie!"

"Lou?"

The voice was so close that he took a startled step away from it.

"Is that you, Lou? Where are you?"

169

Roebuck felt a relief surge through him greater than the physical relief he'd felt earlier.

"Take it easy, Ellie, I'm coming."

He made his way to the campsite, only a few yards away from where he'd been standing.

"I didn't mean to leave you alone," he said, settling back into the leaves that were warmed by her body.

"What in heaven's name were you doing out there in the dark?"

"I thought I heard something in the woods, in the night. I thought it might be a lawman who found us and was going back for help. Whatever it was, I followed it for about half a mile and I'm pretty sure it was just an animal of some kind. Probably a coyote."

Ellie lay back down in the leaves beside him. "I don't see how anybody could find us, dark as it is."

"Infrared glasses," Roebuck said, snuggling up to her. "They have infrared glasses." He wrapped a protective arm around her and went to sleep.

They started out early the next morning, after only a can of peaches and a swig of water for breakfast. The country seemed to get rougher, the woods denser. They would be lucky to make over six or seven miles if they walked hard, all day, Roebuck thought dismally. And he was getting a blister on his heel.

They walked for hour after hour, and it seemed as if they had gotten nowhere. The woods were the same in front of them, behind them, all around them. Well before sundown Roebuck suggested making camp to give Ellie a rest, and they went through the motions of last night, the lean-to, the bed of leaves, the fire, only this time supper out of a can.

Roebuck tramped briefly into the woods to make sure he

wouldn't have to get up in the middle of the night again, and when it got dark enough for the smoke to be unnoticeable, he built a somewhat larger fire that would burn longer into the night.

The vision of that still smoldering campfire comforted him as he closed his eyes and slept.

"I heard a scream!"

"You screamed, Lou. It was you."

Ellie was bending over him, staring down at him with pity and alarm. Roebuck saw that it was light; it was morning. He pressed his hands to his temples, trying to adjust to the sudden shift in time. Just a minute ago it had been dark, except for the reddish, flickering glare. And the suffocating haze . . .

Ellie placed her hand on his shoulder and he flinched.

"You yelled something about a fire," she said in a puzzled voice.

"Fire? A nightmare. I dreamed the woods were on fire, a forest fire."

"Just a dream," Ellie said. "It's morning. We slept later than we should have, I guess."

Roebuck glared up at the sun, as if he had some personal grudge against it. "It must be past ten o'clock." He stood, trying to shake off the effects of last night's dream, the dream that he kept locked within him, that broke its confines during his nights to intrude into his sleep.

"We better get going," Ellie said. "Do you want to eat breakfast?"

"We should have something." He went to the open suitcase and got the thermos of water, half full now, and rinsed the thickness from his mouth.

"How do apricot halves sound?"

171

"I wish to hell I had some coffee," he said.

His only answer was the little hiss of inrushing air as Ellie opened the can of apricots.

That day was a repetition of the last two—at least until late afternoon. They continued to trudge through the crisp leaves and harsh underbrush, wondering now if they would ever see Highway R. At times Roebuck feared they might have been walking in a circle, like the prospectors in the desert who become dazed and die of thirst. Then he would reassure himself. They had been very careful about their direction, and traveling had been slower than they'd anticipated. Highway R wasn't moving; it was ahead of them somewhere, waiting for them like home.

God, but it would be good to get out of the woods, to take a shower and change into clothes that didn't itch. Roebuck vowed to himself that as soon as they made Ironton they would buy some new clothes and stop at a motel just to shower and rest.

He ran his tongue over the cottony dryness on the roof of his mouth.

"Time for a water break," he said. "You must be choking with thirst."

They stopped and got the thermos from the suitcase. There were barely two inches of water left in it.

"We better watch for a spring or something," Ellie said.

Roebuck took a swallow of water and looked up at the sky through the roof of leaves. "You're right. It doesn't look like it's ever going to rain again." He shuddered. "A fire would sweep through these woods like a wind."

Ellie wiped the sweat from her face. "A forest fire's the least of my worries now."

"You wouldn't say that if you'd ever seen a big forest fire.

172

The flames leap five stories high! There's no stopping them; they travel over the treetops."

"I'm still not too worried," Ellie said. "They don't have forest fires that often."

"More often than you think."

There was a slight sound, a very soft, sudden sound, and they both started and turned toward it.

Only the woods.

"It's something!" Roebuck whispered. They both knew somehow that what they had heard was not an animal, that it was a sound unnatural to the harmony of the woods. There was in the deep woods the noise made by things frightened, by things stalking, by things wary or watching. But this had been none of those; this had been the bold sound of something unafraid but unaggressive, outside the ritual of nature. They heard it again, a rising and falling steady sound of something moving through the carpet of leaves. It was moving toward them, but from what direction they couldn't tell.

Then it stepped out from behind a tree.

A boy, about twelve years old, his eyes wide and startled at seeing two people suddenly appear before him. He was wearing a long-sleeved plaid shirt and blue jeans, ragged, and he stood very still and stared at them, waiting for them to make the first move.

Roebuck's head was spinning. Now they were spotted! Now someone could tell the law that they were still in the area, on foot and easy to capture! This wasn't in his plans. This was an aberration that he couldn't tolerate.

The gun was suddenly in his hand, pointed at the boy.

"What are you doing here?" Roebuck asked.

The boy backed up a step, his skinny body tense. He stared from the gun up into Roebuck's eyes and saw a subtle change of light in them, like something turning in deep water.

173

For a fragment of a second, man and boy stood staring at each other, the will of death between them.

"He's only a boy, Lou," Ellie said from beside Roebuck.

"Of course he is," Roebuck said. "I'm not going to hurt him. But what are we going to do? He knows about us now. What in the hell are we going to do?"

"We'll think of something," Ellie said. "We've thought of something so far, haven't we?"

Roebuck motioned with the gun. "Come over here, son."

The boy walked toward them reluctantly, afraid but a long way from panic.

"What are you doing out here in the woods alone?"

The voice was thin and unsteady. "I live near here."

"How far away?" Ellie asked gently.

The boy turned toward her, sensing her sympathy. " 'Bout half a mile."

Roebuck slid the revolver back in his belt. "What are you doing out here alone?"

"Jus' walkin'."

"To where?"

"Nowheres. I jus' like to walk in the woods is all."

"What's your name?" Ellie asked.

"Claude Mulhaney."

Roebuck knew what they must do. They would never be safe once this boy was out of their sight.

"How many are in your family?" he asked, glowering menacingly at the boy to frighten a correct answer from him.

"Me an' my dad an' ma." Young Claude was not nearly as frightened as he had been, and in fact was showing a certain degree of cockiness, the instinctive courage of something cornered.

"Who's home now?" Roebuck asked.

"Jus' my ma."

174

Roebuck made a jerking motion with his thumb. "Lead the way."

Claude didn't move.

Roebuck again drew the pistol from his belt. "Why aren't you moving, son?"

"I want you to promise."

"Promise what?"

"That you won't hurt my ma."

"Nobody'll hurt your mother," Ellie said.

"Nobody's going to hurt anybody." Roebuck waved the pistol. "That's a promise from somebody who's never broken one, son. Now you show us where you live."

Claude gave him a searching look, then turned and began leading them in the direction he'd come from. Roebuck saw that the boy's sandy hair was close-cropped around the neck and ears, as if someone actually had placed a bowl on his head to give him a haircut. He had to admire the courage of the boy in the face of a loaded gun. What might such courage grow into?

They had gone only a short way through the woods when they came upon a path, a winding dirt trail through a corridor of green where the woods thinned to let in the sunlight and there was high foliage beneath the trees on either side of them.

"We're being honest with you," Roebuck said, as they followed the small bobbing head. "We don't expect you to try something cute like leading us in a circle."

"Don't worry," Claude said without looking back. "Long as I got your promise."

"Brigadier generals have taken my word," Roebuck said. "You can rely on it."

"You some kind of soldier?"

"Was."

"Really? In the Army?"

"For a while," Roebuck said, "then I was in the Special Service, a spy outfit."

"You don't look like a spy."

"That's enough yapping," Roebuck said. "You just lead the way."

2

Claude's home was situated at the foot of a tall but not very steep bluff. As he led Roebuck and Ellie down the dirt path on the opposite hill, Roebuck could see a small garden behind the ramshackle house, an outhouse, and to one side a fairly big patch of corn. The house itself was frame with a tin roof. There was another frame building behind it that leaned to one side away from the garden. As they got closer Roebuck saw that both buildings were in terrible disrepair, with peeling, colorless paint, spots of rotting wood, and cardboard where some of the window panes should have been. Some scraggly chickens pecked about in the bare earth before the house and on the wooden porch where a worn kitchen chair sat.

"Stop here, son," Roebuck said, when they were still far enough from the house not to have been seen by its occupants. "You've got my promise, now I want yours that there isn't anybody in that house but your mother."

"There ain't," the boy said sincerely. "I swear it!"

Roebuck lifted the gun that had been dangling in his hand and slipped it inside his shirt.

"Okay, son, let's go."

When they entered, the woman looked up from where she was sitting at the kitchen table. There was nothing on the table before her; she had just been sitting there.

"These here are some people I met, Ma," Claude stammered.

Roebuck nodded at her, smiling. "Mrs. Mulhaney."

She wasn't an old woman, but she had very stooped shoulders and a lock of drab brown hair carefully flattened over one side of her forehead that made her look older. She coughed and touched a wadded handkerchief to her thin lips. "Where'd you meet these folks, Claude?"

"In the woods, Ma—they said they wouldn't hurt you!"

The woman looked blankly at Roebuck and Ellie, her face gaunt and very pale.

"There's no reason for anybody to get hurt," Roebuck said, strangely ashamed at having intruded into the woman's privacy. He looked about him at the small farmhouse's pathetically worn furniture and saw an old wooden radio on a shelf above the yellowed sink.

"There's no use to pretend," the woman said, following Roebuck's gaze, "I know who you are." Her voice was throaty and rich, the voice of a nightclub torch singer insanely out of place. "I'm Iris Mulhaney and this is my son Claude."

"We meant it when we said nobody was going to get hurt," Ellie said.

"I believe you did, ma'am," Iris Mulhaney said, and she bent forward momentarily as a fit of coughing doubled her. "You'll haft'a excuse me." The handkerchief dabbed at her mouth.

Claude went over to stand by his mother. "Ma ain't well. You see there's no call to hurt her, no reason."

Roebuck walked to the sink and turned the tap for a drink of water but got nothing.

"Somethin' wrong with the line," Iris Mulhaney said. "You'll haft'a use the hand pump out back."

"Where's your husband?" Ellie asked, slumping into a torn armchair.

"Works in the city. He comes home on weekends, sometimes not even then." There was no bitterness in the fogged voice, only fact stripped of all emotion, ancient history still happening.

"That means he won't be home for three days," Roebuck said, leaning on the sink.

"Maybe not then."

Roebuck turned the knob on the radio to satisfy himself that it worked, then turned it off. "We don't have any choice but to stay here, Mrs. Mulhaney. You have my promise that we won't cause any trouble."

Iris Mulhaney nodded and Roebuck saw that the lock of hair was combed down over her forehead to conceal a reddish scar, possibly from a burn.

"How long do you think we'll have to stay, Lou?" Ellie asked.

"It depends," Roebuck said, "on a lot of things."

"There ain't much to eat," Iris said in a voice of apology.

"I'll fix us something later," Ellie said to her with a smile. "We might as well make this a vacation for you, Mrs. Mulhaney."

Roebuck turned to Claude. "How far is your nearest neighbor, son?"

"Ain't got no neighbors."

"There must be somebody . . ."

"The Webster place," Iris said, "but I wouldn't call 'em neighbors. It's over a mile."

Roebuck nodded and looked again at Claude. "Are there any guns in the house?"

Claude hesitated.

"We have each other's word," Roebuck said.

"There's an old shotgun, but we ain't got any shells."

"Where at?"

179

Claude pointed to the farmhouse's one other room.

Roebuck went into the room that contained a battered bedroom set with twin beds and saw the shotgun leaning in a corner. He checked to make sure it was empty and carried it back into the main room.

"I'll be back in a minute," he said to Ellie, and he left the house to walk a short distance into the woods where he buried the shotgun beneath some leaves.

When he returned Ellie and Claude were setting the table while Iris sat in the armchair and watched.

"I'll tell you where the gun is when we leave," Roebuck said, and Claude nodded silently.

"Why don't you and Claude go out and pump some water and pick some vegetables," Ellie said, "and I can get the best meal you ever tasted on that woodstove."

"Okay," Roebuck said. "You bring the bucket, son."

By the time they'd finished a delicious supper of hamburger, corn on the cob, and baked potatoes it was dark outside. Roebuck made sure all the shades were pulled before turning on the lights.

"How come you don't have a telephone?" he asked as they were sitting on the worn furniture after supper.

"No real need for one," Iris said. "And they cost money."

"When do you do your shopping, on weekends?"

"Usually. When my husband comes home. There's a pickup in the garage behind the house, but it ain't running right now."

The thought that they might get the pickup truck running and leave occurred to Roebuck, but he knew that Claude would make the mile to the nearest neighbor and a phone before they could get very far. Of course they might be able to tie the boy and his mother so it would take them a while to get loose.

"What's the matter with the truck?" Roebuck asked.

Iris coughed violently. "Lord knows."

"We can look at it in the morning," Roebuck said.

They sat talking guardedly, feeling one another out, until well into the evening. Then Claude and his mother went into the bedroom to sleep while Roebuck sat in the armchair where he could watch both beds from the living room. Ellie slept on the couch with an old alarm clock set for two a.m., when it would be Roebuck's turn to sleep.

They were both still tired when morning came, but Roebuck felt considerably better after stripping to his shorts and washing in the cold water from the pump. He watched Iris fry the eggs for breakfast while Ellie and Claude carried in buckets of water for Ellie's bath in the ancient and useless bathroom tub.

During breakfast they learned that a doctor had told Iris she might have tuberculosis, but that she had received no treatment and had refused to go to a sanitarium.

"What does your husband say about that?" Ellie asked.

"He says a sanitarium costs a lot of money, and he's right."

Roebuck looked across the table and saw Claude stuffing a last bite of egg into his mouth, staring straight ahead.

"This might be as good a place to rest as a sanitarium," Roebuck said. "You've got quiet and a nice garden out in back, not to mention Claude's medical attention."

"The garden ain't much," Claude said soberly.

"It is, considering the soil," Roebuck said. "It looks like rocky Arkansas soil, but it's surprising what can be grown on it if you know what you're doing. And judging by the garden, somebody knows what they're doing."

"Were you ever a farmer?"

"Once."

"Before you were in the Army?"

Roebuck smiled. "I grew up on a farm. When I hit basic training I could shoot better than anybody in the company."

Iris stood and began to clear the table.

"I'll help you," Ellie said, standing and placing her cup and silverware on her plate.

Roebuck pushed back from the table and stood. "Turn on that radio, Ellie, and keep listening for the news while I go outside and look over that pickup truck."

"I'll show it to you." Claude quickly left the table and followed Roebuck out the door.

They opened the rotted double doors of the barn-like garage, one of which was supported crookedly by a single rusted hinge. The smell of grease and stale air wafted out at them from the high-ceilinged darkness.

"This is it," Claude said proudly.

It was an old red Ford pickup, battered and faded, with rusting fenders that looked as though they'd been sledge-hammered.

"How long since it's run?" Roebuck asked.

"Oh, 'bout two weeks. Last time me an' Ma tried to go into town it wouldn't start."

In the dim light Roebuck saw a can of gasoline among some tools at the other end of the garage. He checked the truck's gas gauge and saw that the needle was broken. "Get me that gas can," he said to Claude.

Claude brought him the can and he poured its contents, about two gallons, into the truck's tank. He opened the squeaking door again, released the emergency brake, and put the gearshift lever in neutral.

"You get in back, son, and we'll push it out into the light where we can look at it."

The truck looked even worse in the sunlight. Roebuck got

in, sat on the ragged upholstery and pressed the starter. Nothing happened. He flicked the one knob on the dashboard radio and turned it all the way to his left.

"This old radio work?" he asked Claude.

"Sometimes."

Roebuck climbed down from the cab and slammed the door. "Well, it's not working now."

He walked to the front of the truck and raised the hood. Everything looked greasy, but nothing seemed out of place. The battery was a mass of corrosion.

"How old is this battery, son?"

"Real old." Claude stood up on the dashboard and peered down under the hood at the engine. "Do you think you can fix it?"

"I was a pit mechanic at Indianapolis," Roebuck said, playing with a wire. "After my nerve went and I couldn't race anymore."

"What caused you to lose your nerve?"

"The accident."

Roebuck slammed the hood.

"Wha'd'ya think?" Claude asked, looking up at him.

"Hit the lights."

Claude reached into the cab and pulled the headlight switch. The lights barely glowed.

Roebuck nodded and Claude pushed the switch back in.

"It might start with a push." Roebuck crossed his arms and looked about him. "Do you have a hammer and some nails?"

"Might have," the boy answered, surprised. "Why?"

"We might as well fix those front steps before your mother has an accident."

They went back into the garage and found a hammer and a box of nails.

"There's some boards in the pump house," Claude said, as they were walking toward the front of the house. "I'll go get 'em."

As Claude danced away Roebuck patted him gently on the back and gazed up at the sky. "We better hurry. It's clouding up."

They'd barely finished replacing the rotted boards when a sudden deluge of rain fell, smashing against the tin porch roof in a monotonous roar.

3

Sheriff Boadeen stood behind his office window in Danton and watched the heavy rain flood over the glass.

"It looks like they might 'a slipped through," Will Clacker, his part-time deputy, said behind him. Clacker was a small, potbellied man with only one arm. He'd lost the other arm in Korea and was drawing a nice government pension.

"That's what the State Patrol's starting to think," Boadeen said, still staring out at the rain, "but it'll take another day or so to make up their minds."

"What do you think?" Clacker asked, striking a bookmatch deftly with one hand and lighting a cigarette.

Boadeen rubbed his smooth-shaven chin. "Could be they're still in the area, holed up, that they never even tried to get past the roadblocks."

Clacker nodded. "Patrol's probably thought of that. If they're still hereabouts their car'll be spotted sooner or later."

Boadeen walked over and sat on the corner of his desk. "Probably later." He touched the sore spot on his head where the heavy reel had struck him.

"You got something on your mind, Sheriff?" Clacker asked.

Boadeen jutted out his lower lip and nodded. "Surely do." He walked to the wall map of Clark County. "Seems to me that if they didn't get by one of the roadblocks that they're holed up somewheres in here." He traced an invisible circle with his capped ball-point pen. "Now, in a day or two the State Patrol figures to give up on the roadblocks and search the whole area."

"And?"

Boadeen gave his crooked smile. "I figure we're gonna beat them to the punch."

"It would be better than just waitin' for news," Clacker said, "but that's a pretty big area to search."

"Surely is," Boadeen said, "unless those two are holed up in a house, and we know where every house in the county is and the quickest way to get to it. We can figure out a route and watch the woods while we're following the side roads."

"You're the boss."

Boadeen nodded, still smiling. He didn't really like Clacker, but the man posed a minimum threat to his job. There weren't many one-armed sheriffs.

"When do you want to start?" Clacker asked.

"Soon as the rain lets up."

"It'll take a good while," Clacker said. "You sure we oughta just drop everything else and do this without the Patrol's authorization?"

Sheriff Boadeen looked hard at him. "You've got my authorization." He walked to the bulletin board and stared at Roebuck's wanted poster, now pinned neatly in the upper left hand corner. There were still four sharp creases in it where it had been folded to fit in his uniform shirt pocket.

"We'll find those two if we have to cover every house in the county," Boadeen said. "After all, I'm the one that let 'em slip away."

Outside the rain began to slacken.

4

The rain passed quickly, the dark scudding clouds moving away to the east. Within a few hours the sun had erased all traces of moisture from the baked earth around the farmhouse and the only sign that it had rained was the fresh coolness coming from the surrounding woods.

Roebuck spent the rest of the day with Claude, repairing small things around the farm, mixing a bucket of pitch and sealing the roof where it had leaked during the rain.

All that day Ellie listened to the radio, but there was no new announcement about them. The State Patrol still had their roadblocks up, and it was believed impossible for anyone to have slipped through. They were admitting now, however, the slim possibility that the net of roadblocks hadn't been put up in time, and that the fugitives may have been well away before their route was closed behind them.

Let them believe that, Roebuck thought, sinking into the worn armchair after supper. Let the bastards believe it and pick up their roadblocks and guns and go home.

He slept that night, better than he'd slept in a long time.

It was four o'clock the next afternoon, and Roebuck and Claude were outside trying to find the trouble with the water line, when Ellie called to them from the farmhouse.

"I just heard something on the news!"

Roebuck could tell by her voice that the something had alarmed her. He jabbed his shovel into the ground and walked toward the house with Claude trailing behind him.

"What was it?" he asked as he stepped into the comparative coolness of the house and the screen door slammed behind him.

"The State Patrol's giving up on their roadblocks," Ellie said, "but starting tomorrow morning they're going to make a careful search of the whole area."

Roebuck heard Claude come into the house behind him.

"You sure that's what you heard?"

Ellie nodded.

"Damn!" Roebuck began to pace. "Damn! The bastards won't let up on you!"

"What now?" Ellie asked, as she had asked before.

"Haven't I always thought of something?" Roebuck shouted.

"Don't yell, Lou."

Roebuck hooked his thumbs in his belt and drew a deep breath. Iris was sitting at the table clenching her wadded handkerchief, and Claude was behind him, staring wide-eyed at him.

"We've got a little time, anyway," Ellie said.

"Yeah." Roebuck walked to the door and leaned there, looking outside. "They did give us that."

"You gonna make a run for it?" Claude asked in a small voice.

"I don't know," Roebuck said. He could feel things pressing in on him, as if the woods, the sky, the sun, all were drawing closer, shrinking around him.

"We can't stay here," Ellie said. "That'd be just waiting for them."

Roebuck had to agree to that. "How do you get to Ironton from here?" he asked.

"You take that road there," Claude said, pointing out the door to the rutted, dusty road from the farmhouse. "It runs for about three miles till it hits Highway R. Then you make a right on R and go about another five miles or so."

"It takes about a half hour," Iris said in her straining voice. "It ain't a good road."

"It'll have to be good enough," Roebuck said. He knew also that they would have to trust Claude and his mother, for he would need them to help push the truck to get it started. If the truck would start.

"When we going to leave?" Ellie asked.

"Tonight, just before it gets dark." That seemed to Roebuck the ideal time to make their run for freedom. Not only would there be less chance of being seen in the pickup truck, but they would arrive at Ironton at night and could steal another car when it was dark.

"I'll get our stuff together," Ellie said, smiling her broad and wistful smile. "Seems like I'm always getting our stuff together."

Roebuck held the screen door open for Claude. "We might as well finish trying to find the break in that water line."

The sun was hovering over the horizon when they said goodbye to Claude and Iris Mulhaney.

"I sure hope your throat gets better," Ellie said to Iris as they were walking toward the pickup.

"It will, ma'am."

"Your shotgun's under some leaves by that big rock up the bluff," Roebuck said to Claude. He felt he could trust both these people now, felt they were on his side. They were all battling odds, and people battling odds had an affinity for one another.

Roebuck opened the squeaking truck door and tossed the

189

suitcase into the cab. He turned to Iris. "We trust you not to call the police on us, Mrs. Mulhaney."

"We're law-abiding folks," Iris said, "but nobody'd expect me to send a boy over a mile through the dark woods to get to a phone."

"An' nobody'd expect a boy to go," Claude said with a grin.

Ellie got into the truck and sat behind the wheel.

"Got the key on?" Roebuck called.

Through the back window he saw her blonde head nod.

"Okay, son, let's go."

Roebuck and Claude leaned into the truck together, rocking it at first, then rolling it faster and faster down the slight grade toward the road.

"Now!" Roebuck yelled.

Ellie popped the clutch and the engine sputtered to life, then died.

"It's okay," Roebuck said. "It'll start."

They pushed again.

This time the engine sputtered and broke into an uneven roar. "You'll get your truck back!" Roebuck yelled as Ellie scooted over and he climbed into the cab behind the wheel. "I promise!"

Claude raised one hand in a slow wave and Iris stood watching the setting sun turning the sky blood-red behind them.

The gears meshed with a loud grinding sound.

Roebuck felt like Robin Hood as he and Ellie sped away down the narrow dirt road in the wildly bucking truck, a magnificent plume of dust hanging behind them in the still summer air.

They had gone almost a mile in the rattling truck, driving

as fast as they thought safe, afraid that at any moment something would fly apart on the ancient pickup. The bumpy road was a series of sharp curves, and there was so much play in the steering wheel that it took all of Roebuck's concentration and energy just to keep the truck from veering and hitting a tree.

"Watch out!"

As they lurched around a bend Ellie's scream rang in Roebuck's ear. He twisted the wheel a full turn and a half, sideswiping the car that had been coming from the opposite direction.

He couldn't believe it as he looked out the truck's rear window at the car they had just run off the road. Sitting at an angle in the high weeds at the edge of the road was Sheriff Boadeen's vaunted cruiser, a nasty red scrape down the two-tone paint of its shining side, through the ornate gold badge on its door.

Even as Roebuck watched the sheriff turned and gaped at him, his blue uniform cap crooked on his head, his lips moving in a surprised shout to his deputy who was also twisted in his seat and staring at the truck. The cruiser roared backward across the road as Boadeen attempted to turn it around.

"It's Boadeen!" Roebuck yelled, and he slammed his foot down on the accelerator. Ellie turned in the seat and looked out the rear window as the ancient truck gradually gained speed. They half-slid, half-tilted around the bends in the rutted road, bucking and shimmying violently.

"They're after us!" Ellie yelled as she caught a glimpse of the cruiser's smiling grill through the haze of dust just as they rocked around a corner.

They were rolling now. Roebuck mashed down with all his strength on the accelerator, feeling the mad vibrations of the rattling truck's racing engine run up his leg and through his body. His teeth were clacking together and the seat of his pants was slapping up and down against the hard upholstery as he barely kept the roaring, bucking pickup on the road.

"They're g-g-going to c-c-catch us!" Ellie shouted, bouncing up and down beside him.

"They're n-n-not!" Roebuck screamed back. They heard a popping sound behind them and Ellie grabbed Roebuck's shirt.

"They're sh-sh-shooting at us!" she screamed. "G-G-Goddamn them!"

They smashed over a rut so deep that the truck was momentarily airborne, bouncing down with such a jolt that Roebuck actually struck his head on the cab roof. He tried to steer with one hand as he drew his pistol from his belt, but he fumbled the gun and it dropped to the floor and began clattering around between his feet. In the back of his mind he realized that Boadeen's gunfire would be ineffectual anyway, for the bumpy road wound so tightly that the two racing vehicles were seldom within sight of each other long enough for a clear shot.

Wham!

The truck was suddenly all over the road, then off the road and rocketing through the woods, barely passing between trees as Roebuck braced himself and struggled frantically with the suddenly alive wheel that was writhing in his hands like a coiled snake. They spun sideways as the bed of the pickup ricocheted off a tree, and the truck tilted partway over, paused, then bounced back to sit upright on all four wheels with the engine dead and the radio suddenly blaring. Roebuck rubbed his eyes and turned to see the cruiser flash past with screaming siren.

"They didn't see us!" Ellie yelled over the blare of the radio. "What happened?"

"Blowout! Come on!"

They were out of the truck, running unsteadily through the woods.

"Wait a minute!" Roebuck whispered hoarsely as they crashed through the woods. "I don't hear the siren anymore."

They stood still, listening vainly, then they went forward more quietly.

After moving carefully through the woods for a short distance they both stopped, both hearing the same faint rustling sound at the same time.

"Over here," Roebuck whispered, and he guided Ellie by the arm to some thick underbrush behind two trees that grew close together. They crouched, waiting.

Ellie squeezed Roebuck's hand and pointed. About a hundred feet from them a blue uniform cap with a gold badge was moving slowly just above the brush on the edge of a slight depression. As they watched, the cap disappeared behind some higher brush, then reappeared a few feet away. For a second they glimpsed a slowly moving figure through the trees, bent forward, gun drawn, staring intently ahead. Sheriff Boadeen moving in for the kill, unknowingly stalking past his quarry.

Roebuck knew that the deputy was somewhere near, probably creeping through the woods on the other side of the road. The sheriff must have seen almost immediately that there was no raised dust ahead of him and realized that the pickup had run off the road. Now he and his deputy were backtracking, and Roebuck suddenly realized that they were closing in on the barely audible, static-filled sound of the blaring truck radio.

"Let's go," Roebuck whispered when Sheriff Boadeen was well past them. He took Ellie's arm and they moved through the woods as fast as they could with reasonable silence, parallel to the winding road.

Then they too heard a sound, a low and rhythmic rumble.

"What the hell is that?" Roebuck asked in a whisper, sweat pouring down his face.

"Sounds like a car engine." Ellie bent over, her hands on her knees, trying to catch her breath.

Roebuck felt a sudden elation course through him. "By God, it is! It is a car engine!" Ellie followed him as he began trudging in the direction of the low, steady sound.

They stopped at the edge of the woods and looked all around them. The cruiser sat in the middle of the road facing away from them, shimmers of hot exhaust fumes rising from its tailpipe with every throb of the engine.

We've got to chance it! Roebuck thought, breathing in unconscious rhythm to the quick beat of the idling motor.

He and Ellie exchanged glances, and it was Ellie who stepped out onto the road first, pulling Roebuck after her by the shirt sleeve.

The road was empty for the short distance they could see in each direction.

They climbed quickly into the powerful cruiser, careful not to slam the doors and alert Boadeen or his deputy. Roebuck put the car in gear and with a trembling foot applied just the slightest pressure to the accelerator.

The cruiser moved forward slowly and quietly, around the bend in the road, up a hill and through another curve. Then he gave it more gas and they picked up speed smoothly as the big car took the winding road with ease. They opened both doors and slammed them shut all the way.

Roebuck let out a long sigh, like a sharp wind through the trees.

"That's going to be one surprised sheriff!" he said loudly, and he began to giggle.

Before Ellie knew it, she was giggling with him.

★ ★ ★ ★ ★

They pulled the cruiser off the highway, into a grove of trees just outside Ironton, and walked the last half mile through the darkness of mid-evening. Now they sat on a hill overlooking the strip of lights along either side of the highway and the dotted white lights of residences beyond.

"Where we going to get a car?" Ellie asked.

"I don't know yet, but it's a cinch we wouldn't have gotten much farther in a stolen police car."

"You think we better hurry?"

"We've got time." Roebuck fingered the .38 police special Ellie had found in the cruiser's glove compartment. "Boadeen will never get that pickup running again, and even if he did they couldn't drive very fast on that flat tire."

"Just the same," Ellie said, "I'll be glad when we get out of Clark County."

An unexpected shiver of dread ran through Roebuck. If only Gipp would stop his deadly pursuit at an imaginary line, to turn around and go back according to the rules. But no line, imaginary or otherwise, could stop Gipp, and no rules applied to him.

A long shrill whistle drifted up to Roebuck and Ellie from the town below. It came from a low complex of factories or plants of some sort, with tall smokestacks in bunches of threes stretching up toward the night sky. In a few minutes they saw below them a string of automobile lights leading from a parking lot behind one of the buildings.

"What kind of place is that?" Roebuck asked.

Ellie shrugged her shoulders. "I don't know."

"It looks like the afternoon shift getting off." Roebuck broke off a tiny blade of grass and began chewing on it. "There should be a night shift. Maybe we can get a car off that lot."

195

"That's a good idea," Ellie said, "and it might not be missed for eight hours. But how we going to get it started?"

"I don't know," Roebuck said. "I'll hot wire it or something." He had no idea how to hot wire a car. Actually he had been counting on someone leaving their keys in their car, as many people do in public parking lots. But Ellie had a point. The odds were against his finding a car ready to go on a lot like this.

On the other hand, how hard could it be to change the wires on a car? He would use a dime for a screwdriver and switch a few connections around until he got the right combination. At this point a man had to kind of play things by ear.

"There is a night shift," Ellie said.

Roebuck looked down to see three or four cars going into the lot where the outgoing string of headlights had been. Soon more sets of headlights showed up, driving the same curving pattern around the building to what looked like a well-lighted parking area. Roebuck counted forty-two cars before he and Ellie began walking down the long grassy hill.

They walked quickly but relaxed, their heels digging into the soft, slanted earth. Below them the lights of Ironton, above them the detached tranquility of the stars. The shrill, wavering whistle sounded again, louder now as they were nearing the parking lot.

"I hope to hell there's not a guard or something," Roebuck said.

"It doesn't look like there would be," Ellie said. "This looks like a pretty small town."

"Yeah, but who knows what this place makes? Maybe they manufacture parts for the hydrogen bomb."

They could see now that the low building was bigger than it had appeared from atop the hill. The only windows on the long walls were slit-like affairs near the roof, and every one of them had light streaming from it.

"There's no fence or anything around it," Ellie said in a breathless voice, though there was obviously no point in whispering.

"We'll go around to the side where the parking lot is," Roebuck said firmly.

There was no one in sight on the lot, only the cars in neat rows between freshly painted yellow lines. The lot was discouragingly well-lighted.

"This place is a steel mill," Roebuck said, as he and Ellie stood in darkness just off the parking lot. There was a weightless, nervous feeling in his stomach.

"Do you want me to go with you?" Ellie asked. Roebuck shook his head. That was a hell of a question for her to ask.

"You wait here," he said, and he stepped out into the light and began walking down a row of cars, trying to appear casual, as if he belonged there.

He felt the panic grow in him as car after car had an empty ignition keyhole. Slipping his hand in his pants pocket, he found a dime and rolled it between sweat damp fingers. He was not so sure now that he could get one of the cars started, and he felt terribly exposed on the wide lot, like an outfielder in a night baseball game. He bet that he could have been a ball player if he'd tried, marveling for just an instant that his frightened mind could harbor such an irrelevant thought at a time like this.

The whistle shattered the air with a scream. Roebuck jumped, unable to hear his own frightened shout. Then he realized what was happening and made himself appear unaffected as the shrill blast reached a crescendo and died away. He turned up another row of cars and began walking toward a sleek late model Pontiac, making up his mind that if he didn't spot an ignition key by the time he reached it he would get into it and lie down on the front seat to experiment with the wires beneath the dash. If that didn't work they would just have to steal a car somewhere else.

"Hey!"

Roebuck leaped and whirled toward the voice.

It was a young man, about twenty-five, his tall, lean body dressed in tight pants and a faded blue workshirt. He was about twenty yards from Roebuck and walking swiftly toward him.

Roebuck wanted to run but he was paralyzed with surprise and fright.

"You mean me?" His voice was much too high and not loud enough, as if he were speaking in a drape-lined room.

"Yeah, what are you doin' on this lot? I seen you lookin' in all the cars."

"No, you're crazy. I was just cutting through . . ."

The man stopped about ten feet from Roebuck, looking narrowly at him over the hood of the car that separated them. "It didn't look that way to me."

"Well, you're wrong." As if the conversation was ended, Roebuck turned and began walking off the lot.

He heard footsteps, as the young worker came after him around the front of the car.

"Hey! Hold on, you!"

Roebuck turned, the .38 in his hand leveled at the man's midsection.

Fright and puzzlement crossed the young, handsome face. "What goes on here?"

Roebuck heard the edge of fear in the voice, felt the sudden shift in the delicate balance. He had the power now.

"Stay where you are, Junior." Roebuck's fingers flexed around the gun butt. "Now, what are you doing out here?"

"I work here. I forgot my lunch and came out to get it, that's all."

"Which car is yours?"

The slender man pointed to a late model red Ford.

"Let's get in," Roebuck said, putting hardness in his command.

Roebuck ordered the man behind the wheel, then got in on the passenger's side and sat with the gun nestled in the crook of his elbow, still aimed at his young hostage.

"Look," the man began, "I gotta work . . ."

"Drive, Junior!"

The red Ford pulled out of its parking space with its headlights off. Roebuck ordered the car stopped on the driveway just outside the floodlit area of the lot. Ellie ran out of the darkness and scrambled into the back seat behind Roebuck. He saw the young man's blue eyes follow her blonde figure in surprise, unable for a moment to look away. I'll bet you'd like some of that, Roebuck thought smugly, juggling the gun, if you weren't so scared!

"Who's this?" Ellie asked.

"He's a young fellow who's lending us his car," Roebuck said. "Turn your lights on and drive, Junior."

They drove south for an hour in silence, the young man trying to concentrate on his driving but finding his attention centering on the revolver that was aimed at him.

"I wouldn't try anything if I were you," Roebuck said tersely. "I'm wanted for killing four F.B.I. agents in a shoot-out and I don't have a damn thing to lose."

"Listen," the man said in a scared voice, "this ain't any of my business. All I want is to take you where you want to go and get out of it."

Roebuck noticed the young man's eyes flick to the rear view mirror as he spoke, appealing to Ellie's sympathy.

"She's not a bad-looking woman, is she?" Roebuck said.

The slender man didn't answer, but his grip on the wheel tightened.

Roebuck smiled. "That's a steel mill you work at, isn't it?"

"We bake bread," the man said. "It's a bakery."

"Oh." Roebuck steadied the gun in his hand. "I couldn't tell in the dark."

They had been traveling a desolate strip of highway now for the past ten minutes, a straight gray line between black, borderless fields. Only darkness lay ahead of them.

"Pull over here, Junior!" Roebuck commanded. He saw his captive draw a sharp breath.

"Leave the engine running," Roebuck said when the car was parked on the shoulder of the road. He didn't say anything else for a full minute, watching the fright crawl over the lean, handsome face.

"Nobody's going to hurt you," Ellie said from the back seat. "You just have a good walk ahead of you."

Roebuck got out of the car and motioned for the young man to scoot across the seat and get out on the same side. Ellie got behind the wheel while the two men stood facing one another beside the highway, the revolver between them.

"We better get going, Lou," she said. "A car's liable to come along."

"That's right," Roebuck said. "Back up, Junior." He waited until the lean man was ten feet away before waving the gun for him to stop. Then Roebuck got in the car and shut the door, still aiming the revolver at the young man through the open window. He could see the slender body tighten, tensing itself for the rip of a bullet. The thin, handsome face was drawn, the eyes wide in the moonlight and riveted to the gun barrel.

Roebuck lifted the revolver to point directly at the frightened face, his finger trembling on the trigger.

"So long, Junior!" he screamed as the car roared away. He jerked his hand at the last instant and the gun exploded, firing the bullet almost straight up into the night sky.

The young man instinctively dived to the ground with a startled shout.

"I only scared him!" Roebuck yelled as Ellie picked up speed, her eyes fixed straight ahead on the highway. "I only scared him . . . I . . ." His voice trailed off on the rush of wind into the car.

Roebuck and Ellie were traveling again.

PART FOUR

1

They had driven south long enough. Roebuck wheeled the red Ford to the west less than an hour after they'd left its young owner shaken by the side of the road.

It felt good to be traveling west again, aimed like an arrow toward a land of sun and perpetual summer. Roebuck wondered why he instinctively sensed safety to the west, danger to the east. Why had he run west after Ingrahm's death instead of east to one of half a dozen closer large cities he could have lost himself in? Perhaps that was it, losing himself, ceasing to exist to everyone else and so to himself. The anonymity of a big city horrified him. Then there was the vastness of the west to run to before being confronted with an ocean. Didn't the fear of every animal decrease in proportion to the vastness of the area into which it could retreat?

Roebuck snorted. Animal? He was no animal; he was a man!

As soon as they could, Roebuck and Ellie stole another car, this time off the lot of a large A&P supermarket. They hid the red Ford in the darkness behind the V formed by two huge billboards constructed to face both lanes of traffic. From each billboard smiled the massive sincere face of a political candidate in the upcoming elections. Roebuck wished they could have hidden the cruiser there, to be found in the black crotch of that gigantic political pitch. What an ironic delight that would have been, a final tweak of the nose at Boadeen!

"When do you want to stop someplace?" Ellie asked as they sped along the highway in their new car, a yellow Mercury sedan.

"Late," Roebuck said. "About one or two. We need distance." He squinted dramatically into the onrushing night.

"I think we got away clean." Ellie smiled and glanced backward. "They might not connect this car with us at all."

"Maybe not," Roebuck said wisely. "The way we hid the Ford it might not be found for a long time."

As they drove on, that first flush of freedom from their narrow escape began to wear off of Roebuck, and the worry began to set in again, nagging, pecking, corroding his peace of mind like acid. He sat watching the wavering white center line play out before the headlights of the car, and far ahead the distant red pinpoints of taillights, giving some clue to the twists and turns of the dark road. Roebuck thought with dread of the dangers that lay ahead of them, the vast, efficient machinery of the law, out to get him, out to kill him now or later, the cold business of spilled blood. And somewhere, watching, following, was Benny Gipp. He tried to ignore the headache that began throbbing behind his eyes. Inexorably the joy of sudden freedom was turning to a disturbing sense of naked exposure.

Ellie twisted the rear view mirror and began arranging her hair as best she could with a broken-toothed comb. "I've seen enough woods for a while. I itch all over."

"Yeah," Roebuck said, "you're not too at home in the woods."

Ellie smiled at herself in the mirror as she combed a tangle from a blonde lock. "I did all right, I guess. We didn't get lost or caught."

Roebuck stared straight ahead, listening to the low rasp of the comb through her hair. Was she thinking of that night he'd got lost in the woods? Had she read something in his voice then, sensed the fear in him as he'd worried an animal might?

"You didn't slow me down too much," he said. He glanced over at her with a grin. "All in all you've been worth having along."

She smiled back.

Or was she smiling through him? Roebuck felt again the pressure on his arm as she pulled his sleeve to step out onto the road where Boadeen's cruiser was. She couldn't think he had been afraid. He was only being careful, methodical. There are times for action and daring, but that hadn't been one of them. Suppose the whole thing had been set up by Boadeen, and that he and his deputy had been waiting in the woods on the other side of the road? It had been nothing but a lucky break, being able to steal the sheriff's cruiser. Just like Ellie to step right into a possible trap.

Roebuck whizzed around a brightly lighted tractor-trailer and cut back just in time to miss an oncoming set of headlights.

"Should you drive so fast, Lou? We might get stopped or something."

"No cops along this kind of highway," Roebuck said. "Don't be afraid to take chances. The only reason we got this far is because we dared."

"I guess you're right." Ellie was finished with her hair, so she twisted the mirror back into position and put the comb in the glove compartment. "Look," she said in a pleased voice, "a five-dollar bill." She held it up for Roebuck to see. "It was laying right there in the glove compartment!"

"So what?"

"So we can use it." The childlike pleasure in her voice had given way to vague annoyance. "We're not independently wealthy, you know."

Roebuck didn't change expression. "We've still got plenty of money."

"Less than you think," Ellie said. "Some of our money was in the suitcase we left in that pickup truck."

She was right! Roebuck ran their speed up another five miles an hour. She was always right. Or seemed to be, anyway. He had forgotten the money in the plaid suitcase. How much had it been? Three hundred dollars? Five hundred?

"There was almost six hundred dollars in there," Ellie said.

There was triumph in her voice, Roebuck thought. She was glad they'd lost the money! For the first time Ellie was really beginning to aggravate him.

He reached into his pocket for his wallet and tossed it into her lap. "Count this."

He listened as she flicked through the bills.

"Almost seven hundred dollars."

"That means there was another seven hundred in the suitcase," Roebuck said. "You were wrong as usual."

"I didn't count that money, Lou." She sounded hurt. "You put it there."

Roebuck took a corner too fast. "You know what they say about one basket."

"Well, I didn't say you made a mistake, Lou. It was just a bad break we lost it."

"Tell you the truth," Roebuck said, "when we jumped out of the truck I yelled for you to grab the suitcase. You were closest. I didn't know you didn't have it until we were too far away to go back."

"I didn't hear you, Lou."

"You were excited."

Low silence, the hum of the tires on the road.

"I suppose you're right," Ellie said at last.

Roebuck briskly punched in the car's lighter. "Give me a cigarette."

Smoking seemed to lessen the pain in Roebuck's head. He smoked cigarette after cigarette as they drove on through the night. Ellie had turned on the car radio to listen for news, and the soft, relaxed flow of music from some distant town helped to soothe his nerves. Around them in the darkness the rolling hills were getting shallower, farther apart. The land was un-limbering, stretching out into flatness like a motionless earth wave spewing itself onto a mammoth beach. They were almost into Kansas.

"That looks like a motel," Ellie said, pointing through the windshield at a lighted sign about a mile ahead of them. "Why don't we stop, Lou?"

Roebuck squinted at the blinding beams of approaching headlights, then he winced as the car shot past them with a blast of air and glaring yellow light.

"I was going to pull in there," he said, rubbing the base of his neck where the muscles were stiffening. "You're probably getting tired of traveling."

"I'm just afraid we're going to have an accident," Ellie said. "You haven't slept for a long time."

Roebuck flicked his cigarette butt out the window like a tiny rocket. "I can go a long time without sleep."

They checked into the Wayside Motel, a modern two story building built on a square around a swimming pool. They requested a room on the first floor toward the back. So it would be quiet and they could be near the pool, Roebuck had told the man behind the desk.

"It sure is a little room," Ellie said, looking around as Roebuck shut the door behind them.

She had a way of sizing up every room she walked into, he thought irritably, as if she had to make a scaled, itemized drawing.

"The room is fine," he said, sitting in the one chair and working off his boots. "The room is goddamn fine!"

"Don't get mad, Lou." She walked over and flicked on the light above the double bed. "There's no reason to get mad."

She was right, Roebuck realized. There wasn't any reason.

Ellie tested the mattress with the flat of her hand. "I'm just used to being outside, I guess. Any motel room'd seem small."

Roebuck carried his boots into the bathroom and wiped the dust off them with toilet paper. He'd feel better when he got them shined.

He heard the faint rustle of Ellie removing her clothes, and he walked back in and set the boots by the bed.

"We'll have to buy some more stuff tomorrow," he said, stepping out of his pants. "Food, something to wear . . ." He walked to the door in his jockey shorts and double checked to make sure it was locked.

"We're safe here," Ellie said with a smile. Wearing only panties and bra, she slipped beneath the folds of white sheet. "Like in a cocoon." The smile was still on her face as she closed her eyes.

Holding that picture of Ellie in his mind, Roebuck turned off the reading lamp. He got into bed and made love to her, roughly, forcibly. He slapped, he dug his fingernails into the soft, round meat of her buttocks. And she met him all the way, building, building, biting and moaning into the burning flesh of his neck.

It was over, with long, mournful sighs that seemed never

to fade.

Roebuck rolled onto his back, pulling out of her warmth and wetness, back into the cold, real world. The thermostat clicked and the air conditioner began to hum.

"Lou?" Beneath the sheets her fingertips brushed the side of his thigh pleadingly.

"I was noticing the headlights before we checked in here," he said in a distant voice. He felt a cool wetness between his legs, on his stomach.

"Lou?"

He lay on his back, gazing up into the darkness. "I think there was a car following us." And he settled into sleep-like silence.

2

Early the next morning, before anyone else in the Wayside Motel had risen, Roebuck and Ellie got into the yellow Mercury sedan and drove away. They left the room key attached to the plastic Wayside card on the bureau top, and they left the plastic Do Not Disturb sign hanging on the doorknob.

They sped through the low morning mist that swirled cloudily over the highway and fields. The sun, rising in a sky that was only partially clouded, would soon dissipate the mist as the morning heat increased. But right now the flat land had an unreal quality, and Roebuck felt like a pilot skimming the tops of the clouds as the speeding car broke through the layers of fog.

"We going to stop for breakfast?" Ellie asked beside him.

Roebuck let his arm dangle out the window, straight down against the cool metal of the car door, into the cool mist. "We can stop and eat this morning when we buy what we need. But starting tomorrow we'll travel like before, eating whenever we can in our room."

She didn't answer. He knew she was getting tired of traveling, tired of being pursued. Like a woman, Roebuck thought, to be worn down by the chase.

"This reminds me of a time in Canada," he said, "when four of us were lost, almost out of food, and a pack of wolves was following us. They never got too close, but at night we could see their eyes reflecting the light of the campfire, waiting patiently for us to wear down, to give up."

Ellie smoothed a fold in her slacks. "How'd you get out of it?"

"We began shooting the wolves for food, one by one. There were only two wolves left by the time we reached Anchorage."

"That's in Alaska, isn't it?"

"Near the border. Look!" Roebuck pointed to a roadside sign. "It says to slow down. That means there's a town in front of us. We can do our shopping before people are in the stores."

"If anything's open," Ellie said. "It's not even eight o'clock."

At first the entire town did appear closed, a string of dirty buildings that seemed to have sleep hanging over them. But a service station was open, and there was one of those all-night grocery stores. They filled up on gas and bought two bags of groceries. They would have to buy their clothes later.

By the time they were on the road again the low mist had disappeared, and a clear sky promised a hot day. On each side of them the flat fields of Kansas stretched away, unbroken except for an occasional toy house and a few solitary irrigation pumps, rising and falling as if weary and unable to work faster in the heat.

Roebuck felt more exposed than ever now as he pictured the car from above, crawling slowly across an endless plain, bound by a ribbon of road. He felt like a wingless fly on a white ceiling.

It had been a half hour since a car had passed them from the other direction. How conspicuous they must be, Roebuck thought again. Maybe they should have tried to cross Kansas by night. But then headlights were visible for a great distance in this flat land.

"I suppose we can buy our clothes and get some lunch at the same time," Ellie said. "We have to go in someplace anyway."

"No reason we can't do that," Roebuck said. He was watching a tiny dot on the highway ahead, trying to estimate how far away it was. Amazing, he thought, how long it takes a dot to become a car on this highway. They could have taken the four lane interstate farther north and made better time, but the State Patrol might be watching that highway as a matter of routine! That's what you had to watch out for, their damn routine!

Roebuck saw the dot grow larger and change to the form of a car. Then it grew with astounding rapidity and became a red station wagon that whizzed by them. Roebuck's glance flitted to the rear view mirror to follow the car's shrinkage and disappearance, and his gaze stuck there. Far away, beyond the car that had just passed them, was another tiny dot on the highway.

Roebuck watched the dot for the next twenty minutes. It got neither larger nor smaller. He began to alternate his speed, sometimes slowing to fifty-five, then zooming up to eighty. Still the dot remained the same size, too far away for shape or color.

After the next ten miles the dot was so steadily, so persistently there, that Roebuck's glances into the mirror were only unnecessary confirmations of its presence. It was as if he could see it from the back of his head.

Ellie was dozing beside him, unaware of what was happening.

Roebuck nudged her in the ribs. "We're turning here."

"What?" She rubbed sleep from her eyes. "Turning? Why?"

"This road goes into a town. It's late enough to buy what we need and grab a bite of lunch."

Ellie looked at the dashboard clock, puzzled. "It's only quarter to ten, Lou."

"Damn it, don't argue!" He braked the car and swerved left beneath overhead traffic lights and signs onto a blacktop road. The tires sang. "Be making up your mind what you want to buy," he said, stealing a quick look at her, a sideways dart of his eyes as he checked the mirror.

"How much can we spend?"

"I don't know," Roebuck said impatiently. "We'll spend whatever we need to." Again his eyes darted to the mirror. Nothing.

"I need some makeup," Ellie said, "and another blouse and a few dresses. Maybe some underthings. Some underthings, I guess."

Roebuck saw the town in the distance and speeded up to head for the biggest store so he could park the car in an inconspicuous spot.

The biggest store turned out to be a dimestore. Roebuck swung into a parking area alongside the narrow walk of a side street and opened the door. "Come on."

"How come we're parking here?" Ellie asked as she got out of the car.

"Less likely to be spotted." Roebuck led her into a side entrance of the dimestore.

The clothes they bought were cheap but sturdy. A pair of pre-cuffed dress pants and shirts for Roebuck, slacks and two dresses for Ellie. Then they bought socks, underwear, and whatever incidentals they needed. The whole thing came to only thirty-nine dollars.

"We'll take the front door this time," Roebuck said, carrying the packages.

"But the car's over there."

Roebuck didn't answer. God, would she never stop with her dumb questions! She followed him silently out the front door.

He handed her the packages. "Hold these. I'll be right back to pick you up." Looking straight ahead, he strode toward the corner.

Ellie waited for perhaps five minutes before the yellow sedan pulled around the corner and stopped before her. She put the packages on the back seat and got in.

"What was all that about, Lou?"

"I wanted to make sure nobody was watching the car. I didn't want to put you in any danger."

"What made you think somebody'd be watching the car?"

Roebuck turned onto the blacktop road and drove back toward the highway.

"A car was following us," he said. "I've been watching it for miles."

Ellie's forehead creased in a frown. "The police?"

"Or Benny Gipp," Roebuck said. "The police would close in and arrest us, but Gipp would follow us, wait for the right moment."

"Are you sure the car was following us? Maybe it was just somebody going the same way we are."

"Sure?" Roebuck laughed quickly, nervously. "Yeah, I'm sure. When I slowed down or picked up speed, so did it."

"If it is this Gipp, do you think he'll call the police?"

"Hell no, he won't call the police!" Roebuck was getting angry, angry with her stupidity and her senseless questions. "I told you, he wouldn't want me to get a life sentence and be paroled. And if I was convicted, he wouldn't want someone else to put the noose around my neck, to spring the trap. The bastard wants to do it himself! Don't you understand, it's his pleasure!"

"Lou, relax." Ellie stroked his arm as she looked behind them. "There's no one back there now."

Roebuck sighed, checking the rear view mirror. "No," he said, "not now."

They unfolded the road map they had picked up at the last service station and took to the side roads, still traveling west, but by a devious and more indirect route. Progress was much slower this way, but Roebuck felt it was safer.

"Why don't we stop early this afternoon at a motel?" Ellie suggested. "We know nobody's following us now. Anyway, if this Gipp is after us, it'll throw him off some."

Roebuck was biting his lower lip as he drove. "I don't know if anything will throw him off."

"We have to eat anyway," Ellie said. "We were going to eat lunch when we shopped and we forgot. If we have to stop someplace it might as well be a motel where I can fix us something. It'd be safer."

Roebuck did feel unusually tired, tired to the marrow of his bones, and he wished Ellie would just keep quiet and leave him alone. The very sound of her voice was beginning to annoy him.

"It's because I'm tired," he said.

"What is?"

Roebuck cleared his throat. "I said we'll stop at the next motel."

The motel where they stopped was old, with individual shingled cabins in a weed-grown, rustic setting. It looked cool and safe after the bare heat of the road. Roebuck steered the car through the entrance and under an arbor of withered roses to the office.

After they checked in, Ellie prepared a lunch of sandwiches and cold soda while Roebuck showered. They ate then, and he felt better, more relaxed, more tired. He got up, turned the window air conditioner on high and stretched out on the bed in his underwear.

He closed his eyes, but the darkness wasn't complete.

"Pull the curtains all the way," he ordered, his damp forearm thrown over his eyes. He listened as Ellie crossed the room and drew the curtains. With his eyes pressed closed he heard her walk back, run the sink water for a few seconds, then walk to the double bed. The bed rocked and squeaked as she lay beside him.

Still Roebuck couldn't sleep. He was tired, but his nerves were crying out, not letting him relax deep inside himself. He crossed his other arm over his face. It was the light, he decided, that would not permit him to sleep. There was something . . . unnatural about sleeping in the light. It made a man uneasy when other people could see him sleep. It made him feel vulnerable.

Rolling over on his stomach, Roebuck tried without success to escape the sunlight that seeped into the room between the slats of the blinds, through the skimpy material of the curtains, along the tops of the windows, even under the door.

He reached for Ellie.

3

Ellie shook him awake.

"You screamed."

Roebuck lay on his back, breathing hard. The sheets were tangled about his legs. He didn't remember screaming, but he remembered his dream. The past three nights he'd had the dream, but this time it had been fantastically real, immediate, as if he'd fallen back in time during his sleep.

He fastened his gaze on the closed door, expecting at any moment to hear an alarmed knock.

"Was it loud enough for anyone else to hear?" he asked, realizing for the first time that Ellie had a very tight grasp on his hand.

She nodded. "If there's somebody in one of the cabins near us they must have heard."

Roebuck looked up at her. "If somebody comes, you go to the door. Tell them I stepped on a nail. They'll believe that."

"Why don't I just tell them you had a bad dream?"

Roebuck didn't answer, and neither of them relaxed until a full five minutes had passed and it was apparent that no one was going to investigate Roebuck's sudden scream.

"No one heard," he said to Ellie. It's as if it hadn't happened, he thought, freeing his legs from the twisted sheets and sitting on the edge of the bed. "Why don't you fix us some coffee?"

"I thought you might want to skip breakfast, Lou. It's nine-thirty; we must have been tireder than we thought."

"Yeah," Roebuck agreed. He didn't tell her that he'd hardly slept at all since they'd gone back to bed at ten after a late supper last night. All those hours in bed had to do him some good, though, whether he'd had his eyes open or not.

"Fix the coffee anyway," he said. "You probably need it." He got up and slipped into his pants, almost losing his balance as he stood for a moment on one leg. His head throbbed with pain as he stooped to pick up his boots and went into the bathroom.

Roebuck stood leaning over the washbasin, listening to the hiss from the tap on the other side of the wall as Ellie ran water into the coffeepot. He turned the cold faucet handle on the washbasin and watched the trickle of water meet the sloping white porcelain and swirl down the drain.

The cold water on his face revitalized him somewhat, and he hurriedly combed his hair and brushed his teeth. Then, posing, he smiled at himself in the medicine cabinet mirror, examining the frown lines and puffy eyes of his reflection. The mechanical smile sagged. The man in the mirror looked so different! If he were grayer he'd look like an old man. Lack of sleep, Roebuck thought. Only lack of sleep. Picking up the bar of soap, he ran it edgeways across the smooth mirror, leaving a broad white X that touched all four corners of the glass. Then he squared his shoulders and turned away from the mirror. He got the can of shoe polish he'd bought yesterday, sat on the toilet bowl lid and carefully began to polish his boots.

After coffee and some packaged donuts for breakfast, they left the motel to drive west again, winding over narrow and shimmering side roads, speeding like a free-scared thing over stretches of highway until they came again to another self-imposed detour. Now Roebuck began to picture the car as a huge yellow beetle, crawling across Kansas to evade a thousand natural enemies.

Hour after hour, mile after mile, Ellie continued to aggravate Roebuck. The thing between them festered, for she would never defy or disagree with him, never give his challenges something on which to beat themselves. His frustration grew.

"Look behind us!" he rasped at her, speeding down a flat and endless stretch of highway. "I told you to keep looking behind us! There are things I can't see in the mirror."

Dutifully, she twisted in her seat and looked out the rear window. "The highway's empty, Lou."

"Good thing," Roebuck muttered. "See if you're bright enough to remember to look back there every five minutes or so."

Ellie didn't answer. Roebuck reached over and turned off the radio so violently that the knob almost twisted loose in his hand.

"That goddamned thing is getting on my nerves!"

"I thought you might want to listen for the news."

"You thought, huh?"

Again she met him with one of her receding silences. They were nearing the state line before Ellie spoke. "Do you think you oughta have that gun laying on the seat, Lou?"

"Nobody can see it," Roebuck said. "It's up against my body."

"Just the same, there's probably a law . . ."

"Law!" Roebuck snorted the word with half a laugh. "Don't you understand we're wanted for murder?"

"It's not that, Lou. I mean, it just seems to be taking a

chance, calling attention to us, to have a gun out in plain sight if somebody does come up to the car. Maybe a truck driver could even look down and see it."

"Law!" Roebuck spat the word out again, as if he hadn't heard her last statement. "I'll tell you about the law. If I had this gun in my pocket it would be a concealed weapon, understand? But here, right out where it can be seen, it's not breaking the concealed weapons law. Don't you see that?"

Ellie's voice was helpless. "I didn't know, Lou. I'm no lawyer."

"You sure as hell aren't! But I did go to law school for two years, so believe me, I know a little something of what I'm talking about."

"All you have to do is tell me, Lou." Ellie sat primly with her hands in the lap of her new green dress.

She was acting like what she was now, Roebuck thought. A ten-dollar pickup who liked to be pushed around. What had he ever seen in her that made him want her so? What did he still see in her? Why didn't he just stop the car and shove her out? She was one problem he could get rid of easily.

He thought about that, and he decided that she was still good cover, would still come in useful if the law did force a showdown.

"I told you, you tramp, take a look now and then out the rear window!"

Ellie obeyed, but he saw the anger, the reddish flush at the roots of her blonde hairline when she turned back.

"If I bother you, Lou, all you have to do is let me out at the next town. I can make my own way."

Roebuck was surprised. So she would actually leave him. "You wouldn't go if I did try to get rid of you," he said. "I'd have to drag you out of the car."

"I don't want to go unless you want me to. But if you tell me to go that'll be it."

She didn't sound so sure now, he thought. The hell of it was that he didn't want her to go, and she had a lot of nerve threatening him like that. He knew what she was.

Taking a banked S curve, he paid more attention to his driving than was necessary. "You let Boadeen have you, didn't you?" he said abruptly, surprising himself that the words came so easily. He had that on her, though; he had known it all along.

"Yes," she said, as if admitting to something of little importance. "I did that for us, to keep him from getting suspicious and investigating. And if he did get onto us, I thought he might not do anything for fear of getting himself in trouble."

Roebuck's breathing was coming harder. "It didn't work too well, did it?"

"I didn't know he was that rotten."

"He was that rotten! He didn't do anything you didn't! And are you trying to tell me you didn't enjoy it?"

Ellie's hands were out of her lap, resting lightly on her knees. "I enjoyed it some, I admit that."

Roebuck slapped the seat beside him. "How the hell do you think that makes me feel?"

"I didn't think you'd find out," Ellie said calmly, "or I wouldn't have done it."

"At night you say you love me and the next day you're letting that bastard take your pants off! What the hell kind of woman are you?" The words were rushing from Roebuck in a stream of bitterness, his voice tight, tears brimming his eyes. "There was only one other woman who ever did that to me, in Singapore, a high-class girl from the Wing family! A little bitch is what she was, like you, goddamnit! She was going to marry me and I found her in bed with my best friend and his brother! I knew a man who'd take care of her! The last time I saw her she was on a Mongolian slaver's junk sailing off to God knows where and what!"

"I did it for us, Lou, us!"

Roebuck narrowed his eyes and looked straight ahead. She didn't seem ashamed. That was the thing about it.

"You're a whore," he said in a controlled and vicious whisper. "A cheap, hick town whore!"

Even that didn't seem to stir Ellie as she sat very still, not looking at him. "You didn't have any trouble picking me up, Lou. It started out as a business proposition."

"You admit what you are, then? A small town, bar-hopping slut?"

Her voice was tolerant, as if she were explaining something to a child. "I never said I was anything else, Lou."

Ellie was quiet, across the state line, into Colorado. What bothered Roebuck was that she didn't seem at all upset about the conversation they'd had. Of course, Roebuck had understood all along what she was. That was part of her appeal to him. Ellie was the kind of woman a hard-bitten fugitive from the law should have; she was part of the cast for his present role, like Gipp chasing him across the country, like the gun on the seat beside him and the moustache he was beginning to cultivate—props, all of them. He was beginning, only beginning, to understand that, to face it.

His eyes went slowly to the rear view mirror, checking the empty road behind him. The fear of Gipp was there, so why couldn't Gipp be? Running from Gipp made Roebuck feel like a character in a movie he'd once seen, where a private detective traced the man who killed his partner all the way from New York to San Francisco—only this time the hero and villain were reversed.

Ellie sighed, leaning back in her seat and staring up at the yellow upholstery on the car's ceiling.

"You aren't ashamed of what you are," Roebuck said. "I don't understand that."

"Ashamed?" Ellie closed her eyes. "Why should I be ashamed?"

Roebuck didn't answer.

"I never told you," Ellie said, "but I tried marriage—twice."

"What happened?"

"My first husband turned out to be a drunk. That's when I started going out with other men, and we got a divorce. Marriage worked for a while the second time; then I started going out again. I liked going out with other men; I couldn't help it. Al found out and divorced me. He wouldn't have had any trouble finding correspondents if I'd contested it. It was my fault and I didn't much care." Her voice wavered and Roebuck saw her hand clutch the material of her dress. "Except for my little girl. Al's family got her."

"If you loved your girl, why didn't you stay home?"

"Because I couldn't, Lou. You called me a whore, and I guess I am one. I can't change. I accept myself as what I am, and I'm . . . you know . . . content."

Content. Roebuck didn't completely understand that, but he envied it. Ellie accepted what she was, and so she was somebody. It was the source of her strength, knowing what she was. "Whore," that was her label. She might wish it was something else, but that was her label. Oh, people were classified, by society, by God, by themselves. Everybody was something that marked him or her—thief, housewife, cop, con, queer, drunk, wife beater, businessman, tramp, pimp . . . The list went on. People fell into their niches, were held fast there. They were labeled, to themselves and to everyone else, and sometimes they didn't like what they read on their labels.

Ellie's voice was gentle, a confirmation of what he'd been thinking. "You knew what I was, Lou, really."

"Yeah." Roebuck passed his hand over his perspiring face, as if wiping away a vision, "I knew."

"And you loved me anyway."

"How could I?"

"Everybody loves somebody anyway."

"Maybe they do," Roebuck said.

The mountains appeared before them suddenly, shockingly. Around them the land was still low and rolling, and like weird, unsymmetrical pyramids built on level sand, the mountains loomed out of place and purple in the distance. One second they were an idle thought in the back of Roebuck's mind; the next second he felt he could stretch out his hand and touch them.

"They're still far away," Ellie said. "They fool you, like mirages." She turned to Roebuck. "If you want to stop soon, Lou, I'll fix us some supper and go out and get a bottle somewhere. You'll feel better."

"Okay," Roebuck said, staring at the distant mountain range, "that sounds good." The mountains reminded him of a roller coaster at an amusement park he'd gone to once as a school boy. Everybody in the class had been afraid to go on that roller coaster; he'd been the only one who'd volunteered. He'd gone not only once, but over and over, roaring through dips and turns, listening to the screams, feeling the rise and fall tear at his stomach, proving his courage to himself and his timid classmates, finally and forever.

He knew now why some people went on roller coasters, pretending they had courage, taking a hundred-thousand-to-one chance to reassure themselves and their girls. Comparing courage with going on a roller coaster was like comparing love with going to a whorehouse. Roebuck felt a twinge of alarm at the thought and looked at Ellie, almost afraid she'd read his thoughts.

As they drove the mountains loomed ahead of them as before, magnificent and unchanging, like a fantastic mural against a canvas of dimming blue sky.

"There's a sign that says Clinton's Motel's five miles away," Ellie said.

"I see it." Roebuck rested his arm on the rolled down window. "That's where I'd planned on stopping."

Clinton's Motel was like a thousand others, low, square, with a garish neon sign that blinked a slumbery invitation.

In the dead silence of the turned off engine Roebuck tucked the .38 in his belt beneath his shirt and got out of the car. He felt an unexpected cool passage of air as he stood there, like a chill emanating from the faraway mountains. Making sure the revolver was wedged firmly in his belt, he entered the motel office.

4

Roebuck felt immediately ill at ease at Clinton's Motel. The desk clerk had given him a strange look when he'd signed the register, a penetrating gaze from hooded blue eyes. And now that they were in their room Roebuck was even more uncomfortable. Everything in the tiny, ultra-modern room was square and sharp-angled—everything but the people. Roebuck felt his own human softness and vulnerability in contrast to the hard, precision angles and clean, cutting lines around him.

After a quick drink from the bottle of bourbon Ellie had bought at the motel lounge, he lay on the firm bed, feeling out of place and uneasy, his stockinged feet hanging over the edge of the mattress. It was silly, he told himself. These four walls concealed them just as the walls of any motel room. "You want to rest before we eat?" Ellie asked, stepping over to examine the bathroom.

Roebuck told her he wanted to. He toyed with the notion of apologizing to Ellie for the things he'd called her, but damn it, they were true! Besides, she was acting as if it hadn't happened. It didn't bother her, being called what she was.

The occasional whine of a passing truck invaded the quiet room, and now and then the resonant slapping of the motel pool's diving board sounded. The window air conditioner was drawing in a faint chlorine scent from the pool to hang

225

cool and clear in the atmosphere of the small, sparsely furnished room, giving it the antiseptic air of an operating room.

Roebuck heard and felt Ellie stretch out on the bed next to him, but he kept his eyes closed and let everything become distant. He descended into sleep.

It was pitch-black in the room when Roebuck opened his eyes and fought his way up, up out of sleep like a man struggling to the surface of dark water.

The lamp by the bed came on and he slumped back limply, lying with his fingertips pressed for reassurance against the firmness of the mattress beneath him.

Ellie's voice came to him, as comfortingly real as the light and the mattress. "What did you dream this time?"

Roebuck folded his hands behind his head, expanding his chest to breathe in the too-cool air in the room. He held his breath as long as he could and then let it out in a long sigh. "The same dream," he said. "It's always the same dream."

"It must be a bad one."

He was quiet, letting the reality around him implant itself, taking the place of the more horrible reality he'd experienced in his sleep.

"Why don't you tell me about it?" Ellie said. "Tell me about it and you might not dream it anymore." She touched his bare arm, and the touch was like a lifeline.

"I'll always have that dream," Roebuck said, "even when I'm awake." Since they'd left the cabin at Lake Chippewa the dream had become a presence in him, a swelling, shadowed thing that grew and grew.

"I don't guess you can be blamed for your dreams," Ellie said, "awake or asleep. For the things that come into your mind when you let your guard down."

Roebuck didn't answer.

"Tell me about it," Ellie said.

He had never told anyone about his dream.

Her fingers, peaceful, compelling, caressed his arm. "Tell me about it . . ."

"I was eleven," Roebuck said. "I was raised in Arkansas on a little farm something like the one we stayed at with Claude and his mother, not enough land to really make a living, and what land there was all rocky and dry. And tilted. No matter what you did on the land, plowing, tilling, seeding, it was always on a tilt. There were only a few buildings, a frame house, barn, chicken coop . . . all falling apart, paint peeling. We lived there, though, me, my dad and my two older brothers, Mark and Frank. They were my half brothers, really, from my dad's first wife, and five and six years older than me. I remember when I was a lot younger asking my dad what happened to my mother. He told me she'd died in childbirth, and he'd been drinking ever since.

"But he was only just starting to drink.

"Time passed, and my dad began to harden toward me, like when I'd ask to go someplace with him, 'Don't need you to help carry feed, Louie Boy.'

" 'All I wanna do is watch, Pa. Mark can carry the grain if you want.'

"He rubbed his chin, all covered with whiskers, then pushed me in the back with his fist. 'Come along, then, damn you! An eleven-year-old boy can carry his share at that!'

"I was eleven when he started to really beat me. I guess he figured I was old enough that nobody would report him. It was a long piece of harness leather that he'd use, and he'd keep it tucked in his belt and call me a son of a bitch and zing it at me for no reason at all. I showed Mark the welts on my legs and back one time, and he didn't say anything. When I

227

showed them to Frank, though, he put some stuff on me that he got at the drugstore. Frank was my favorite, but I idolized both my brothers. An eleven-year-old boy is proud of his older brothers, and I was more so because I couldn't be proud of my father.

"He beat me more and more, Pa did, until I tried to stay away from him, out of his reach for whole days at a time. Then he'd look at me with a hate that ate away at me. As if when he couldn't reach me with the leather strap he'd make marks on my body with his eyes.

"He was my natural pa, no matter what he did, and I knew I should love him, but I couldn't. Still I felt something for him, through the pain and hate, through the shame. Even when he'd come out of the house all drunk and lash away at the animals and chickens with his leather strap, screaming and red in the face until he had to sit down. Even then when he was sitting there in the hot sun looking around at what he'd done to the animals I'd feel something for him. He was my natural pa.

"It got worse. Pa was either ignoring me altogether or swearing and beating me like one of the animals. Frank would tell me to be patient, and he'd talk to Pa sometimes, long talks they'd have out in the fields or in the mornings before Pa started to drink. But I didn't like to see it, because that's when Pa would blow up and swear at Frank. He never hit him, though, like he did me.

"Then one day it came out. Pa was especially drunk and especially mad at me. He whistled the strap twice across my back and then he screamed it at me. 'Bastard! You ain't mine!' He let loose again with the strap. I didn't understand.

" 'You belong to some over-the-road trucker that lived over in town! You're your filthy ma's!' His eyes were sad and he began to mumble. '. . . No blood of mine. Git to the barn . . .'

"He always told me that, to sleep in the barn. Frank and Mark were away on a hunting trip, so I was alone with Pa and I was afraid.

" '. . . Son of a bitch!' he moaned at me.

"I caught one more lick on the back as I broke for the door.

"When I was out in the barn I thought about what Pa had said. I didn't understand it exactly, but I saw that he must have hated my ma. I fell asleep crying, like I did more often than not.

"It was late when I woke up, and dark and hot in the barn. I was in the loft, where it was still and hard to breathe, so I climbed down onto the barn floor and went outside.

"The lights were all out in the house, and as I stood there staring at it, at that cold dark house, the hate in me for Pa just got bigger and bigger. I can remember standing there under the moon, shaking with hate. It was like I was still half asleep, or dreaming. I went back into the barn and got a can of coal oil and some matches: I don't think anything but hate was going through my mind as I walked toward the house.

"The fire caught right away, so fast it scared me. It lit up the night as I stood there and watched it, knowing Pa was sleeping drunk inside. I could hear the town fire bell ringing, far away.

"They came in a hurry. There were headlights all over, and a red pumper and men with buckets. There was nothing I could do. I stood and watched.

" 'What happened, Lou?'

"It was Grady, a big bald man who was the Volunteer Fire Department chief.

"I think I mumbled that I didn't know, that I'd been sleeping in the barn. Grady yelled some instructions to his men, but it didn't do any good. The house was burning like a cardboard box. Another man I knew, Quentin Dibbs, came up and wiped his forehead.

" 'Whooeee! There's no way to get in there, Grady. Too damn hot!'

" 'I know,' Grady said, watching the flames. 'It's too late.' He looked down at me. 'Your pa and brothers in there?'

"I just stood there, not even thinking.

"Dibbs bent over and stared at me, his face all black with soot. 'Shock,' he said. 'I do believe that boy's in shock.'

"I started to say something when I heard the scream. It was Pa's scream, and every man at the fire stood still for a moment, listening. It came from inside the house, inside the flames, like nothing you ever heard.

"Then somebody came running out the door, black, burning, on fire. Only it wasn't Pa, it was Frank!

"He died right there, holding onto the burning porch rail. They rushed to him and got blankets around him, but I could see he was dead and just leaning there.

"After they dragged Frank away they continued pouring water onto the fire, mostly for sport, because everything was beyond saving anyway.

" 'Whoeee!' Quentin Dibbs was yelling. 'Smells just like a barbecue!'

"Grady's hand closed on my shoulder and squeezed harder and harder, so hard that it hurt. My eyes were stinging from the smoke. The breeze shifted and I was choking on the sweet grayish haze. I screamed, just like Pa did . . ."

Ellie's fingers were entwined in Roebuck's.

"The neighbors all thought the fire was an accident," Roebuck was saying, "and they all said how lucky I was to be sleeping in the barn. I never told them otherwise, that I set the fire, that I murdered my father and two brothers. I went to live with an aunt, and I had to live that lie. From then on it became hard for me to tell the truth or to see the truth about anything. Except in my sleep; in my sleep the truth always found me."

Ellie got up, hunted the bottle of bourbon, and poured them each a drink straight over some ice cubes.

"It was a long time ago," she said, returning with the glasses to sit on the edge of the bed.

"What matter?" Roebuck said. "I'm a murderer. No matter what other people think of me, I know that's what I am. I've always tried to run away from it, even convincing myself that the fire was accidental. But I could only convince myself up to a point." He took a drink. "My whole life is a lie."

"Well, now you've told the truth," Ellie said gently. "If you murdered, you're a murderer. There's no changing that. I guess you just have to face it and live with it."

"Running away from the truth has become a habit with me, a compulsion. Oh, it's not as hard as you think—so much of the goddamn world is behind our eyes!" Roebuck lifted the glass to his lips and drained it, sloshing some of the liquor down his chin.

For the next hour they drank steadily, seriously, as if it were some strange kind of religious communion, an unspoken agreement to get drunk as soon as possible.

Ellie refilled their glasses. "Face it," she said in a voice made thick by the liquor. "Face it and you can live with it. That's the only way, Lou. I know."

Roebuck hurriedly lifted his glass, letting the cold bourbon bite at his throat. "It's all been a rotten lie and still is. I murdered Ingrahm too; it was no accident. I don't know why I did it, but I did. Killing is in me, deep in me! If you hadn't been there I would have killed Boadeen, crushed his head in. And you'll never know how close I came to shooting that boy we stole the car from."

"But you didn't kill them, Lou. You can control it." She tilted back her glass.

Sleep or liquor or both was making Roebuck's head whirl. "I can't control it! Everything's a goddamn lie, an act! Don't you see, it's all part of my desperado act! Kidding myself that I've got guts, that I'm innocent, the gun I carry, imagining Gipp is chasing me across the country, even you, all part of the act . . . to keep me from facing myself . . . !"

Again the neck of the bottle clinked against the glasses. Ellie stroked Roebuck's cheek in long, comforting caresses. "You don't have to suffer, Lou. Just admit it to yourself. Easier to live with the truth than run from it, believe me." Her words were running together. She turned and lay with her head propped on her pillow, holding her glass unsteadily. "You know, you can't change it."

"I know," Roebuck said softly. "It's like a label on me. Everybody's marked as something. The mark of Cain . . . on the inside of our heads, and we put it there ourselves . . ."

"Admit it and live with it," Ellie mumbled, not realizing that her glass was tilted and the little remaining bourbon was spilling to the floor. "Only way, only way."

Roebuck let his head press back against the bed. He had admitted it for the first time, to Ellie and to himself. Through the growing effects of the bourbon he did feel a sense of release, of freedom. There was a madness in the world of dreams, and a loneliness. He lifted his glass and found that it was empty, but he didn't care. He had shown himself to himself, and to someone else.

". . . Murderer, murderer, murderer," Ellie was whispering softly into her pillow. "Who gives a damn . . . ?"

5

Roebuck awoke by slow degrees, taking in the angular furniture of the motel room as he lay on his stomach, his head turned to the side and pressed deeply into the pillow. He remembered last night, and a warm relief passed through him. Strange that a man hunted for murder could feel relief, but Roebuck was suddenly free of so many things. For the first time he had acknowledged his true self, and the illusions had disappeared like shadows exposed to the sun. No longer did he have to strike his poses, worry about Benny Gipp, lie to himself every minute of the day about the deaths he'd caused. Murderer: a fact faced easier in the light. Roebuck was clear to himself now; he didn't like everything he saw, but there it was and he couldn't change it.

But why couldn't he? The idea ran like a thin wire into Roebuck's brain. Now that he knew himself, accepted himself for what he was, didn't that give him the strength, the power to change himself?

He struggled to sit up in bed, feeling for the first time the unpleasant effects of last night's bourbon. Ellie was still asleep beside him, a wisp of blonde hair covering one of her closed eyes. By the light filtering through the blinds, Roebuck estimated that it was past nine o'clock. They'd have to be leaving soon, though right now all he wanted was to sit with his back pressed against the cool wooden headboard and let

233

himself come fully awake.

Ellie stirred beside him, rolled onto her side, and nestled her head in the crook of her arm. He watched her awaken, her one visible eye above the smooth flesh of her arm fluttering, then opening slowly.

The gray eye was vague at first, unfocused, then it fastened itself on Roebuck's face. For an instant there was an uncomfortable dropping sensation in his stomach; something had changed in the eye, deep in the black of it. Then Ellie raised her head and smiled at him, with both eyes. "Morning," she said drowsily.

Roebuck leaned down and kissed her on the forehead.

"Is it late?" she asked.

He nodded.

"How come you didn't wake me up?" She extended her arms in a languid stretch.

"I don't know," Roebuck said. "Somehow it didn't seem important to get an early start this morning."

"You're not so afraid anymore, are you?" There was still sleep in Ellie's voice.

"No," Roebuck said, "not like I was."

Ellie rolled onto her back with a sigh. "You're not the first person to ever kill."

She was right, Roebuck thought. She had brought that fact home to him, and for the first time in his life he didn't feel alone. He got up and began dressing.

"People don't realize how easy it is to live with yourself once you know you can't change," Ellie said, throwing back the sheet and sitting with her legs apart on the edge of the bed.

Roebuck hesitated, buckling his belt.

"Want me to put on some coffee?" she asked behind him.

"Why don't you think you can change?" Roebuck asked.

"You are what you are." Ellie laughed a sad low laugh. "You're born that way, I guess."

Roebuck turned to face her. "Ever think of trying to change again?"

Ellie's wide mouth turned down and then up, as if confused at the signals from her mind. "I've had my try, Lou. I just know it can't be done."

"Maybe you're right." Again he saw that fleeting look, deep in her eyes, and he couldn't or wouldn't identify it. "No need to put coffee on this morning," he said. "Let's chance a restaurant."

After they'd dressed and closed the motel room door behind them, Roebuck breathed in the fresh air and felt oddly at peace, in harmony. He and Ellie got into the car, and he pulled out onto the quiet highway. Before the gleaming yellow hood the Rocky Mountains loomed, touched by morning haze.

As they sped toward the unmoving mountains the thought continued to burrow into Roebuck's mind: why couldn't he change? He had faced what he was, and seeing the horror of it, wasn't there a compulsion to change, a compulsion he wouldn't admit to himself? No, he would admit it to himself. Was this the irresistible impulse to confess he'd heard and read so much about, the criminal's desire to purge himself of his sins, to punish himself? Whatever it was, Roebuck knew that it was fast becoming a part of him. He couldn't fully realize his own imperfection without trying to change it, to balance it.

"Why do you suppose, so many murderers turn themselves in?" he asked aloud. "Knowing what's in store for them?"

"I don't know," Ellie said. "Maybe they just get tired."

"It does tire a man out," Roebuck said, "worrying about every possible slip. A man afraid sees danger everywhere." He looked sideways and he recognized the thing he'd seen in Ellie's eyes. It was fear, undeniable fear bobbing to the surface like a cork. It suddenly jolted Roebuck. He had confessed to her, and she was afraid of him.

Not that he'd do anything to harm her. But in her fear would she do something to protect herself? Had Roebuck something to fear from her?

The thought of Ellie turning him in was completely unacceptable to Roebuck. He pushed it to the back of his mind and looked up at the distant mountain peaks.

"Scrambled eggs are going to taste mighty good," he said.

"Anything for a change," Ellie replied, staring straight ahead through the windshield.

They ate breakfast at a clean, near empty truck stop. When they were finished they sat talking over coffee, and Roebuck was aware of a new tension between them, a weighing of words. Their conversation seemed to be constructed brick by brick to conceal what each of them was thinking. Ellie waited in the car while Roebuck took the bill to the cashier.

They drove on slowly, each lulled into quiet by the hypnotic, twisting highway and the mountains that seemed larger and were appearing to the side of them.

At Roebuck's request they stopped for an early lunch at one of the roadside rest parks along the highway. It was no more than a small clearing with picnic essentials—stone barbecue pit, wooden table cemented into the ground, lidless green trash barrel.

Roebuck backed the car in toward the woods. They sat at the picnic table in the shade of a gigantic pine tree and Ellie opened a can of peaches and some potato chips. With the edge of his hand, Roebuck brushed some ants off the rough wood of the table, glancing up as a car swished by on the highway.

They ate silently, Ellie staring into the woods that started behind a smooth rock formation, Roebuck looking down at the overlapping tire tracks in the hard earth.

He finished the last of the peaches and tossed the empty can into the metal trash barrel. The echoing clang of metal on metal seemed to awaken something in Ellie for a second and their eyes met.

"Can't change, huh?" Roebuck said.

Instead of answering she crumpled the potato chip bag and rose to throw it away. Roebuck watched her walk, watched the sway of her hips and the compact rhythm. When she returned she stood on the other side of the table.

"Sit down," he said, taking her hand and pulling her around the end of the table to sit next to him.

"It's quiet and private here," he whispered in her ear, "and the woods are cool." He sensed something within her drawing away from him.

"We have to drive, Lou. Don't forget who we are."

"I'm not forgetting. I can't. But we have time."

"I guess we do," Ellie said, standing again, "but I'm not much in the mood."

Roebuck turned on the bench seat and leaned back with both elbows on the table. "Why not?"

She shrugged with an attempted smile. "I don't know. I suppose because it's the middle of the afternoon."

"That never bothered you before."

"It's the woods, too," Ellie said. "I've had enough of the woods."

"Or enough of me."

"Maybe I'm just used to you now, Lou. Things cool off

some; ask any married couple."

"I've been married," Roebuck said, toeing the cement at the base of a table leg. "Things don't cool off that fast."

A sudden breeze passed them, rippling Ellie's skirt and hair, stirring the dust from the beaten ground.

Roebuck crossed his outstretched legs, setting one shining boot atop the other, and looked at her. "You're afraid to go into the woods with me, aren't you?"

For a moment he was thrown by the surprised expression on her face, but her eyes weren't surprised. "Why should I be afraid?"

"I have every reason to kill you," Roebuck said, "now that I've confessed murder to you. You weren't sure before, but now you know. And you said yourself people can't change."

"But why would you have to kill me?"

How convincing she was, Roebuck thought.

"Because you're afraid of me," he said. "You might turn me in out of fear. And because you're afraid of me, the smartest thing for me to do would be to get rid of you. It's what's known as a vicious circle."

Ellie came to him and sat beside him. She rested her hand against the side of his face and brushed her lips against his. "Well, that circle's broken," she said gently. "You're one man I'm not afraid of."

"You know I've murdered."

"And you know I don't care."

Roebuck stared at her, his face creased against the sun. "I'd care if I were you."

"You're not, though," Ellie said. "We're all ourselves." She stood and folded her arms, her slender body hunched as if she were cold. For a moment she stood that way, looking into the silent woods, then she turned and walked to the car.

6

Roebuck knew now that Ellie was afraid, and that her fear was a real danger. For the first time he wondered if the idea of murdering her was creeping into his mind. He knew Ellie. She wasn't exactly immoral; she was simply Ellie. It occurred to Roebuck that she might think she should turn him in. She loved him now, but that love was disintegrating along with their mutual trust.

He glanced at her as he guided the car up a winding mountain road. Danger. All the while he'd been looking behind him, fearing what might be drawing nearer, danger was sitting next to him in the car, lying beside him at night. Life had always dealt with Roebuck that way: misfortune from an unexpected quarter.

They stopped that night at the Mountain Crest Motel, a futuristic, semicircular building erected on a site carved out of the side of a mountain. The motel appealed to Roebuck. It was high, aloof, secluded. From the window of their room the dimming view stretched to a faraway invisible horizon.

After dinner in the motel's restaurant they had a few drinks and returned to their room. The distrust had been growing between them, pushing them apart. In the motel room the strain of their silence became almost unbearable, so

they avoided it by sitting transfixed before the flickering un-
reality of the TV, absorbing themselves in the two dimen-
sional dreams and problems of the six-inch figures that
moved and talked across the screen. The National Anthem
was their lullaby.

Sleep was impossible for Roebuck that night. He lay in the
faint light and watched Ellie sleep, secure in her positive
identity and unchangeability. Then he turned away from her,
staring at the blankness of the wall and listening to the even
rhythm of her breathing.

At three a.m. he got up to go to the bathroom, and as he
flushed the toilet his gaze fell on a bottle of disinfectant on the
floor beneath the washbasin. The bottle was half full of thick
amber liquid that killed and cleaned. Wasn't that what Roebuck was looking for, purity and oblivion? He sat on the edge
of the bathtub with his elbows resting on his knees, staring at
the bottle.

DIRT-GONE, the label on the disinfectant read, THE
STRONGEST INDUSTRIAL GERM KILLER ON THE
MARKET! Roebuck wondered if it would kill the long-ago
planted germ in him. He stood wearily, so that the washbasin
blocked his view of the bottle, and studied his reflection in the
mirror, running his fingers over the bristly moustache he'd
started a few days before. Quickly his hand moved to the light
switch, snapping the bathroom into darkness. He found his
way back to the bed and stretched out on the mattress with
his eyes open.

Roebuck already had his pants on the next morning, and
was struggling into his boots, when Ellie awoke and sat
straight up in bed. She turned her tousled head as if to bring
the strange room into perspective and then stared at him with
sleep-puffed eyes.

"How come you're getting dressed so early?"

Roebuck said nothing, finished putting on his boots and stood.

"Where are you going, Lou?" She asked the question as if she knew the answer, only wanted him to say it if he must.

"To give myself up."

She looked at him as if he'd hurt her. "Are you joking?"

"I've been joking all my life."

"Well, this one isn't funny, Lou. You better not do what you said. The best you'll get is life in prison. They might even give you death, let you sit in a cell for months and then strap you into the chair, electrocute you!" She scooted back to lean against her pillow. "You can't mean what you say!"

Roebuck buttoned his shirt.

"Why do you want to, Lou? Are you tired?"

"Maybe. Or maybe I just want to balance the scales on myself."

"Don't talk crap! Nothing can change the fact you're a murderer! Your chancing death in the electric chair won't change that!"

"It will to me. I can see what I am, and I can do something about it."

"You can't!" He was almost finished dressing and she was getting frantic. "You'll be sorry after you do it! You know you will!"

He moved toward the door.

"Don't be an ass, Lou! Nothing can make up for what you did! Nothing!"

Roebuck hesitated, and then he turned to face her. He began walking toward the bed and he saw the fear rise in her like a bloated corpse rising to the surface of smooth water. "If I'm what you say I am," he said in an even voice, "if I really can't do anything about what I am and will be, then I ought to kill you."

Ellie's mouth opened as his hands clamped about her slender neck, blocking her breath. Roebuck stared down at her, digging his thumbs into the warm flesh of her throat, feeling the rush of her pulse beneath them. He hadn't intended to kill her when he'd walked to the bed; he'd only wanted to frighten her. He tried to think, tried to loosen his grip, but he had to listen to the old, old voices in his blood, the voices that whispered to kill.

He watched as her complexion changed to red, then a mottled purple.

When her eyelids began to flutter Roebuck jerked his hands away, and Ellie fell back onto the bed. She lay staring up at him, taking great gasps as if she were trying to eat the air.

"You don't like to admit it!" Roebuck screamed hoarsely. "You don't like to admit you can do something about yourself! That's the truth you're running away from!"

He didn't look back at her as he walked out the door.

Roebuck was more sure of himself than he'd ever been in his life. He knew what he should do, must do, would do! He had reality by the balls!

The people in the room next to them had heard and were looking out through the blinds, and toward the motel office a man was standing staring down that way. Roebuck didn't give a damn. He strode to the car and got in, slamming the door. He looked about him as he twisted the ignition key. The morning was new and clear and beautiful. Beneath the glistening yellow hood the engine caught the first time, and Roebuck pulled out onto the mountain highway.

It was a winding road, a steep road that arced down the mountain in great sweeping spirals. Roebuck hadn't driven very far on it when he looked into the rear view mirror and saw the car behind him. The car was big and shining black, of a make he didn't recognize.

Fear went through Roebuck like a blade of ice. "Oh, Christ!" he whispered.

Behind the windshield of the dark car two round lenses caught the glint of sunlight and shot it at Roebuck like sparks of rifle fire. The car was close enough for him to see the square, hard features of Benny Gipp quite clearly.

Roebuck twisted the wheel, taking a curve with squealing tires as he almost brushed the wooden guard rail that marked an endless fall. The rhythm of his hammering heart beat in his ears. Had Roebuck's own new self double-crossed him? Had he not fantasized a vengeful and pursuing Gipp, or was he fantasizing him now? Had Gipp really been after him all along, waiting his chance, to get him alone? Reality had broken out of Roebuck's world of fantasy.

Roebuck was speeding as fast as he dared now down the winding mountain road—faster than he dared! The black car maintained exactly the same speed, the same distance behind him, as if they were two toy cars, one trailing the other by a piece of string. "Oh, Christ!" Roebuck said aloud, squirming in his seat. He could smell the Mercury's brakes burning as he rode the pedal to make the twisting, dangerous turns, taking panicky glances in the mirror to see the big car still near his bumper, Gipp's shining spectacles still aiming rays of light at him. And strangely, even when the steep and winding road took them away from the sun, the lenses still seemed to catch the brilliant light.

Roebuck screamed in fright as he lost control for a second and the car careened off the wall of the mountain, bouncing chunks of rock down the road in front of him. "Oh, Christ!" He struggled over the steering wheel, whipping the car back to the center of the road with a screech of rubber, just ticking the guard rail on the other side. His speed was building, and still the black car kept pace, turning smoothly, not even leaning on the curves. The steering wheel, hot and slippery from perspiration, was vibrating in Roebuck's clenched hands and the distant horizon was rotating madly before him as he pressed down even harder on the accelerator with his right foot, trying to stay on the road by slamming at the brake with his left. Again he crashed into the side of the mountain, sparks flying from the crumpled yellow metal. The car rocked, jolted him from side to side, and in the rear view mirror he caught a glimpse of the black car still speeding smoothly behind him as if riding a cushion of air. He screamed again, not even hearing himself over the roaring engine and screeching tires.

The car was vibrating crazily beneath Roebuck now, impossible to control. It caromed again off the mountainside, rolling and veering in mad fishtail patterns with a dizzying life of its own.

Then suddenly the steering wheel turned freely in Roebuck's hands, for he had hurtled through the guard rail into space.

Roebuck held onto the wheel as the car flew outward and nosed over, and as he rose gently upward off the front seat he saw below him a seemingly endless, sloping fall to earth. Through his horror he realized the car would bounce several times on the way down, and his last thought as he began his fall was that if by some miracle he should survive, what a tale he would have to tell.

But on the first bounce the car exploded into flame. Then bounce after bounce it disintegrated, fiery bits of it falling away to tumble and lose momentum on the sloping mountainside. Roebuck never actually reached the valley below.

DNA

I don't think what happened to me's ever happened to a woman before, which is why I'm sitting here in the shade of this live oak tree, talking into this recorder.

People need to know about this, and I need to put it all out in some kinda order so maybe I can understand it better. I don't know if you'll believe me, but I swear it's true down to the last word.

You probably read about part of it in the papers or saw it on the TV news, how a man name of Jerome Bodeen was set free from the state penitentiary after serving eleven years of a forty-year sentence. It was this slick attorney Jack Weld that got him turned loose, and who put me into a kinda prison of my own.

When I heard on the news about Bodeen's release, and why he got out, I went numb, and then I purely didn't know what to think. I still don't know. Maybe this, talking it all out, will provide me with some kinda sign or at least ease my mind. That's the theory, anyway.

Reporters started calling the very same day the news broke. They'd been thinking ahead and already had learned my identity, where I lived, my phone number. Probably that slick attorney gave it to them weeks, maybe months ago.

Bodeen himself, I've got no idea what he thought and

245

what he felt when he was set free. I still wonder about that, and about lots of other things.

Eleven years ago last June fourteenth I was raped. Now, this was no date-rape in-the-least-way-gentle kinda thing. It was one of those cases where the victim was chosen at random and ill-treated. I had never met Jerome Bodeen until he walked up to me, smiling like he was about to try and sell me insurance or a used car, and then his smile disappeared and it began.

I'd left my husband Dan watching a stock car race on TV in our apartment while I walked over to Quik-Pik Market for some diet pop, which we were out of because both of us drank the stuff like it was water. The truth is, maybe I shouldn't have gone out dressed the way I was, with my shorts and tight top and sandals that showed how I'd just painted my toenails bright red. At least that's what Bodeen's lawyer said at the trial. He said it so good I half believed it myself.

At Quik-Pik I bought three of those liter-size plastic bottles of cola and had the clerk put them in a plastic sack so I could use the handles, since I was going to carry them back to the apartment. I was never strong, so the weight of the bottles helped me make the decision to walk through the woods behind Quik-Pik and cut the distance to the apartment nearly in half. I'd never been through there at night before, but there was a moon full as a pie plate that evening and the dirt path was wide and clear.

Halfway back to the apartment, I paused and saw that the red and green Quik-Pik sign behind me was still visible through the trees. Off ahead, I could barely make out some of the lighted apartment windows of our building. Time to turn back if I was uneasy, I thought. What airplane pilots call the point of no return. I remember the crickets were screaming loud and shrill while I was standing there, like they were trying to warn me of something.

But I shrugged off my nervousness and walked on. That's when a friendly male voice mentioned what a nice night it was, in a tone like we were supposed to meet there in the woods and I was expected by a pal I'd known for years.

But I knew we'd never met. I squinted in the dappled moonlight that filtered down through the trees and saw this big man with a beer gut, a bushy head of hair, and a full beard. He was wearing jeans and a dark-colored T-shirt without even short sleeves. My heart jumped and I was scared at first. Then I saw his friendly smile and I figured this was going to be okay, he was just somebody else who'd decided to take the shortcut and we'd pass each other and that'd be that. You know, strangers in the night, or ships that pass.

I didn't look into his eyes as I stepped aside to let him go past, and he moved well off to the side too. So polite and proper. If he'd been wearing a cap, I bet he woulda tipped it.

Fine, I figured with relief. Nothing to be scared of.

Then his hand was over my mouth and I dropped the plastic sack and he was dragging me off the path. It was that sudden, like a matter of a few seconds. I tried to bite his hand but couldn't manage to do that before he socked me in the stomach with his free fist and all the air whooshed right out of me and between his fingers.

I ain't gonna hurt you if you do as I say, is what he told me, but I panicked and tried to yell even though I could hardly catch my breath.

That's when he slapped me hard, cutting the inside of my cheek on my teeth, and kept on slapping me on both sides of my face and shaking me. I remember seeing the full moon up above, dancing around among the leafy branches like it was a helium balloon being jerked back and forth on a string.

I didn't remember much of what happened after that,

except in dreams I could barely recall on waking. And I admit that's the way I wanted it. I didn't have any desire to remember.

I did recollect laying there wearing only my halter top, which was twisted up around my neck. I stayed there without moving for a long time, hurting everywhere, and listening to the crickets scream we told you so, your fault, we told you so.

Dan finally wondered what was keeping me and went to Quik-Pik, where the clerk told him I'd been there an hour ago and bought three bottles of pop and left. He'd come the long way and hadn't seen me, so he got worried and made his way along the trail through the woods and found me. Dan shouted loud enough, he bellowed angry enough, so a customer who'd just driven up to Quik-Pik heard him and had the clerk call the police. Maybe if I'd been able to yell that loud the whole thing woulda been cut short or wouldn't have happened at all, even if I was dumb enough to take a shortcut through the woods at night, and dressed the way I was. In a way you could say it was because of me that it did happen.

The cops were fine. They listened to my story on the spot while an ambulance was on the way, and one of them, a policewoman named Erika, rode with me to the hospital. All the way she kept telling me that tonight hadn't been my fault, that I wasn't the one who should feel guilty. It was just a natural reaction in some rape victims, a psychological thing that caused more suffering needlessly. Don't make yourself a victim again, is what she kept saying. Don't let them rape you again with your own guilt, or you'll be lost.

They tested me to make sure I'd really been raped, confiscated my underwear and a pair of dirty men's underpants they'd found nearby in the woods, and there was the evidence.

Everybody at the hospital treated me swell, and Dan, even

though he was angry, acted like I was made of delicate crystal that might break. They were going to send me home from the hospital after treatment that night, but Dan said the hell with the insurance coverage, we'd pay for the extra time, and insisted they keep me under observation, which they did, not knowing we didn't even have insurance. I think Erika might have had something to do with that. She was professional and all, but she was mad too, almost like she'd been raped right along with me. I found out later she had been raped when she was in high school, so when she kept assuring me I'd get through what was happening and everything would be all right, I believed her maybe because she'd been through it herself and I could sense that.

But she'd never been through what was waiting around the corner for me.

The police had acted fast and picked up a suspect, a man on a motorcycle that had broke down a mile away from where the terrible thing had happened to me. He was driving through on his way to California, he'd told them. He had no alibi for the time of the attack, and there was no one to vouch for him. He said he was estranged from his family back in Chicago. They verified that, all right, and it turned out he had a police record, including a conviction just the year before for beating up his girlfriend.

Soon as I saw him the next morning in that lineup with those five other men I knew he was the one. I knew, and no mistake about it. A Lieutenant Hammacker with the police was obviously happy I was so quick and so positive. It would make everything easier, he told me.

So they charged Jerome Bodeen with assault and rape and I told the prosecution I'd testify against him. So would the Quik-Pik clerk, I found out, who'd sold Bodeen a six-pack of beer forty-five minutes before she sold me the cola, and hadn't liked the way he'd looked at her. Only two beers were with Bodeen when the police picked him up down the road from Quik-Pik.

A month later was when I found out I was pregnant. Dan said he'd make arrangements for an abortion, and at first I said okay. I was kind of drifting mentally then, ready to agree to almost anything. And Dan had been so gentle.

Then I got to considering things. I know women who've been raped aren't supposed to think this way, and believe me, I was as full of hate and rage and hurt as any of them. But my feeling about being pregnant changed. Maybe if I hadn't blocked so much of that night out of my memory, if I'd actually remembered the rape itself, I wouldn't have felt that way.

Maybe that's why I told Dan I wanted to keep the baby.

He tried to gentle me out of it at first, but I resisted. I figured, why should I be a victim again? I wanted to have this baby, and it was my choice.

Dan and I had long, violent arguments. I don't mean he ever hit me, but he shouted and came close. And I came close to hitting him. The more he tried to argue me into an abortion, the more I wanted to keep the baby. It didn't have anything to do with how I felt about abortions themselves. It was more me, how I felt about my baby. So we'd argue, sometimes most of the night, then Dan would leave angry for his job at the plant and I'd lay there alone still mad at him, and furious at myself for getting into this kinda mess. But I couldn't be mad at the innocent baby, that I thought I could already feel moving inside me, though I know now it was way too early for that.

Five months later, when Bodeen's trial started, I was very obviously pregnant. My condition didn't help Bodeen, even though he turned up at the courthouse clean-shaven and in a cheap blue suit and white shirt. He looked like one of the lawyers. Though not his own lawyer, whose name was Charlton, and who was young and wore a cheap suit and a ponytail fastened tight in back with a rubber band and had a gold stud in one ear.

But a high-fashion suit and a million-dollar defense team wouldn't have helped Bodeen. He had no alibi. He'd been in the Quik-Pik. He'd been wearing underwear when the police had picked him up, but he coulda gotten some out of his suitcase strapped to the back of his motorcycle. And his were the same size as the briefs found in the woods at the crime scene. And the victim had pointed him out in a police lineup the day after the rape. That was more than enough for the law in Opamawa County.

Case closed.

It was only a matter of how many years the judge'd sentence Bodeen to serve after the guilty verdict. And that turned out to be forty years. Because of the vicious way he'd beaten me up, the judge said. Bodeen and Dan glared at each other when the bailiffs escorted Bodeen out of the courtroom.

My job, Dan told me that night, was now to put the whole thing behind me. Behind the two of us, he said.

I knew what he meant, talking about the two of us. But I was in my third trimester by the time the trial was ended, and I wasn't about to have an abortion. Maybe I wanted something good to come out of what happened. And Dan and I had been trying for the last year for me to get pregnant and we got no results. Maybe we never would. Whatever my reasons, the ones I knew and didn't know, I decided the thing to do was for me to go ahead and have this baby. Dan didn't see it that way, but the arguing stopped and was replaced with stony silence. Sometimes it seemed days would pass with us barely talking to each other.

I wasn't surprised when he left me six months after Dale was born.

Dan did the proper thing and stayed with me till he felt it honorable to leave. I will give him that. He was a good husband, but it was too much for him, to have to raise the son of the man who raped his wife. He tried to love Dale but he couldn't. And after a while he couldn't love me, so one morning he was gone. It was simple as that. He went off to Louisiana and worked in an oil refinery, I found out later, when he came back so we could get legally divorced. I didn't ask for child support for Dale, but the judge ordered Dan to pay anyway. Which he did for a while, before he got remarried in Rome, Georgia, to a woman with three children, and needed the money for himself and his new family.

Me, I was happy and loved Dale as much as any mother ever loved a child. How he came to be conceived, well, one look into his eyes and that didn't matter to me. The night of the rape was becoming less and less real, falling away into the past. I wanted the memory to fade. I thought of it as a healing.

When the money from Dan stopped, I never went after it. I was making enough to get us by, working at a place that reprocessed used tires. The work was hard, but it was steady, and so was the pay. It wasn't easy, but I found good day care for Dale, and the two of us moved to an apartment not far from where we'd lived with Dan. I still shopped sometimes at Quik-Pik, but the clerk who testified at my trial was long gone, graduated from the state university and married someplace up north. The place isn't even called Quik-Pik anymore but has some hard-to-pronounce foreign name. It was a new world and a hard one, but Dale and I learned to live in it.

Things were made lots easier after I met Nick Blake. I'd seen him before, eyeing me over his beer in Grodin's Bar, where I stopped on Friday nights with some people from work, and finally he just came over and asked me to dance to a slow country-western song.

Neither of us was much as dancers, so we just stood and kinda swayed with the music and talked. And before the song was over, I'd given him my phone number. Six years had passed since the rape, and I thought it was time to do something like that.

Nick was a skinny guy and not bad looking, with thinning brown hair that meant he'd probably be bald by age forty. He dressed nice but sort of cheap, and he worked as the night bartender at a lounge called Victor's, a few miles outside of town. It was the best job he could find as he'd just moved from Texas, where he'd gotten into some kinda trouble that had to do with drugs, and which he didn't talk much about. I know Nick sounds like a loser, but he wasn't an addict and he didn't deal, and he was good to me and, just as important, good to Dale.

He understood my problem after I told him what had happened, and in bed he was gentle with me in all ways, and was in fact the gentlest man I could imagine. He got real fond of Dale, and the two of them would go to high school basketball games and play catch in the vacant lot back of the apartment building, and sometimes go fishing together upriver, tying an old canoe Nick had bought to the top of his Ford station wagon. I'd watch those two together, thinking that my life, which had been just bearable before Nick, had became good.

It went on that way for several years, until I got the phone call from Jerome Bodeen's attorney, not Charlton but the fella named Jack Weld. It was a shock when he first identified himself as representing Bodeen. I mean, what would Bodeen, who I hadn't thought of directly in years and who was nameless and faceless now in the prison system, want with an attorney?

I soon found out. This social service law firm was reviewing cases where they decided the evidence wasn't strong, using the new DNA science to make sure the wrong people hadn't been convicted. And their digging into the past had brought to light someone who claimed to have seen Bodeen sitting drinking beer next to his motorcycle, a mile down the road from Quik-Pik, at the exact time I was raped.

Nick was mad and said I oughta fight and not do anything the lawyers said, but I figured the thing to do was to cooperate and end the thing as soon as possible. The physical evidence from Bodeen's trial was long gone. So what they wanted was a sample of Dale's blood to see if there was a match with Bodeen's. I learned that while DNA can't actually prove some man is the father of a child, it can absolutely disprove it.

I figured there was nothing to lose here, and I could get this over with and push it back into the past where it belonged. So at the lawyer Weld's expense, I made a doctor's appointment for Dale for a regular physical checkup, part of which was the taking of a blood sample.

I'd pretty much put the whole thing out of my mind, when a few months later I saw on the TV news that Bodeen was proved innocent by DNA and was to be released from prison.

I might as well have been struck by lightning. Had I really sent the wrong man to prison all those years ago? Was I guilty twice, of walking through the woods late at night wearing shorts and a tight top, almost inviting a rape, of not yelling for help when someone was close enough to hear? Then guilty again of pointing at the wrong man in the police lineup? I'd been so sure! I'd seen Bodeen's profile so clear in the moonlight when he'd raised himself up off me for a few seconds and turned to listen in case he'd heard a sound. I could still remember the jut of his bearded jaw, his thick neck and the tilt of his nose, the yellow moon caught glistening in the corner of his wide eye. I'd been positive it was Bodeen!

But they say DNA doesn't lie. It's a science and you can't argue against it.

What had Bodeen thought about me all those years in prison? What was he thinking about me now?

For the first time in years, I tried hard to remember the details of that night, to figure out where I might have seen it wrong.

And memory eventually came, slow at first but persistent, like an animal that had been stalking me all this time. I heard again the crickets screaming, saw the moon through the branches, felt the pain and the terror and the guilt.

But there were things I couldn't quite picture for sure, so the doubts came along with the memories. And then the dreams began. And Nick would hold me at night and try to comfort me. Then, though we'd been living together happy for years, he insisted on us getting married. And we did the next week at the home of a Justice of the Peace two miles off the interstate, a little white house set near a grove of cotton-wood trees.

Only days after that, we started adoption proceedings for Dale to make Nick his official father.

But the dreams kept coming. And for a while, the news media stayed on the story of Jerome Bodeen. They kept showing the tape where he walks out of prison and hugs some woman who wrote to him every week, then he hugs his lawyer Weld, then talks into a bunch of microphones about how he never gave up hope because he knew he was innocent. When they showed where he was living now with the woman who'd wrote him all that time then met him the day of his release, in the town of Maysville about a hundred miles east, I decided to drive there and explain to him, ask him to forgive me. Then maybe the dreams that came to me almost every night would stop.

It turned out they didn't live in Maysville itself, but in a trailer about a mile outside town, not far from the furniture manufacturer that had given Bodeen a job after prison. Just over a hill from the trailer was the highway, and you could hear the big trucks whining and gearing down for a grade.

The trailer was dilapidated and starting to rust around the rivets, and it had a big butane gas tank for heating or cooking setting near one corner. It was a blue and white trailer with wood lattice work around its base to hide the wheels and axles so it would look more like a house. There were about ten other trailers there on concrete pads, and there were thick woods all around them.

I could hear crickets screaming, but I couldn't make out what, and I tried to block them out of my mind as I got up my nerve. Then I went up to stand on the hard steel steps I could feel through the soles of my shoes, and knocked softly on the metal screen door.

It was my hope that the woman would answer my knock, and she might understand and kinda clear it with Bodeen for us to talk. We might sort of ease into this.

But he came. Bodeen himself.

I was standing lower than him on the steps, which made him look even bigger when I saw his form in the dimness behind the screen. Fear made me cold inside and my legs started to tremble. I hadn't counted on feeling like that, though maybe I should have.

I tried to introduce myself but wound up only stuttering.

Finally Bodeen told me in a deep, sad voice that he knew who I was.

I saw the woman appear in the dimness behind the screen

and stand next to him, a little behind him. What's she want, is all she asked.

I came to say I'm sorry, I told both of them.

Neither of them said anything till the woman spoke up and told me that wasn't all I wanted.

I knew what she meant. What she was waiting for me to say. Why I'd really come there.

I want your forgiveness, I said.

I can't give you that, is what Jerome Bodeen told me, and shut the door inside the screen.

I stood alone for a while on the metal steps, listening to the crickets screaming, feeling the tears tracking down my cheeks, wondering what to do next.

There was nothing I could do but leave.

After that day, the dreams got worse, and they came more often.

Nick, who had always been a beer drinker, began to drink more during this time. And we always had eaten too often and too much at fast food places. I'd put on some weight, but he was at that age in men where they tend to get heavier fast. Nick had been so skinny, but now he was becoming husky and had even developed a big stomach paunch that sagged over his belt like a grain sack.

And one day in the lot behind the building, while I was watching him and Dale play catch with an old tennis ball, I noticed how the sunlight shone in his hair and there was a red tint to it, like there's a red tint to Dale's hair.

I didn't say anything to either of them, but I went inside and was sick. I don't think they even noticed when I left.

After that's when I began stopping in at Grodin's on weeknights again, and drinking more than I should. I received some warnings at work from a foreman I know didn't like me because of what had happened with Bodeen.

At night I'd lay there next to Nick and I'd wonder if it could be true, what was trying to get a hold on my mind and cause me so much pain.

Nick would ask me what was wrong, but I couldn't tell him. He'd hold me close, trying to make my fear go away, but now it felt different when he hugged me up tight to him. And I knew he could sense that.

I tried to act like everything was normal, and for a while I pushed away the idea, telling myself I was going crazy. I cut back on the booze and tried to put the past where it belonged, in the shadows at the back of my mind.

Then one night when we were making love, I looked up at Nick's fleshier face, feeling the heft of his weightier body on me, saw how his hair was all mussed and sticking out from his head. Then he raised himself up off me and looked to the side for a few seconds, and I saw the jut of his jaw and the tilt of his nose, and the light from the TV at the foot of the bed was caught like a moon in the corner of his eye.

I was looking again at the man I saw that night in the woods. I knew it for sure, and it was simple as that.

I didn't let on that anything had changed, just laid there still as I could get, small as I could get, being somebody else someplace else in my mind.

Next day I called and made an appointment with the lawyer Weld who had got Bodeen out of jail, then called in to work and told them I was sick. After dropping off Dale at school, I drove in to the city to see Weld.

He was silver-haired and handsome and neatly dressed, like I'd seen him on TV, only much younger and smaller in person. I recalled the tape of Bodeen hugging him outside prison, looking only slightly taller than Weld. Bodeen must be shorter than I remembered or he appeared to be at the trailer, I thought, sitting down in a chair facing Weld's desk.

Weld's office wasn't what I thought it would be. It wasn't much more than a cubicle in a messy place with a lot of other folks working there, some of them looking like college kids. Lots of volunteers searching for the truth, in such a place. And wasn't that what I was doing here?

Weld was surprised when I told him I believed the real rapist was Nick, that he'd thought he was safe with Bodeen in jail, then had got the urge to see his son. I figure he dieted, or maybe had been sick and lost a lot of weight, and of course he'd shaved off the beard. And I'd only seen him once at night, so he didn't think I'd recognize him. He made it a point to meet me at Grodin's, and he got next to me so he could get to know his son Dale. Then one thing led to another.

Weld told me I might be right, but if I was, it was the damndest thing he'd ever heard of, a rapist coming back as somebody else to marry his victim and be a father to the son conceived in the attack. I told him I'd been damned for years and wanted to be free of it, and there was only one way that could happen. I needed to know for sure. Then I told him there was a way I might be able to find out. DNA? he asked me with a smile. I told him he was the expert, wasn't he?

I didn't say anything about it to Nick, because I didn't have to. And we already had Dale's DNA from Bodeen's trial. What I did was borrow Nick's toothbrush when it was still wet, wrapped it in a towel, and took it to this doctor who was waiting in a car with Weld. I could see they both really wanted this DNA thing to work, not for me but because they wanted to be in the news big time.

When I phoned Weld the next week like we planned, he sounded disappointed on the phone. I thought at first there'd been something wrong with the saliva sample, but that wasn't it. The test results were back, he told me, and they didn't rule out that Nick might be Dale's biological father. Trouble was, they also didn't prove for sure that he was the father. It was a question of odds, Weld said, and that wasn't good enough for the law.

That's DNA for you, Weld told me. It was like I could see him shrug over the phone.

After that he lost interest in me. I was just the villain in an earlier adventure again, the evil or silly woman who'd been responsible for sending an innocent man to prison.

I didn't have any choice then but to confront Nick with what I knew. So when Dale was outside playing, I sat down opposite Nick at the kitchen table and told him I had something important to say and to put down his beer for a minute.

When he got over what I was supposed to think was shock, he put on a big act, like he thought the idea was crazy. But the more he talked the guiltier he seemed. And the more I looked at him, the surer I was that the first time we met wasn't in Grodin's Bar, but was in the dark woods behind the Quik-Pik Market the night my whole life got changed. He admitted he couldn't prove to me he was somewhere else that June night all those years ago. Then he asked if I could prove where I was any other night in June of that time.

I couldn't, but I squeezed the trigger anyway.

The noise of the gunshot seemed to ring in my ears forever.

Now, after all those years, I don't even know if any of it was real. Dreams and what happens when I wake up are all the same to me. Was I ever that pretty young wife something terrible happened to that night in the woods? A part of me has trouble believing any of it ever happened at all. What I think and what I say isn't to be trusted. I've heard them whisper that about me. But maybe talking about it into a tape recorder like this will help me to get things straight, help me to know if it really did happen.

Dr. Mindle says it will help, so maybe it will.

If there ever really was a rape in the woods behind the Quik-Pik Market.

If the man who sometimes visits me here is really a grown-up Dale.

If Jerome Bodeen is really innocent and a man named Nick is really dead.

If there really is a Dr. Mindle.

What I think, what I say, isn't to be trusted.

IMAGE

"This is a car battery," Jack Olson said, "but sometimes it's used to get people started talking. Once they get running off at the mouth, they don't wanna stop."

He was a large man with a sad face and he was wearing a neat suit he wouldn't want to get messy. Nicko Doyle, standing just inside the shack's open door, was an even larger man but with the features of a malevolent leprechaun, complete with protruding, pointed ears. He was wearing old chinos and a sweatshirt. The man tied to the chair guessed Nicko, who'd carried the car battery inside, would do the work.

The shack was five miles outside of town, well back in the woods, and had no electricity. That was why they needed the car battery. They needed the shack because it was to hell and gone and no one would disturb them.

Vern, the driver who'd brought them here in the black Ford Bronco the battery had come out of, was somebody the man in the chair had never seen before that day. He was a wiry little guy who walked hunched over with his elbows tucked in and had an injured expression in his watery blue eyes. He walked into the shack now and closed the door behind him. He was wearing old clothes, a rubberized white butcher's apron, and was carrying a metal tool box and some jumper cables with large alligator clamps. So he'd be the one, and not Nicko.

The man in the chair knew they'd figured out who he was—or more accurately who he wasn't—and they'd brought him to the isolated shack because they didn't want to gag or silence him in any way while they tortured him. The whole idea was that he'd be talkative when he wasn't screaming.

Sad-faced Olson ambled over to him and bent down so he could look him in the eye. "You lied to us for over a year," he said, "but you were only doing your job. It's a job I wouldn't have on a stick. You got a streak of character in you. We respect that. We're not animals and don't want you to suffer more'n you have to. We do want you to tell us what you know. The more you tell, the less you suffer."

"He'll tell everything," Vern said. He drew a hobby knife with a razor blade from his pocket and began cutting away the clothes of the man in the chair. "I'm better at my job than he was at his."

Within less than a minute the bound man was wearing only scraps of cloth, his wingtip shoes and black dress socks. He couldn't help it; he began to tremble and lost control of his bladder as Vern raised the lid on the tool box.

"You guys wanna stay and watch?" Vern asked, glancing up over his shoulder.

"No," Olson said. "It's hot in here and it already smells. I'll wait outside."

"I guess I'll stay," Nicko said.

Olson left the shack and used a white handkerchief to pat perspiration from his forehead. Then he walked down a narrow dirt path that he knew led to a small creek. When he was about out of earshot, he lit one of the thin, dark cigars he often smoked and watched a hawk or a buzzard circle in the eastern sky. The creek made a pleasant trickling sound, like time passing.

Twenty minutes of it passed before he saw Vern and Nicko making their way down the path toward where he was standing in bright sunlight. Vern was no longer wearing his butcher's apron.

"Get everything?" Olson asked, when they were closer.

"He admitted he was undercover F.B.I.," Nicko said. "Real name was Frank Stokes."

"Can we be sure he was telling the truth?"

Vern smiled. "I'm like a priest in the confessional. Everyone tells me the truth."

"He knew damn near everything about our operation," Nicko said, "enough to put us away till the sun gets cold."

"So now we know where we stand," Olson said.

"Not quite, I'm afraid," Vern told him. "There's this." He held up Stokes' wallet, open to reveal a photograph of an attractive dark-haired woman in her twenties. She was smiling with her mouth open wide as if she'd just heard a good joke.

"Any other photos?" Olson asked Vern.

"No. They seldom carry photographs of people they love, but sometimes they can't resist. It's lonely work they do."

"And risky," Nicko said with a nasty grin and a glance back at the shack.

"So who is she?" Olson asked, nodding toward the photograph. "His wife? Girlfriend?"

Vern looked embarrassed. "He refused to tell us."

"Some things you don't even tell your priest, I guess," Nicko said.

Olson stared at Vern. "You were brought in because you were the best in your profession."

"High muckety-fuckin'-muck," Nicko said.

Olson looked disgusted. "He was supposed to tell you everything."

"And he did—or would have if he hadn't died before I could get it out of him." Vern pointed at Nicko. "Your buddy wanted me to keep boosting the current in the jumper cables. It must have arced to his heart."

"Bastard didn't have a heart," Nicko said. He snatched the wallet away from Vern and stared at the photograph. "She's one fine lookin' piece, whoever she is."

"The kinda woman," Olson said, "who if she asked you at the right time, you'd tell her anything."

"She might know what Stokes knew," Nicko said uneasily.

"You want me to stay around town for a while after I clean up here?" Vern asked.

"For a while, anyway," Olson said. "Bayview's not that big a city, population maybe a hundred thousand."

Vern said, "Lots of my business is because of pillow talk."

Kate Adams unlocked the glass front doors of Speed-Stop Market and went inside. Since it was only a few minutes after sunrise, she switched on the overhead fluorescent fixtures. Then she dragged in the heavy stack of morning newspapers and cut the tight nylon band on them so people could get to them.

After the band had snapped free, she straightened up and held the scissors as if about to stab someone, a serious rather than enraged expression on her heart-shaped face. She stalked to her left then her right, now smiling sweetly but insanely, then threw back her head and laughed, pretending to stab herself in the chest with the scissors. She was twenty-two and had narrow hips and wide cheekbones, and plenty of ambition. An acting career awaited her beyond Bayview. She was sure of it. She often used the store's surveillance video camera for what she considered cameo performances, but of course never when there were customers. In the evening, before leaving the store, she'd review the tape and try to iron bugs out of her technique—too much hand and arm movement, wider smile next time, improve posture, and for God's sake do something about that hair. She knew that to advance in her chosen career she'd have to find in herself the very best Kate Adams, her consistent image for screen and stage.

A gray pickup truck had pulled into the lot and parked near the door. Larry, a wallpaper hanger who came by every morning, climbed out of the truck and came in the store. He was a tall, lanky man about thirty, with unruly black hair and bad teeth. "Super Slurp," he said, smiling at Kate.

"I don't know how you can drink these things so early in the morning," Kate said, working the machine to draw a large foam cup of the store's special carry-out beverage. She added a little more strawberry syrup to the carbonated water, the way she knew Larry liked it.

He used a plastic straw to sip. Smiled wider. "Any more luck landing acting jobs?" he asked.

"Sort of." She got a damp paper towel and wiped down the machine, which seemed always to be sticky.

"What's a 'sort of' acting job?" Larry asked.

"It was modeling work, really."

Larry showed his crooked teeth. "Kate, Kate . . ."

"Not that kind of modeling job," she said, wondering if he was really kidding her. "Photographs."

"Sure, for guys who pretend they have film in their cameras."

Kate found herself blushing, which wouldn't do for someone who planned on a major acting career. "Listen, Larry—"

"Don't get all mad and flushed," Larry said around his

straw. "I know you meant for catalog pictures, something like that."

"It was for a picture frame distributor right here in Bay-view," she said. "You know, like when you buy a frame there's always somebody's photo in it so it shows better."

"Yeah, glamour shots, like you'd want your wife or husband to really look. So when I go to the dollar store to buy a frame for my latest award, you might be in it."

"Might be," Kate said. "And not just new picture frames. New wallets, too."

Lois Stokes was an attractive blond woman who seemed to have aged twenty years since yesterday. That was when she'd been informed her husband Frank was dead, and learned the way he had died. She was wearing a brave face today, but she had yesterday's eyes.

F.B.I. Special Agent Willis Ames and Agent Ralph Camporini sat in the living room of her modest west side tract house, sipping the coffee she'd just brought them. Willis was a lean, hatchet-faced man from Maine, with touches of gray in his hair and bushy eyebrows. Camporini was a short, hefty man with a vertical scar on his right cheek that made him look remarkably like old newsreel images of Al Capone. Nobody in the Bureau called him Al Capone.

It was too warm in the living room, and the smell of something left too long on the burner wafted in from the kitchen. It wasn't an appetizing scent. Lois sat across from the two agents, on the sofa, gripping her white ceramic coffee mug with both hands as if it was the thing most precious to her in the world. Willis found himself confused about whether he wished Agent Stokes had left children.

"It took you almost a week to find his body," Lois said dully of her husband, looking into the steaming mug instead of at Willis and Camporini.

"He was found by luck," Willis said. "If those campers hadn't decided to pitch their tent—"

"I know!" She cut him off, still staring into her coffee as if it were hemlock she was considering drinking. Then she raised her head and looked at Willis and he was startled by the change in her, the fierce light in her eyes. "I want Frank's killer found. What he did to him—" Words snagged in her throat, temporarily choking her. "I want the bastard found!"

"We think there was more than one," Camporini said in a soft voice.

"Did your husband give any indication of where he might be going the last time you saw him?" Willis asked, knowing the answer. Undercover agents did everything possible to keep their families out of their work, out of danger.

"Frank didn't share his work with me," Lois confirmed, staring back down at her coffee.

Willis thought she might be about to break into uncontrollable sobbing again, as she had yesterday when they'd tried to question her. He and Camporini stood up and moved awkwardly to the door.

"If there's anything we can help you with . . ." Willis said.

"Find them!" Lois said.

"We will, Mrs. Stokes," Camporini assured her, before they went out.

Willis saw that Camporini's dark eyes were moist. He was the first agent to see Stokes' body after the campers had discovered it in its shallow grave.

"Find them!" they heard Lois Stokes say again in a tight voice, as the door swung shut on the hot, quiet house.

"I seen her," Nicko had said to Olson and Vern. "I went to this place for cigarettes and a Super Slurp, and there she was, grinnin' and sashayin' around like she was in a play or movie."

"You sure it was her?" Olson asked.

"If it wasn't her, it was her spittin' image. I watched her through the window for a while, till she noticed me. Then some customers went in. I waited a while and went inside so I could get a closer look at her. She was standin' there bigger'n shit, punchin' the cash register an' gabbin' with the customers, smilin' just like in her picture."

"You didn't do anything dumb, did you?" Vern asked. "Anything that might make her suspicious?"

"Naw, I just asked if she was F.B.I. Agent Frank Stokes' wife or girlfriend."

Vern stared at him the way he'd stared at Stokes before starting in on his work. Nicko felt it all over his body.

"None of us are gonna do anything dumb," Olson told him. "We got no room whatsoever for dumb."

"And no time," Vern added.

Olson said, "What the hell's a Super Slurp?"

Kate was alone that night behind the counter at Speed-Stop when the big man with the pointy ears came in. He'd been in before, she was sure. And even surer that the nattily dressed, sad-faced man she noticed waiting for him outside had been in before, only half an hour ago.

The big man grinned at her. "Got any *American Honey* magazines?" he asked. "An' I don't mean somethin' for beekeepers to read. This is one of them kind with the clear plastic around them so you can't look at the pictures inside without buyin' it."

"I know," she said. She glanced at the teenage boy who'd just come in. He stood in a slouch and started to read a car magazine near the door.

"I've gotta go in back for that kind of magazine," she told the big man. "But I'm sure we've got them. Just a minute."

She was gone less than half a minute, not long enough to use the phone, even if there had been a phone back there.

She returned without the magazine—which the store never carried—and shrugged apologetically. "Sorry, that one's sold out." She noticed that the teenage boy had left. The man waiting outside glanced into the store. Behind him, a black off-road vehicle had pulled up and stopped but didn't turn off its lights.

"It don't matter," the big man told her. "You come with me now."

Kate tucked in her chin and gave him her Lauren Bacall from-down-under stare, figuring it might intimidate him. "I beg your pardon," she said archly.

He grabbed her by one arm and dragged her over the counter.

When she was crammed in the black Bronco with Vern and Olson, he returned to the store only for a minute to make sure there would be no trace of him having been there.

Then he got in his white Neon rental car and drove toward what Olson had called the rendezvous point.

"This woman," Willis said to Lois Stokes as he held up a photograph, "have you ever seen her?"

Lois looked briefly at the photo, then at him. "Yes. Her picture was in my husband's wallet."

Willis wasn't surprised. Undercover agents often carried photos of people other than their loved ones, not only to help establish fake identities, but to misdirect anyone who might harm them. Usually they were snapshots of strangers thousands of miles away who couldn't be traced.

"Who is she?" Willis asked.

"I have no idea. Neither did Frank. He bought a cheap little picture frame someplace and cut the photo that came in it down to wallet size. He figured she was some model off somewhere who nobody would recognize."

"He was half right," Camporini said. "She's a local model."

It took Lois a few seconds to realize what that might mean. "My God, you'd better—"

"It's too late," Willis said. "She was abducted last night from her work at Speed-Stop Market. A teenage boy saw a large man drag her from the store and force her into a vehicle containing two other men."

"When we found out she was a model," Camporini said, "and remembered we found your husband's wallet with no identification or photos in it, we thought we better check with you."

"That poor girl was taken by the men who tortured and killed Frank, and she can't tell them what they want to know."

"They'll only ask her some basic questions," Willis said, "to find out what your husband might have told her. How much he knew that he didn't tell them. Who else he might have told."

Lois didn't ask what would happen to Kate Adams then. She'd identified her husband's body and she knew.

"We've had someone watching this house," Camporini told her in a gentle voice.

Lois didn't understand at first.

"One thing your husband didn't tell them was his address, or anything about you," Willis said. "If he had, they would have come for you and not Kate Adams." He didn't add that once Stokes' killers were sure Kate Adams wasn't his widow, they'd resume their efforts to find the real Mrs. Stokes. And in a city the size of Bayview, they would find her.

After leaving Lois Stokes, Willis and Camporini stopped at a service station and Willis used the phone. They were hoping to learn that Kate Adams' abduction was caught on the store's security camera videotape. But the lab informed him that the abductors had been too smart for that. The video camera was smashed, its cassette missing.

Kate watched the man she'd heard them call Vern enter the barn. The deserted farmhouse she'd noticed driving in was ready to collapse. The barn was in slightly better condition, but neither building would have electricity. She was sure that was the reason for the car battery Vern had taken from the Bronco then carried in and placed on the floor; it would be dusk soon, and they'd need light in the barn.

The big one who'd been in the store, Nicko, walked around behind her and yanked the duct tape from her mouth so abruptly she yelped with pain.

"Don't take her lips off with the tape," Olson, the sad-faced one in the suit, said. "She's gotta use 'em to talk."

"I don't know anything about what you asked me," Kate told them. Her words were slurred because of the tingling pain in her lips.

Olson reached inside his suit coat and her heart almost stopped. Was his hand going to come out holding a gun?

But it wasn't a gun, it was her photograph, the one she'd posed for during her latest modeling job.

"That's you, isn't it?" Olson asked, holding the photo out so she could see it clearly.

Despite its lack of success so far, Kate tried to stay in her Lauren Bacall mode. Scared, but cool and a little defiant. "Sure, it's me. I told you I'm an actress-model. I posed for that photo so they could use it to help sell picture frames."

"It wasn't in no frame when we run across it," Nicko said.

"Somebody's cropped it. Look close and you can see the edges aren't evenly cut."

Olson held the photo toward the light filtering in through cracks between boards and studied it. "She's right about that," he said.

"So your husband or boyfriend trimmed it so it'd fit in his wallet," Vern said.

"I don't have a boyfriend!"

"That's hard to believe," Nicko said, stroking her hair.

"Those photos are all over the place," Kate told them, jerking her head to the side and making Nicko grin. "Look in any department store in town, if you don't believe me."

Olson walked over to the barn door and stood in soft sunlight, his head bowed. Then he cursed and kicked at the plank wall. Barn swallows or maybe an owl fluttered overhead, startling everyone.

"Drive the Neon into town, Nicko," Olson said. "Shop for some picture frames."

Nicko looked at the Bronco battery, then at Kate. "You ain't really gonna believe her, are you?"

"No," Olson said. "That's why you're driving into town."

"We won't start without you," Vern assured him.

That seemed to mollify Nicko.

Vern tossed him a ring of keys, and he stalked out.

They listened to the sound of the Neon starting and driving away.

"He won't be gone long," Vern said. As he spoke, he pressed the duct tape again over Kate's mouth, mashing hard to get adhesion and bruising the insides of her cheeks against her teeth. "A geek like him's got plenty of incentive to get back here."

And he was right. Less than ninety minutes had passed before they heard the Neon drive up and park near the barn. Its door slammed, and Kate heard footsteps outside.

Nicko came in carrying a cheap plastic picture frame about four by five inches.

"Same damned picture," he said, showing Olson and Vern what the frame held, "only she's sittin' next to a vase of flowers in this one that was cut out of the other."

The three men stared at Kate, at her image in the photograph, then went outside. She sat still and heard nothing for a few minutes, then heard them arguing. Their voices rose so they were yelling at times, but she couldn't figure out what they were saying.

Then Vern and Olson came back into the barn. Beyond them, she could see the big one, Nicko, standing near some trees. Even though night was falling, Kate could see that he had his hands stuffed in his pockets and was glaring at the barn with his head lowered, as if sulking.

"Won't need this, after all," Vern said, and picked up the car battery.

Kate was relieved. They believed her at last. Whatever good they thought she might do them, they knew better now and would release her.

His arms stretched straight and his shoulders hunched to support the heavy battery, Vern trudged toward the open barn door. It was getting dark outside fast now, and within seconds she could barely see him. She could no longer see Nicko at all, or even the trees he'd been standing near. She did notice it was going to be a bright, clear night, with a big half-moon and a wide scattering of stars.

Olson moved close to her. "I'm no damned animal," he said, almost in a whisper. "I got a daughter of my own somewhere." Then he smiled reassuringly and reached inside his suit coat again, and she thought he was going to withdraw her picture.

Instead he pulled out a gun.

"She wasn't tortured," Willis said, watching the medical examiner do a preliminary on Kate Adams' body where it had been discovered in the barn. "You know what that means?"

"Means they believed her story," Camporini said. "And we both know what that means."

Lois Stokes sat nervously on her living room sofa. Some of the coffee she'd been drinking had sloshed out of her cup onto the back of her hand. She barely felt the burn, instead becoming acutely aware that the hand was trembling. She knew what Willis and Camporini were going to ask her to do. She knew she'd say yes.

"The men who killed your husband also killed Kate Adams," Willis was saying. "They'll come for you. You can play it safe and leave—"

"Or I can stay here and be live bait," Lois said.

"We'll do everything possible to ensure your safety," Camporini told her.

"But it's true, you'll be bait," Willis confirmed.

Lois smiled at him, knowing he was at least leveling with her, knowing that the Bureau and the Bayview police couldn't possibly guarantee her safety.

"I'll stay here in Bayview," she said, "in this house. For as long as it takes."

She was no longer trembling, but she was still afraid.

Within a few days she was able to see them, at least some of them. When she walked outside to pick up the newspaper, a car would pass. The driver, always a man, never glanced at her, a still-attractive woman wearing a robe. When she went for groceries, she noticed some of the same shoppers in the supermarket, younger women without children and with an alertness about them, though they never acknowledged her presence.

She made sure her doors and windows were locked at night, as instructed, and though she never saw anything beyond darkened panes of glass, she knew they were out there, watching over her like guardian angels with guns.

And she knew if she was aware they were there, so might be whoever came for her.

What woke her at three a.m. on Wednesday of the second week was a faint clinking sound, like glass falling but not breaking.

By the time she'd come fully awake and sat up, she knew it was too late. The small, taped section of window pane cut away to unlock the sash had fallen to the floor after the man had entered her bedroom.

He stood now at the foot of the bed, a gigantic figure that seemed to make the dark shapes of everything else in the room smaller and insignificant.

Lois reached over and switched on the bedside lamp.

He grinned down at her in the sudden light that hurt her eyes. He was wearing dark clothes, even a black or navy blue stocking cap. His teeth were bad and his ears were pointed. In his left hand was a role of silver duct tape. In his right was a large knife.

He raised the hand holding the tape and held a thick forefinger before his lips, signaling for her to be silent.

"Time for you to come along with me," he said.

"Why?" Playing for time, trying to control her fear.

"Because we wanna know what you know and who else you mighta told."

"Then?"

"Then we bring you straight back here. A little question an' answer session's all we're lookin' for."

The casual sincerity in his voice chilled her. She could almost believe him, this man who had killed or helped to kill her husband and Kate Adams.

He held the knife out and took a step toward the bed. "There's no need to shake like that," he told her. "Just walk with me out through the back yard to where we got a car waitin'."

Lois wondered where her protectors were. What had happened to her guardian angels? How had the man slipped past them? She tried to control her gaze so it wouldn't slide toward the door, tipping him off that she was waiting for help.

"What if I say no?" she asked.

The big man shrugged. "You're comin' one way or the other. It's no big deal either way for me. Don't have to be for you, either, if you come along nice. Get it over with, get back here, catch a few more hours sleep. This'll all seem like it was a dream. That'd be the easy way. The hard way, you don't wanna think about."

She emitted a quavering sigh that was almost a whine. "All right," she said meekly.

She bent over stiffly from her sitting position on the bed and reached for her white fuzzy slippers. Where was Willis? Camporini? Her husband's fellow agents who had let him down and were now failing his widow? She could not survive this alone! She knew it with a certainly that froze her heart.

She slid her foot into her left slipper, unable to resist a glance at the door. Where were they?

The intruder was sharp. He saw her eye movement and his grin widened. "I might be big," he said, "but the Army taught me how to move around small, 'specially at night. And how to use this." He waved the knife. "I hate to see you covered up more'n you gotta be, but you can put on that robe and then we're leavin'. I always try to be a gentleman around ladies. You'll see that before the night's over."

"At least I'm glad of that," she said, leaning down for her right slipper. Through its toe she used her husband's Bureau issue Sig Sauer 9 mm handgun to shoot the gentleman.

Willis and Camporini entered the room in Bayville Police Headquarters where Nicholas (Nicko) Doyle sat with his attorney at a small oak table. Doyle's right arm was in a sling. Lois had shot him in the shoulder and the bullet had smashed his collar bone. He'd still been writhing on her bedroom floor when agents attracted by the shot had stormed into the room, seen the knife still in his hand, and subdued and handcuffed him before realizing he'd been wounded. Nicko's attorney, a man named Gray, had indignantly pointed out that their actions had permanently disabled the shoulder.

"I want to know the specific charge against my client," Gray said. His head and pock-marked face looked too small for the shoulder pads of his chalk-striped blue suit. Like a mean little kid playing dress-up with his father's clothes.

"It's murder," Willis said bluntly.

Nicko and his attorney appeared confused.

"You told me it was attempted murder when you read me my rights," Nicko said.

"It's changed."

"But I didn't kill that woman! She's still alive!" Nicko rose half out of his chair. "I only broke into that house to commit burglary! I used the knife to help pry open the window, that's all. I wasn't gonna kill nobody. Believe me, it ain't my style!"

Willis shrugged. "We're talking about two different women. You're being charged with the murder of Kate

Adams. And I'm sure you'll cooperate to avoid also being charged with murdering Federal Agent Frank Stokes."

Nicko sat back and looked wary. Gray's posture changed slightly, but his face gave away nothing.

"A witness saw you leave the convenience store with Kate Adams in tow," Camporini said to Nicko.

Nicko and his attorney put their heads close together and conferred in whispers, then sat back.

"I read about the Adams case in the papers," Gray said. "You have a teenage boy who thinks he saw something from across the street. Any identification of my client would be highly suspect."

"We have more than that," Willis said.

Nicko rubbed his sore shoulder gingerly with his free hand but still appeared unworried. He was remembering how he'd removed the cassette from the store's security camera and taken it with him, but not before smashing the camera for good measure. He'd wiped the camera clean of prints and then stamped on it, and he'd been careful not to touch anything in the store other than the girl. He'd even wiped the door handle on the way out. He was positive he'd left no fingerprints.

"I don't think I need to talk to you about anything I don't wanna," he said with a confident smirk.

Willis nodded to Camporini, who walked across the room and removed a videocassette from his suit coat pocket.

"It's a bluff," Nicko assured his stone-faced attorney.

Gray looked off in the distance and said nothing.

Camporini switched on the small TV and VCR in the corner and inserted the cassette.

The screen flickered and a black and white security tape began to play. It was the kind that always showed the date and time in white letters at the bottom of the picture. There was

279

Kate Adams, smiling and striking poses, walking slinkily with a hand on her hip, tucking in her chin and staring at the camera. A screen test, in case anyone was interested.

Then she was at the cash register, waiting on a series of customers.

Cut to Kate watching a slouchy teenage boy thumb through a magazine.

Then, unmistakably, Nicko Doyle entered the store. He approached the counter and said something to Kate, who then excused herself and turned around, leaving the frame. A few seconds later the tape went blank.

"Kate Adams was a model and aspiring actress who used the store's security tape to perfect her technique," Willis said. Nicko and his attorney were staring hard at him now. Nicko had begun to perspire. "You must have come on too strong and frightened her, Mr. Doyle," Willis continued. "And maybe she knew you'd looked through the window and seen her mugging and posing for the security camera. Before she waited on you she went to the back room and removed the old cassette and replaced it with a blank. She knew you'd probably smash the camera and take the cassette if you were up to no good, so she hid the cassette she'd removed so there'd be a record of what happened up to that point."

Camporini pressed the rewind button, then the pause.

And there again in black and white, above the printed date and time of Kate's abduction, was the clear image of Nicko Doyle staring at her with an expression usually seen on wolves regarding sheep.

Willis sat down at the table, directly across from the shaken and perspiring Nicko. "Three things: You didn't kill Frank Stokes alone. You didn't kill Kate Adams alone. You can possibly escape death by lethal injection if you answer all our questions so you give us the others."

Nicko looked at Gray. Gray looked at Willis.

"We'll deal," the attorney said.

Willis nodded, not reminding anyone he'd said "possibly."

He hadn't actually lied. The Bureau had an image to maintain.

S.O.S.

Dr. Mona Pilsing was frowning.

Across from her sat station manager Harvey Wellstone, staring at her with concern from behind his wide desk. He said, "You must take some time off, Mona."

Dr. Mona—as she was known to the many listeners of her radio call-in psychological aid show "Dr. Mona Cares"—merely glared at him. She was a waspishly thin woman with a lean, lined face that had endured three cosmetic surgery procedures that had improved the firmness and symmetry of her features yet had somehow made her appear older than her forty-five years. Her flesh was like parchment, and her wise blue eyes looked as if they might emit rays that would etch glass. Right now, they were making Harvey Wellstone squirm.

"I am not responsible for that man's death," she said.

"Of course not, Mona. But you are the one who advised him to leave his wife and move in with his mistress."

"Only to save his marriage," Dr. Mona said. "His wife was out of control with her credit cards and refused to communicate with him about their expanding debt."

Wellstone sighed. "She used one of her cards to buy a shotgun, Mona."

"I didn't pull the trigger," Dr. Mona said. She breathed

deeply and centered herself. "This is a classic example of responsibility displacement."

"The station's worried about a lawsuit."

"And ratings that mean big advertising revenue," Dr. Mona pointed out.

"Of course, Mona. This is a business and I don't deny we're looking at the bottom line. But there are those who say instant psychological advice over the radio on the basis of a phone call can be harmful, even dangerous. Now they have an example. It would be best if you went on vacation for a month. We'll rerun Frank Lee Speaking programs in your time slot."

Mona grimaced. Frank Lee Speaking was the radio name of the station's youth movement, a pimply-faced redheaded boy who had an unimaginative opinion about everything. "My audience won't stick around to listen to cockeyed theories voiced by a child who doesn't remember the Reagan era."

"Still," Wellstone said, shifting in his leather chair as if he might avoid Dr. Mona's fierce stare and prevent burns in his clothes, "we think it would do you good to rest for a while and get in touch—"

"I am in touch with my feelings!" Dr. Mona snapped.

"—with the station now and then to see what's happening," Wellstone finished.

Dr. Mona leaned forward in her chair, her brow furrowed, her eyes angry. Wellstone was such a fool to even suggest she was losing control. "Let's be clear on this, Harvey. I am not responsible if some weak-willed wife who finds it easier to shoot her problem than to solve it lacks a psychological trigger lock and stirs herself from her pathetic zeitgeist of her own making long enough to fall victim to her id and react negatively to her husband's rational act by acting irrationally."

"That's clear enough, Mona," Wellstone said, "to convince me of the rightness of my decision. You don't think you're under a strain and need rest, but I've thought so for a long time. Even before this shooting incident. You're out of control. And that's dangerous for the station. While our attorneys iron out this problem, you're going to be safely out of reach of the media, with a lot of other stressed-out people finding relaxation and renewal—on a cruise."

Dr. Mona had never been on an ocean-going vessel. As the bus from the airport approached the docked ship, the immensity of the Sea Frolic surprised her. The cruise ship's pristine white hull loomed like a building wall over its berth in San Juan, Puerto Rico. Passengers who'd already boarded and white-uniformed crewmembers swarmed on the upper decks. Flags with champagne glass emblems or the bright gold Benington Cruise Line logo snapped in the breeze.

No sooner had Dr. Mona boarded than a smiling steward directed her to her outside cabin on B-Deck. Her suitcases were already on board and lined side by side at the foot of the bed, so she wasted no time in unpacking and hanging her clothes in the tiny closet.

The cabin itself was larger than she'd anticipated, with a suitable bathroom and plenty of built-in drawer space. There was a comfortable looking bed with a royal blue spread embossed with the insignia of the Benington Cruise Line that had appeared on the flags and travel brochures. The drapes were a matching blue with gold flecks. Dr. Mona stepped around the small writing desk and opened the drapes to find herself taking in a view of San Juan as if she were observing it from a fourth-story window. The city looked more peaceful than it had when the travel agency bus transported her to the docks. And a light haze hung over it—not pollution, she was sure, but a faint fog caught by the sun and made magical.

Two hours later, Dr. Mona watched the dock and city recede then gradually disappear as a low ribbon of land into the bright horizon line of the ocean. The Sea Frolic had left port and set course for its first stop in the Caribbean, the sunny island of Curacao.

Dr. Mona experienced apprehension as she felt the great power of the ship's engines throb through the floor beneath her feet. Panic disorder threatened. But she sought and found her calm center, then left her cabin to explore the ship.

She was surprised by the luxury of the Sea Frolic. Everywhere she looked were thick drapes and carpets, tasteful decor, much rich wood paneling and strategically placed mirrors to make large areas appear even larger. There were elevators to carry passengers between decks, and softly upholstered chairs to lounge in air-conditioned contentment while the sea slid past outside tinted windows. Were it not for a nautical touch here and there, Dr. Mona could have imagined herself in a luxury hotel.

She'd signed for early seating at dinner, so after a nap in her cabin, she went up to the cavernous plush dining room and was led to a table by an unctuous maitre d'. Several other passengers were already seated and introducing themselves. There were three elderly women from Seattle, traveling together; Dr. Mona didn't quite catch their names over the background noise in the dining room. Next to her sat a mustached man and his frumpy wife; Evers or Nevers, she thought their names were. A detestable couple from Indianapolis with two teenage girls sat across from her. Dr. Mona didn't bother to try to understand their names. When she introduced herself as Dr. Mona Pilsing, one of the Seattle women opened her mouth and stared. Then she squealed that she listened to "Dr. Mona Cares" on the radio as often as she could.

Not often enough, Dr. Mona thought behind her polite smile.

The waiter arrived to take their orders, interrupting all adulation. As he pointed out items on the menu to the teenage beasts from Indiana, the three Seattle women gossiped and stared at Dr. Mona. She was sure they were talking about that foolish man being shot at the hands of his more foolish wife after reacting foolishly—

"I recommend the cold banana soup as an appetizer," a waiter was saying to her.

Dr. Mona stared up at him. "Yes, I'll have that. And the trout almandine."

Fish? She seldom ate fish. Why had she ordered fish? Was she really not herself lately, as the idiot Wellstone assumed?

She wondered less about the question as the appetizers were placed on the table. By the time her soup bowl was empty, she had rediscovered her sense of self.

Dinner went smoothly enough, though the conversation was banal. As she excused herself and rose from her chair, Dr. Mona was glad no one had asked for a free consultation. But as she walked away, she was sure the obnoxious couple with the beastly daughters would ask her advice before the end of the voyage. Maybe she'd recommend that they file for divorce and fight over who wouldn't get custody of the children.

Dr. Mona stopped walking and gripped a brass handrail. Why had she thought such a thing? Maybe Wellstone was right and she did need a rest, a long sea voyage to get her own psyche straightened out.

Then she centered herself and shook off the thought. She was the same Dr. Mona she'd always been. That was the bottom line. No one could convince her otherwise because no one knew her better than she knew herself.

Having found her comfort level, she continued toward the

casino to kill time until the scheduled evening floor show in the lounge, a dance troop of some sort.

She was impressed by the size of the ship's casino. There were blackjack and crap tables, keno, roulette, over a hundred slot machines. The place was alive with voices, bright colors, the clinking of coins and the tinkling music of machines rewarding small, selfish dreams. The voices and laughter further cheered Dr. Mona. She got a roll of quarters from the cashier's cage and sat before one of the gleaming slot machines.

She wasn't normally a gambler, and it took her a while to figure out what this was all about. The idea seemed to be to match rows of number sevens with images of various kinds of fruit.

"I'm sorry, but I was playing that machine," said a voice on her left.

Dr. Mona turned and saw a short, plump man in a skimpy white dinner jacket. He had a porcine face, oily skin, and tiny, nasty dark eyes. She had never seen anyone who reminded her so much of a pig.

"There was no one here when I arrived," Dr. Mona said.

"That doesn't matter," the man said impatiently. His flesh-padded eyes fairly glittered, as if he were regarding warm mud after a meal. "I only left for a moment to get change."

Dr. Mona looked around at the rows of slot machines, several of which weren't being played, and decided it was a time for constructive assertiveness. "There are plenty of other—"

"I was working on this one," the porcine man said. "I have money invested in it and it's about to pay off."

"How could you possibly know that, Porky?"

"What'd you say?"

"I said how could you know when a machine is about to pay?"

287

He stared at her for a moment, his shoulders bunched and tense. Then he said, "I got a system. I'd explain, but it'd be too hard for you to understand." He was throbbing in his eagerness to return to the machine.

"Gambling is compulsive," she told him. "It can easily become an addiction. Often it's linked with a sense of loss stemming from a deprived childhood. There are psychological techniques for breaking the bonds of—"

He glared at her. "Get lost, lady!"

As he gripped her shoulder to try to remove her from the stool in front of the machine, Dr. Mona stood up and ground the spike heel of her shoe into his instep. He squealed precisely like a pig and jumped back.

"I can hurt you worse than that," she told him in a hoarse voice that frightened even her.

Porky started to say something then saw what was in her eyes and was quiet.

"There are plenty of other machines for me anyway," he mumbled after a few seconds.

She stepped close to him, her face hard, the flesh beneath her right eye dancing. I am not out of control, she told herself. She locked gazes with the man and whispered, "Get in touch with yourself, who you really are."

"Huh?"

"Be your own best friend," she hissed fiercely.

He stared at her in confusion as he backed away, then walked hurriedly toward the blackjack tables.

He was wrong about the slot machine with the sevens and fruit. Dr. Mona played it for more than an hour and lost twenty dollars.

The floor show in the lounge later that evening was awkward and mistook energy for talent. The dancers were followed by a stand-up comedian who joked about how all the honeymooners on board were rocking the boat so hard he was seasick before it left port. That made Dr. Mona glance around the dim lounge. The comedian seemed to be right about the number of honeymooners. There certainly were a large percentage of moon-eyed men with adoring females at their sides. Some of the love-sick fools looked too young to drive cars much less marry. Unfulfilled lifestyles seemed inevitable.

The comedian, Bucky something or other, was telling a joke about honeymooners, sex, and a psychoanalyst as Dr. Mona finished her drink and left the lounge.

The next morning she decided to work harder at relaxing.

It wasn't easy. She had no desire to take part in a limbo competition, watch a short film on how to treat sunstroke, or observe the contest in the pool to see which honeymoon couple could stuff the most ping-pong balls into each other's swim suits.

When she returned to her cabin in disgust, she saw a large envelope on her bed. It contained an invitation to dine at the captain's table that evening. The dinner would be in a private room, and she and other "notable personalities" on board would be present.

At lunch a few hours later, the women from Seattle jabbered enviously when Dr. Mona told them why she wouldn't be joining them that evening for dinner. Dr. Mona watched them with contempt from behind her polite mask. Celebrity really threw the idiots' switches.

Then she silently reprimanded herself for entertaining such a thought. It was celebrity that made troubled souls tune to her radio program and enabled her to help them and her other listeners. She was a good person, not someone who deliberately did harm. Helping people was what she was about. It was her identity and the currency of her self-worth. She centered herself and smiled across the table at the giggling Seattle women. They weren't really so terrible. Why had she been thinking such dreadful thoughts about people lately? Was there a disconnect in her emotional mechanism? Or was it the Feng Shui of her cabin? Whatever the reason, she didn't feel good about herself, and that was something she could hardly bear.

As soon as she returned to her cabin, she switched the covers and pillow on the bed so that now she would lie facing the door. She removed her shoes, stretched out on the bed, and let her eyes take in the cabin from this new perspective.

Much better, she thought. The Feng Shui. She decided to take a nap so she'd be at her best for dinner with the captain.

This was an improvement over her company in the dining room.

Captain Waveschmidt was a tall, bearded man with a barrel chest who looked as if he could command a ship with physical presence alone. He and his crew all wore neat white uniforms resplendent with gold braid and insignia. The other honored guests besides Dr. Mona were a young actress who had appeared in rental car commercials, a Hollywood producer with a compulsion to name drop, and two women who worked at the cruise line's European office. After drinks and strained but polite small talk, everyone enjoyed a delicious dinner. Dr. Mona sat on the captain's right.

"I must confess," he said, "that I hadn't heard of you until my purser raved about you this morning, Doctor. That is due to my busy schedule in other parts of the world where American radio seldom reaches."

"Don't be embarrassed, Captain," Dr. Mona said around

a mouthful of asparagus spear. "I've never been on an ocean liner until this one. It's beautiful, and the size of a small city."

"We're very much like a city, even with our own on-board radio station. Which brings me to my invitation: would you consider letting some of our passengers phone in to your own commercial-free shipboard program some mornings? You would of course have complete freedom. I realize you're on holiday, but we thought it might be fun for you as well as for your fellow travelers."

Dr. Mona didn't hesitate. She was not out of control. She did not need a rest. What had happened to the fool's husband had not been her fault. She smiled warmly at the captain and said yes.

Dr. Mona's first program was the next morning, before the Sea Frolic docked at Curacao. She sat in the ship's wonderfully intricate communications room, wearing earphones and a headset microphone. After the last announcement enumerating island attractions, she was introduced by the communications officer, talked for about five minutes, then began taking calls. She was pleased to see a dozen lights wink on immediately on the switchboard, indicating calls from cabins about the ship.

"I didn't have the money to buy new clothes and I feel underdressed at the ship's dinners," said a woman named Louella.

"It's not what you wear but how you wear it," Dr. Mona said. "If you carry yourself with self-esteem and pride, others will think your clothes outshine their own. It's human nature, Louella. And it wouldn't hurt to pick up a few colorful shells on the beach and glue them onto some of your clothes. People will think you're clever."

Louella thanked her, and a man named Bing from

291

Oklahoma was on the line.

"My wife's spending too much money and I don't know how to control her," he said.

Another numb-headed woman with too many credit cards, Dr. Mona thought angrily, wishing she had a frequent-flyer mile for every call like this she'd received. "Talk to her reasonably, Bing, and point out that you two have another life at home. Then be specific about some things she might have to give up later if she continues to overspend on your vacation. Sometimes specificity is what you need to make your point. And always remember, communicate and your relationship will flourish."

"Hmm. Well, thanks, Dr. Mona."

"And if she won't listen, Bing, point out that it's a big ocean where she'll have to do a lot of swimming to find her credit cards if you toss them over the side. Be proactive, Bing."

"Hmm. Well, yeah . . ."

Nincompoop! Dr. Mona thought. She could tell by his voice he wouldn't have the nerve to threaten his wife, who was probably an expert in passive resistance.

Ginny from Iowa was on the line: "I'm sure my husband's having an affair with another passenger he knows from high school, Dr. Mona. We're all going to be together for two weeks on this ship, and I don't know what to do. I'm at my wit's end."

Easy to believe, Dr. Mona thought. "You have to do something, Ginny. That's key. Take control of your life. Talk to your husband, then to the other woman if you must."

"We're on our honeymoon," Ginny sniffled, "and he spends most of his time with her in the pool. They're doing things underwater, I know!"

"Buy goggles, Ginny! Find out what they're doing. Don't

be a willing victim. Problem solve. Getting this all out in the open would be so life-affirming for you. Believe me, when things are exposed to the light, the shadows disappear. So might your problem."

Ginny thanked her profusely before hanging up.

Several men called asking how they might increase their chances of a shipboard romance. Women called wondering how they might extend a shipboard romance into a long-term commitment. A man complained that his fellow diners wouldn't talk to him. A woman called protesting the tradition of women being first, like children, into the lifeboats if the ship was going to sink.

"I'll tell you how I feel about that if the ship starts to sink," Dr. Mona joked. She used humor sometimes to make herself more human and accessible.

Bing from Oklahoma again: "You sure about throwing those credit cards overboard, Dr. Mona?"

"Of course, Bing. Take control of your life."

"Of my wife?"

"Of your life, Bing. Don't be manipulated by evil passive resistance and people whose own lives are running wild with surrender to impulse and foolishness. Do you deserve a life-time of debt?"

"Nope."

"Remember then, be proactive. It's essential not just for you, but it's a step toward your wife's self-actualization. Then she'll take control of her own life and you two can be happy. Right now, she's standing squarely in the way of your happiness, Bing, and she holds a credit card in each hand. If you expect to harvest the fruits of life, you have to shake life like a tree."

"The wife'd kill me if I shook her," Bing said with a chuckle.

"You only think that, Bing. And it's what she wants you to think. But it's up to you. If you don't have a sail and a rudder, you'll drift toward the rocks. Do you understand?"

"This is a steamship, Dr. Mona."

"Don't try to hide your anguish with humor. It's time to dip your oars into the water and give yourself direction."

"Yes'm."

After Bing hung up, Mona took a few more calls then saw that her allotted half-hour was at an end. She was smiling when she left the communications room. It felt good to be on the air again, and she'd done just fine, despite what that pea-brain Wellstone thought about her mental state. And what was nice about doing this little daily program was that she could enjoy her celebrity, but still most of the passengers didn't know what she looked like. She would have enough anonymity to have time by herself and relax on the cruise.

Dr. Mona went on shore and enjoyed herself touring the picturesque island and having a lunch of shrimp and fruit and a tropical drink with rum in it. Before going back aboard the Sea Frolic, she bought a wide-brimmed straw hat with a bright yellow ribbon to tie beneath her chin when the breeze kicked up. She was napping peacefully in her cabin when the ship set sail for their next stop, the island of Tortola.

During Dr. Mona's half-hour radio show the next morning, Ginny called again: "I bought goggles, like you suggested, Dr. Mona, and took a good look when we snorkeled on the island. That woman and my husband are doing things underwater!"

"Then you must confront them, Ginny."

"I don't think I can," Ginny said, beginning to sob. "I'm afraid. And I'm so miserable!"

"They're not making you miserable, Ginny. You are."

"But the situation—"

"You can change the situation if you'll be proactive and take control. This is your husband, Ginny, not hers. You have a confrontational issue here and you must communicate and deal with it if you're looking to save your relationship. The woman is a threat that must be removed."

"But he's cooperating."

"Then get everything out in the open, tell him to make his choice. And if he chooses her, make sure he knows that as far as you're concerned, he's history."

"I always hated history. I failed it in third grade."

"That's your inner child talking."

"But we didn't get married because I was—"

"Ginny, you're using oblique subconscious avoidance techniques."

"I guess I am, Dr. Mona."

"Don't be an enabler. Talk about these things, the two of you. Or better still, the three of you."

"Me, my husband, and my inner child?"

"I mean the other woman. Let her know she's breaking up your marriage before it has time to get started, and you won't stand for it. You might be surprised to find she backs down. It's human nature, Ginny."

"I guess it is."

After Ginny, a woman from Rockport, Illinois, called and said she couldn't stand her traveling companion and didn't think she could bear being stuck in the same small cabin with her for the next two weeks. She'd asked to be moved but was told there were no more cabins available.

"Then there's nothing you can do short of shooting her," Dr. Mona said.

"Yes," said the woman. "I know that now. Thank you, Dr. Mona."

Dr. Mona signed off and went to the dining room for

breakfast before going ashore.

Unlike at lunch and dinner, there was open seating at breakfasts. Dr. Mona sat at a table with two elderly couples and a young family from Miami. The talk was of a man and his wife who'd been too late to get back on board when the ship had left Curacao. Dr. Mona thought it served them right. They could shop until they were sun-struck on the island while they tried to arrange other transportation. It might teach them how cause and effect played a role in their life experiences.

But while Dr. Mona was sipping a second cup of coffee, a woman sat down near her and asked if she'd heard the news. A man named Bingham Bradford had thrown his credit cards and then his wife into the sea and was under arrest for murder on Curacao.

"Did he go by the name Bing?" Dr. Mona asked.

"I think so," the woman said. "He told some of the other passengers he thought his wife married him because his name sounded like a cash register."

Dr. Mona couldn't help but believe the wife had gotten exactly what she deserved. There was also no doubt in her mind that she hadn't been instrumental in the woman's death. She certainly hadn't instructed Bing to murder his wife, whatever the man's interpretation of what she'd told him. He was the one who'd killed his wife, and that was the bottom line.

Dr. Mona went on shore and shopped for some duty-free perfume. She wore her straw hat with the yellow ribbon, which made her even more unrecognizable. But a few people from the Sea Frolic stared at her strangely in the streets and tourist shops.

After lunch at a charming combination shell shop and restaurant, she returned to the ship for an afternoon nap. That numbskull Wellstone had been right about one thing: a cruise was undeniably relaxing.

She'd awoken and was propped up in bed, fully dressed except for shoes, reading a copy of *I Feel Good About Myself and You,* when the lamp flickered as a resounding Whump! traveled through the ship.

Dr. Mona looked about, then continued to read, until several minutes later when she heard activity in the passageway outside her cabin. Curious, she got up and went to the door.

Half a dozen people were standing in the passageway, yammering excitedly about something.

"What happened?" Dr. Mona asked.

A woman with wild blond curls and even wilder eyes stared at her. "Didn't you hear? Someone cut an electrical line that ran near the swimming pool so that it fell in the water. Six people were killed."

"It was the line that supplied power to the Limbo Lounge," a man in a flowered silk shirt added. He was holding a yellow drink with a paper umbrella in it and appeared inebriated.

"Honeymooners were in the pool having the ping-pong ball competition," wild woman said. "You know the contest where they stuff as many ping-pong balls as possible into their swim suits."

"I believe those are table tennis balls," the man with the drink said.

Wild woman ignored him. "I heard it was a jilted woman who caused all the trouble, hacked through the line with a hatchet from one of those fire-control boxes. Odd part was, her husband wasn't even in the pool. He'd just climbed out and he's okay."

"They already got the bar in the Limbo up and running again," the man said, raising his drink. "Service is amazing on these cruise ships."

Dr. Mona stood dumbfounded.

Ginny! The woman who'd electrocuted everyone in the ship's pool had to be Ginny, trying to wreak vengeance on her new husband and his lover.

Dr. Mona walked to the end of the passageway and found that power hadn't yet been restored to the elevator, so she climbed the stairs to the pool deck.

Alongside the pool lay several still forms beneath beach towels. Crewmen were loading another onto a stretcher. Knots of people were standing about talking to the ship's officers. The men looked grim and many of the women were sobbing.

Dr. Mona saw Captain Waveschmidt talking to half a dozen passengers and went to him.

"Is there any way I can help?" she asked. "I mean professionally, to make it easier for the passengers to cope."

Everyone was silent. The captain drew a deep breath and stared at her.

"It would be better if you went to your cabin," he said, stroking his beard. "I'll be in touch with you when we finish sorting out things."

Dr. Mona nodded and withdrew, though she didn't agree with the captain's assessment. Some of these people needed counseling, even if they were uninjured. But she could understand why he was upset. He was the ship's captain and was ultimately responsible for what had happened. Maybe when he came to her she could help him to distinguish between professional and personal responsibility and counsel him in his anguish.

She'd been in her cabin about fifteen minutes when there was a light knock on the door. Captain Waveschmidt come to enlist her help.

But when she opened the door, Porky from the casino pushed inside.

He was wearing swimming trunks and was fatter than he'd appeared with clothes on. And hairier. His stomach bulged over the elastic waistband of his wildly colored trunks. He raised a bulky arm and leaned against the wall, blocking Dr. Mona's path to the door. Her attention was caught by thing white attached to the seat of his trunks. At first she thought it was a fake bunny tail. Then she realized it was a half-melted ping-pong, or maybe table tennis, ball stuck to the material.

His mouth grinned at her but his little pig eyes were malicious. "You've been talking to my wife Ginny on the radio," he said.

Dr. Mona knew what he wanted and her mind whirled, seeking words that might save her. "You're both still alive," she said. "You can save your marriage and each other with a life-affirming approach. However you felt about the woman in the pool—"

"I'm not concerned about either one of them," Porky said. "After you left the casino another woman sat down and won six thousand dollars on the slot machine I'd been feeding quarters to for hours. I was going to keep working that machine until it paid off. It was my machine, but you stole it from me, and someone else got the triple sevens and the banana and my six thousand dollars."

"No, no," Dr. Mona said, backing away.

"It won't do you any good to scream," Porky said. "Everybody just rushed to C-Deck where some stupid woman shot her cabin mate."

"I wasn't going to scream. I want to help you. You're acting out. This a classic case of grief transference. You're not responsible for the other woman's death. It was Ginny who electrified the pool."

"Six thousand dollars," Porky said, lowering his arm and moving toward her. "That's the bottom line."

Dr. Mona backed farther away until she felt the bed against the backs of her legs. She summoned all her confidence. She knew better than anyone how to deal with distressed people, understood how to reach them. "Please calm down and try to center yourself. Despite what's happened, you can still achieve self-actualization and contentment if you listen to me and be pro—"

But Porky's hands were at her throat, his thick thumbs digging into her larynx. Dr. Mona's confidence level plunged. She tried to scream but no sound emerged save the muted crunching of cartilage.

As gathering dimness carried Dr. Mona from pain into death, she was aware of Porky's flushed, contorted face close to hers, the laserlike gleam in his eyes, his voice hoarse with madness chanting, "Closure, closure, closure . . ."